D0359696

MURDER IN ABBOT'S FOLLY

MURDER IN ABBOT'S FOLLY

FOLLY

A Marsh & Daughter Mystery

Amy Myers

This first world edition published 2011
in Great Britain and in the USA by
SEVERN HOUSE PUBLISHERS LTD of
9–15 High Street, Sutton, Surrey, England, SM1 1DF.
Trade paperback edition first published
in Great Britain and the USA 2012 by
SEVERN HOUSE PUBLISHERS LTD

British Library Cataloguing in Publication Data

Myers, Amy, 1938-
  Murder in Abbot's folly.
  1. Marsh, Peter (Fictitious character)–Fiction. 2. Marsh,
  Georgia (Fictitious character)–Fiction. 3. Private
  investigators–England–Kent–Fiction. 4. Fathers and
  daughters–Fiction. 5. Murder–Investigation–Fiction.
  6. Detective and mystery stories.
  I. Title
  823.9'14-dc22

ISBN-13: 978-0-7278-8039-0 (cased)
ISBN-13: 978-1-84751-385-4 (trade paper)

All Severn House titles are printed on acid-free paper.

Severn House Publishers support The Forest Stewardship Council [FSC],
the leading international forest certification organisation. All our titles that
are printed on Greenpeace-approved FSC-certified paper carry the FSC logo.

MIX
Paper from
responsible sources
FSC
www.fsc.org   FSC® C018575

Typeset by Palimpsest Book Production Ltd.,
Falkirk, Stirlingshire, Scotland.
Printed and bound in Great Britain by
MPG Books Ltd., Bodmin, Cornwall.

Remembering
Carol
who loved Jane Austen's novels

ONE

'Another raspberry fritter? They would most certainly have been a favourite of dear Jane's.' Dora Clackington beamed, holding out the plate of burnt offerings towards Georgia. 'I shall be taking oodles of them to the Gala on Saturday.'

Georgia Marsh braced herself. This social pantomime was growing more agonizing by the minute, and only her father's presence was making it bearable. 'Thank you,' she said, as warmly as she could, as she took a fritter. If Jane Austen had indeed dined on these, she pitied her greatly. 'What Gala is that?' she asked politely.

'At Stourdens,' Dora said in tones of reverence. 'An annual event held in Jane's memory, and this year is a very special one.'

'You simply have to come,' Elena contributed brightly. 'After all, there was a murder there once.'

Peter Marsh avoided Georgia's eye. When her father had diffidently broached the question of coming to Edgar House this evening, Georgia had been appalled. It was bad enough to learn that Elena – her mother and Peter's former wife – was in England, without having to meet her for the first time in some years in the presence of virtual strangers. Georgia dimly remembered Dora and Gerald Clackington from her childhood and they were pleasant enough, but Dora's effervescent jollity was making it harder, not easier, to cope with the situation.

Georgia decided to make a determined effort to keep the conversation flowing. 'Whose murder?' she asked Elena.

It was unlikely that Peter would be any more interested than Georgia was in the answer. Just because father and daughter worked together on cold murder cases didn't mean that they automatically pursued violent death at every opportunity. Nevertheless, it was an impersonal topic and therefore to be welcomed.

Even now she could hardly believe she was engaged in small talk with her mother, who was chattering gaily (nervously?) as though the last fourteen years had never happened. Elena had telephoned out of the blue to tell Peter she was staying in Kent with her great friends Dora and Gerald at Edgar House in Harblehurst, not far from Canterbury. Would he and Georgia come to drinks there the following night, Elena had pleaded.

Georgia had fumed when Peter had broken the news, and he had fallen very silent. Now she felt ashamed of her initial reaction as she noticed how those elegant manicured hands were twisting together on Elena's lap. This was an effort for her mother too, as well as for Peter. Elena was over sixty although her fine features and model-like figure would seem to belie any advancing years.

In theory, the difficulties between them had been ironed out some time ago, but nine months earlier Elena's second husband – whom Peter and Georgia had both liked – had died at their home in France. It had been the Clackingtons whom Elena had summoned to help, and it was not for another month that Elena had told her daughter and former husband of her loss. The wound at being so disregarded still lingered with them both and only added to the uneasy relationship that had existed between them since Elena had walked out. She had been unable to cope with the double blow of Peter becoming wheelchair-bound only a year after the loss of their son Rick.

Why was she back here so unexpectedly? Georgia wondered. Just to pay a visit to the Clackingtons? Georgia doubted that, and although not a word had been said about future meetings while Elena was here, she was beginning to have misgivings.

Peter must have decided to join in Georgia's valiant efforts to keep the conversation going. 'I know Stourdens, of course,' he said, 'and I do remember something about a murder. Remind me, whose murder?'

'Robert Luckhurst, the then owner.' Gerald Clackington cleared his throat in embarrassment, as though murder were a man's topic, not fit for ladies' ears. 'It was in 1985. Found shot in Abbot's Folly – that's an eighteenth-century monstrosity in the grounds of Stourdens. Thought at first to have been by one of the villagers, who were presenting some kind of protest, but in the end the chap who owned this place went down for it. You'll know that this used to be a roadhouse before we took it over. He'd lost the licence for it – given to his wife instead – and he blamed Luckhurst who was on the council at the time. Mind you, there was a lot of gossip about his being fonder than he ought to be of Luckhurst's wife.'

'The very idea,' Elena said indignantly. She spoke so enthusiastically that it was clear she too wanted to keep the conversation away from the personal. 'I *knew* Amelia Luckhurst. You remember her, Peter darling, don't you?'

To Georgia's amusement 'Peter darling' didn't look as though he had a clue who Amelia was, or didn't want to. References to their joint past made him uncomfortable.

'Gerald and I are so thrilled to see you all here together,' Dora hastily cooed. 'Elena is delighted you could come, aren't you, darling? So very nice.'

Georgia mentally ran through all the emotions churning away inside her, but 'nice' didn't apply to any of them. Nevertheless, she managed to smile brightly and agree that it was.

Dora and Gerald must be in their late fifties, she estimated. In her youth Dora must have been a pretty, doll-like girl, and her soft gentle features, excitable body language and speech, and pink frilly chiffon outfit suggested that she had not moved on. Gerald still seemed the manly adoring protector he must always have been to her. He was almost Dickensian in his upright bearing and stiff formal manner. Not unfriendly, far from it, but reserved. His wife, on the other hand, made Georgia think of David Copperfield's childlike wife Dora, who might have grown to be rather like Dora Clackington, anxious to please by the only methods she knew. Then she reproached herself for making such swift judgements. First impressions were not always right.

'Do come to Stourdens on Saturday, Peter,' Elena urged. 'You and Georgia would be able to find out more about that murder case.' Her nervousness was becoming more apparent. 'You might even have handled it, darling.' Peter had been a DI before a shooting incident in 1995 had put him in a wheel-chair for life.

'No. It's coming back to me though.' Peter seemed as keen as Georgia to stay on neutral ground.

What else could they do in these circumstances? Jane Austen would doubtless have handled it more smoothly, although similar emotions must have been seething away in her characters' hearts under the mask of polite behaviour demanded by the society in which they moved.

'If the case was as cut and dried as you say, Gerald,' Peter continued, 'that would explain why it's not at the top of my brain's filing system any longer.'

'What happened to Amelia?' Elena asked. 'I'm afraid I've lost touch.'

Gerald obliged with the answer. 'She moved away, just like the killer's family. Tanner was his name, Frederick Max Tanner, generally known as Max. Wife's name was Esther. We dealt with her when we bought this place. Way back it was a coaching inn, the Edgar Arms, so named after the family who built and lived in Stourdens for a century or two. It would have been on the main London to Canterbury Road. No bypass then. You probably came here in its later days, Peter, and you too, Georgia.'

Georgia had a faint recollection of having been brought here as a child for a Boxing Day meet, where the mysterious Stirrup Cup and red jackets, referred to as pink, defied any satisfactory explanation. She sometimes wondered whether those early unsolved mysteries had fostered in her the desire to tackle puzzles, which in turn had led to Marsh & Daughter's cases. She and her father now investigated cold cases – which were usually far from cold when the truth was known – and then recorded them in a series of books which was published by her husband, Luke Frost.

Because of its origins, Edgar House had an unusual layout, so Gerald had explained. A timbered medieval building at heart, parts of it had been extended and restored over the years, and this had resulted in its now having two long wings to the main house. One of them, Dora had told Georgia with pride, had been the local Assembly Rooms. Georgia had only seen the front building so far, formerly the inn's bars. The old arched entrance through which carriages would have clattered into the yard had now been converted to become the entrance hall of the house. The large living room, in which they were sitting, had been on its left and must have been the main bar. At the far end of the room a corridor led, Georgia guessed, towards the kitchen area and the side entrance through which Gerald must have guided Peter, as his wheelchair had not taken kindly to the steps at the main entrance. Georgia had come in that way – to be pitchforked straight into Elena's arms. Whereas Elena had been overcome with emotion, Georgia had felt frozen to the spot, and then mentally kicked herself for mishandling the situation.

'I just about remember the inn, but I don't recall meeting Tanner,' Peter said. 'The case is coming back to me though. Didn't he continue to protest his innocence after being convicted? I suppose that's natural, but was there any doubt about the verdict?'

'Doesn't seem to have been,' Gerald grunted. 'Anyway, he must be out of prison long since. His wife moved away after selling the whole caboodle to us. Being a big pub off the main road by that time, she couldn't find anyone to take over the licence. Rather fancied having a go myself, but Dora wasn't keen.'

Dora looked prim. 'Not at all suitable, Gerald.'

For him or for her? Georgia wondered meanly. She couldn't see Dora Clackington taking easily to the role of publican's wife. Far too much hard work and far too many long hours. Gerald, on the other hand, might have made a good stab at playing Mine Host.

'We simply jumped at the chance to acquire the property, however,' Dora continued.

'Such a wonderful building,' Elena said instantly.

Georgia agreed, but nevertheless she was puzzled. The conversion from pub to private house must have cost the Clackingtons a packet, and although the building was interesting, there must have been many others on the market that would not have required so much work. Dora and Gerald, however, seemed to her a couple who had always expected their comforts.

'Oh no.' Dora looked mysterious. 'Because of *her*. There are connections, you see.'

'To the murder of Robert Luckhurst?' Georgia was confused. Had she missed something?

'No, to dear Jane.' Dora waved a hand around the room, settling the question. Georgia had picked up on her hosts' enthusiasm for Jane Austen as soon as she arrived. It wasn't difficult. The walls boasted Regency prints and reproductions of the famous Jane Austen silhouette and the two portraits, and the bookcases were full of what looked like early editions of her works and Austen biographies and commentaries. Dora's eagerness implied more than a normal commitment, however.

'Jane Austen herself had links to the inn?' Georgia asked.

Dora looked smug. 'Modest ones, not to be compared with Stourdens. However, we can claim the honour of *The Watsons*.'

'Who were they?' Peter enquired.

Elena tittered. 'The title of one of Jane Austen's unfinished novels, my love.'

How *could* she? Georgia fumed as she saw Peter's face at her mother's put-down, intentional or not, and she found it hard not to retaliate. Instead she asked steadily, 'Was it set in this pub?' She instantly regretted the reference to a 'pub'. *Not* the right word to use to Dora about Edgar House, even if Gerald had done so.

'Certainly it was,' Dora replied stiffly. 'Part of it at least. The Assembly Rooms where *The Watsons'* all-important ball takes place are clearly ours, on the first floor of our longer wing. The castle where Lord and Lady Osborne reside in the novel is based on Stourdens, where the Gala is to be held on Saturday. I'm sure you must have visited it.'

Georgia had. It was near a hamlet called Dunham several miles away from Medlars, the house she shared with her husband, Luke. Dunham was only a mile or so from Godmersham Park, which Jane Austen had frequently visited, as the elegant Palladian mansion was owned by her brother Edward. Stourdens was also an elegant Georgian mansion, but in dire need of restoration. Set in grounds that shielded it from the Ashford road, the house itself could not be visited, but the gardens were opened once or twice a year to the public under the National Gardens Scheme. This was more for their Humphrey Repton design than their modern maintenance, however. To Georgia, judging from the outside of the house, which was all she could see during her visit to the gardens, it was in sad need of tender loving care – and presumably, therefore, of cash. She had a vague memory of having briefly met the current owners, and she had pitied them their plight.

'It was here at Edgar House, of course, that it all began,' Dora added firmly.

'It?' Peter queried. He was not particularly interested in Jane Austen, and Georgia could see the struggle he was having in fixing his mind on anything but the fact of his former wife's presence.

'Jane's great love affair, which ended tragically,' Dora informed them in a low sombre voice. 'She had begun to pour her heart out about it in writing *The Watsons*, but the effort proved too much for her, poor darling, and she abandoned the novel.'

It was a long time since Georgia had read Jane Austen's unfinished works, and she had to fish around in her mind. 'Isn't it at the ball in the Assembly Rooms where Emma Watson dances with a little boy to save his pride?'

'Yes, indeed.' Dora said, seeming a little put out, as though none but she should be in command of Austen knowledge. 'It was here that Jane met her true love, a story she intended to celebrate in *The Watsons*; at the point Jane laid the story aside, only the first meeting had taken place. Love had yet to come. It is known how she intended to end the novel, however, because her great-grandniece recorded that Jane's sister Cassandra had known how Jane had intended to continue the story. Emma Watson would be happily united with the gentleman who loved her, despite the fact that Lady Osborne had cast desirous eyes upon him with wedlock in mind. Alas, there had been no such happy ending in Jane's real life. *The Watsons* was intended to record a happiness that was denied to her in her own life.'

Peter seemed genuinely interested, to Georgia's surprise. Whereas the murder of Robert Luckhurst had failed to arouse his curiosity, Jane Austen had apparently struck a chord. 'But why did she abandon the novel?'

Dora wagged a provocative finger at him. 'Ah, you detectives.

There's no holding you back. Shall we tell them the full story, Gerald?' she asked skittishly.

From his expression, Georgia interpreted Gerald's answer as a thundering 'no', although he managed to restrain it to a mere, 'Better not, Dollybird.'

'Oh, please,' Elena begged.

'Not until Saturday, darling,' Dora replied mysteriously. 'After that it will become public knowledge, but we can't pre-empt Laura's great day.'

What on earth was all this about? Georgia wondered. This story of a great love affair was news to her, but then she was no expert on Jane Austen's life. She could see Peter's patience fast evaporating again, and he must have decided that enough was enough.

'I'll make a guess, shall I?' he asked jovially. 'Jane Austen murdered her lover and left his body in the folly.'

Elena gasped, but Gerald and Dora merely seemed bewildered. 'Oh no, nothing like that,' Gerald replied.

Peter looked somewhat abashed. 'I'm sorry, Elena. If you knew Amelia, you must have known Robert Luckhurst too, and so I should not be making jokes about him. He doesn't seem to have been a particular friend of yours, though,' he added awkwardly.

'No, darling. He was very reclusive,' Elena replied. 'I hardly knew him and I knew Amelia only a little better . . .' She hesitated. 'Not a very happy marriage, I'm afraid.'

'So the rumours that she sought fresh woods and pastures new in the way of gentlemen friends might be true?' Georgia said.

'Oh, no.' Elena looked shocked. Then she must have caught Peter's eye because she giggled. 'Well, perhaps. Just occasionally.'

Something tugged at Georgia's heart. Some distant memory of Elena laughing one magical day in Georgia's childhood when they had been picnicking on the downs. All of them: Elena, Peter, herself – and Rick. Peter had slipped over and landed with one hand right in the middle of the jelly. Judging by Peter's expression, he had some similar memory.

'With Max Tanner?' he almost snapped at Elena.

'I never knew. I really didn't know her well.' Elena retreated, perhaps alarmed at the shared moment of intimacy.

Nonsense, Georgia told herself, nonsense. She was imagining this emotional tension, perhaps because she wanted to – but what did that imply? Change the subject quickly. 'What happens at this Gala?' she asked.

Dora needed no urging. 'It's going to be such fun. Laura Fettis, who owns Stourdens, is my greatest friend – except for you, Elena,' she added diplomatically. '*Such* fun. I am sure she will show you the Stourdens Jane Austen collection which dwarfs our own modest memorabilia.' She put her finger to her lips. 'But I must say no more about that until Laura has spoken. I *can* tell you about the Gala itself, though. There will be Georgian cookery demonstrations and a buffet of Georgian food – and shuttlecock. You must all play shuttlecock, you really must. There will be riding, fencing, and of course *dancing*. Naturally, you must all come in costume.'

Dora beamed, and Georgia saw Peter's face fall. She shared his feelings. To be clad in period costume was not something she warmed to. 'And bring your dear husband, Georgia,' Dora added, oblivious to their reactions. 'After all, as a local publisher he should be present. He might even discover another Jane Austen.'

'I'll ask him,' Georgia said, trying to imagine Luke dancing the cotillion while checking out hopeful authors.

'Costume,' Peter muttered. 'I'm afraid breeches and swallowtails are somewhat beyond me.'

'But you must come, Peter,' Elena said firmly. Georgia saw him hesitate, and her misgivings returned now that it seemed certain this was not going to be the last they saw of Elena on this trip to England. Nevertheless, Georgia was all too conscious that there was a gulf between them that had to be faced and somehow crossed, which could not be achieved by retreat. Was seeing Elena again on Saturday going to help that problem disappear? No, in Georgia's view. At best Saturday would produce the sort of situations that Jane Austen's novels depended on, in which private emotions were frustrated by social demands. At worst the day might bring forth far more than frustration. Stourdens was not only a place where Jane

Austen had seemingly suffered great unhappiness, but also one where twenty-five years ago the owner had been murdered.

Neither of these factors should cast its shadow over the Stourdens of today, and yet not wanting to back away from meeting Elena again was the only reason that she had not pleaded an earlier engagement for Saturday. Stupid, Georgia told herself, because the murder of Robert Luckhurst was a case that had been solved, and the killer was probably free by now. Still proclaiming his innocence? She couldn't help wondering.

Going home to Medlars brought its usual comfort. Georgia felt a lift of the heart when she pushed open the heavy wooden door into the old house, a door that almost seemed to be welcoming her home with a 'Cheer up, I've seen many problems far worse than this'. She could hear Luke in the kitchen, probably already cooking supper, so she dropped her shoulder bag and hurried to join him. A wave of pleasure swept over her as she hugged him – which seriously impeded his risotto and resulted in a cascade of rice grains landing on the floor. After dealing with this emergency, he listened patiently to her account of her evening before speaking.

'I can't wait to see you in bonnet, bulging panniers and white muslin dress. Got any old pillow cases you can wear?'

'I'll find something,' Georgia said hollowly. 'Anyway, don't laugh. You're coming with me. They all want to meet the famous publisher.'

He groaned. 'Famous publisher not want to meet them. Count me out. I hate costume events.'

'I need support, Luke,' she pleaded. 'Elena will be there.'

He pulled a face. 'Point reluctantly ceded. What's her game?'

'I don't know, but there's a hidden agenda somewhere. All my antennae are waving.'

'She is your mother,' he said gently. 'Suppose she wants to return to England?'

Trust Luke to put into words her secret fear. 'That's a scary thought.' And that was putting it lightly.

'Because she might interfere with Marsh & Daughter's work?'

She considered this. 'Perhaps,' she admitted, 'but it's more than that. I can't forget the way she walked out because she didn't want the responsibility of looking after Peter.'

'Perhaps she can't either, but you should all be able to move on now that Rick's disappearance has been solved. That's no longer lying between you.'

Rick had disappeared on a walking holiday in France, and for fourteen years there had been no clues as to what had happened to him. Then two years ago, thanks partly to a tip from Elena on a possible witness, they had followed the trail to a boating tragedy on the Danube in which he drowned. Georgia had finally managed to get Peter to accept that that was fact and not theory. Elena's current visit seemed to have nothing to do with Rick, and yet Georgia was afraid that even her presence might trigger Peter's doubts again. And as for Luke's suggestion, surely Elena would not wish to return permanently to England? She had not needed her former family when her husband died last year, so why should she now? The question mark hung in the air like a sword of Damocles, until she firmly banished it.

When she reached Marsh & Daughter's office in Peter's home in nearby Haden Shaw on the Friday morning before the Gala, Peter began without ado: 'Max Tanner. Press references. A few stray ends. DI Hamlyn took the case. Remember him?'

'Dimly,' Georgia replied, relieved that Peter seemed to be throwing himself into the Luckhurst case. She had spent the day before reading the proofs of Marsh & Daughter's current book, but she had been worried that Peter might be brooding about Elena. 'Solemn and sarcastic comes to mind,' she added.

'Spot on. I'd like to get one up on him.'

'Hasn't he retired by now?'

'That won't spare him.' Peter paused. 'Might be worth our giving that Jane Austen Gala a go on Saturday.'

She took the bull by the horns. 'Is this about Luckhurst or Elena?'

Another pause, longer this time. 'Let's find out what she's up to, daughter mine. Meanwhile, let's assume it's about Robert Luckhurst.'

The subject of Elena was clearly closed, and on the whole, Georgia reflected, remembering Luke's advice to keep it cool, that was a good thing. Was Peter seriously considering taking on this case, though? So far, probably not. Marsh & Daughter had their own 'rules' for choosing new cases, and this one did not qualify. She suspected that Peter was merely using it as a distraction from Elena, and if so, there was no reason she couldn't do the same.

'You said there were a couple of loose ends over the Tanner conviction,' she prompted him.

'Yes. For instance, why should he choose to take his revenge for a lost licence twelve months after losing it?'

'There was another reason for the murder,' Georgia reminded him, 'if it's true that he and Amelia Luckhurst were an item.'

'Worth bearing in mind. Luckhurst seems to have been a funny sort of chap,' Peter reflected.

'Don't tell me he was the Stourdens Jane Austen fan?'

'An understatement. I rang Dora and badgered her into telling me more. He seems to be of the obsessive collector genus.'

'Expensive hobby when Jane Austen is the subject.'

'Not if you're handed down the goods by your father,' Peter said. 'But the Luckhursts owned Stourdens from the middle of the nineteenth century, so it seems odd that we are only hearing about this collection now. A question mark, don't you think?'

'It's possible. Lots of old mansions still have unexplored attics full of goodies. It just needs an enthusiast to inherit – and Robert Luckhurst seems to have been just the chap. Any idea what the collection consists of?'

'None, so we're left with the Clackington Claptrappers' heavy hints. Anyway, it's hardly relevant to the Luckhurst murder because theft wasn't the motive for it. Not a mention of theft in the trial reports or from what Dora could tell me. Jane Austen's archive was in the Folly when Luckhurst was killed, but it wasn't touched. So we have to look elsewhere for a motive, if we exclude the ones we know about. And there seems no reason to do that at present. Tanner seems either to have planned his crime very oddly or to have been seriously unlucky in having so many potential witnesses turn up.'

'Explain please.' She knew he liked nothing better than explaining. Anything to stop thinking of tomorrow and meeting Elena again. Georgia was painfully aware that her reluctance to think about her mother might be linked to emotions whose origins were too deeply buried to want to unearth, as well as those springing from more obvious causes.

Peter obliged. 'It was Saturday sixteenth June. Tanner and Luckhurst were mates of a sort, because they belonged to the same classic car club, which met every month at the Edgar Arms and had a summer annual beano at Stourdens. Apart from that one day, Luckhurst was severely reclusive, being paranoid about having his precious Austen collection pinched. Which, as I told you, it wasn't.

'What happened was this,' he continued. 'Just as the classic car owners were getting into their serious technical jargon stride, their numbers were swelled by a protest group of twenty or thirty Dunham residents complaining about the closure of a footpath across Stourdens' land. It had apparently been used by farmers for time out of mind, and a diversion had been agreed through the woods. That wasn't much help to the farmers, though, as only the path that led through Stourdens was wide enough to take farm machinery and animals – which it had duly done for ages past, with no objection being raised by the Luckhursts. Robert Luckhurst was a councillor, however, and had taken it into his head to decide that the footpath in question was a threat to his precious collection. Unfortunately, the protest group was not a peaceful reasonable deputation, as it was led by a determined hothead, one Tom Miller. He soon winkled out that Luckhurst had fled from the classic car line-up to take refuge in his beloved Abbot's Folly.'

'Just what *is* that? Gerald just said it was a monstrosity.'

'Patience. I gathered from Mike Gilroy that—'

'I knew it!' Georgia said resignedly. 'You just had to get on the phone to him, didn't you?' Chief Superintendent Mike Gilroy had been Peter's sergeant in his police career days, and to Peter he still was. Mike was extraordinarily patient, but Georgia had no intention of letting Peter take too much advantage of this.

Peter had the grace to blush. 'One more call wouldn't upset

him, and the records must have been easy to access. I was
working there at the time, for heaven's sake. Anyway, since
you ask,' he continued firmly, 'this mock folly was a—'

'Isn't that a contradiction in terms? All follies are mock.'

'Wrong. Follies were beginning to parody themselves
towards the end of the eighteenth century, and this one is
apparently hardly a ruin. It's a gothic horror, and Robert used
it as a study. On the day he died, the protesting horde swept
through the grounds to it and found Tanner there talking to
Luckhurst on a mission of his own. For whatever reason, in
due course the protest group retreated, but Robert was found
shot an hour later. He'd been dead at least half an hour. Tanner
had witnesses who swore he returned to the main house with
the protest group, but then went straight back to the pub.
According to him, the real villain had been the village toughie,
Tom Miller.'

'What good would killing Luckhurst do for their cause?'
Georgia objected.

'I presume that Amelia might have been seen as the softer
touch in the footpath battle. It never came to be an issue,
however, because it was revealed that Tanner's chief witness
was an outsider who had done more time than Big Ben.' A
pause, then Peter added, 'I wonder if Amelia Luckhurst is
going to be at the Gala?'

'She can have my ticket,' Georgia muttered.

'Not keen, eh?'

'No, for obvious reasons.' She didn't have to spell them
out. 'Plus the fact that I have to conjure up a Jane Austen
outfit not only for myself but for Luke too. How are you going
to cope? Can I help?'

'No need. I rang Kate.'

'Who's she?'

'Costume Kate, Ltd. She hires them out.'

TWO

Georgia forced herself to rise early on the Saturday morning. It was either that or diving under the bedclothes and claiming a sudden dose of flu. She was not, but not, looking forward to this Gala. Even Peter was more interested than she was in seeing the folly where Robert Luckhurst had died, but she still saw it only as a distraction from Elena's presence.

'At least it's not raining,' Luke observed, regarding his image gloomily in the mirror. He had an uncommon knack of echoing her own reservations, Georgia thought. At the moment these were concentrated on her costume. The sheer stupidity of donning Regency dress on a Saturday morning in the twenty-first century was taking its toll. Dora had eventually conceded that Regency, for Gala purposes, could be taken in its broader sense of beginning from about 1800 rather than from 1811 when the future George IV formally became Regent during the mental instability of his father. After all, Georgia had pointed out (having done some hasty research), Jane Austen was visiting Kent well before 1800.

She had therefore opted for the earlier fashion of a high-waisted open-fronted dress over a silk underskirt, rather than the later straight clinging classical-style dresses of muslin or lawn for which her figure was hardly a bonus, being tall but not sylphlike. Besides, she had been too mutinous to follow Peter's example and hire a costume, and an ancient long silk nightdress seemed to serve the purpose well, with the help of some speedy work on an out-of-date red evening dress. Nevertheless, she had eyed the result with some dissatisfaction the previous evening, until Luke solved the problem by fishing out a rather dashing scarf, which he deftly turned into a pseudo cap with a sprig of grapes attached.

'High fashion then,' he informed her. 'Looked it up in a book.'

With the long gloves apparently so essential, the outfit looked passable, although showers were forecast.

'I'm sure umbrellas were invented by then,' she said, fixing on the cap and grapes and adding an artistic ribbon she had tracked down in her meagre haberdashery supplies. 'At least for women. Not sure about men. Anyway, we can pop one in the boot.'

'I think Sheridan had something to do with popularizing umbrellas for men, but I doubt that ran to fold-up National Trust brollies,' Luke observed. 'They were probably so huge that they required a servant to run alongside carrying it aloft. Just at the moment I'm out of servants.' He gave another disparaging look at the Luke Frost Famous Publisher image of pantaloons hastily improvised from grey trousers tucked into long grey socks fished out of their walking gear drawer, a flashy waistcoat and an outgrown tailcoat from his past, plus – a great find this – an ancient opera hat.

'I do not feel an up to the knocker Regency gent,' he announced nevertheless. Being Luke, he had consulted a book on Regency jargon in case it came in useful at the Gala.

'How do I rate as your bit of muslin?' she retorted.

Luke laughed. 'Bang up. Ah well, let's get it over with. At least we're allowed to take a car. I thought we might have to hire horses.'

'We could walk,' Georgia threatened him. 'The Regency folk were great walkers.'

'We'll take the car and tell them it's a landau.'

Dunham itself consisted of little more than a pub and a few cottages on the Canterbury to Ashford road with farms and farmland stretching into the hinterland. Just past them Georgia spotted the lane that led only to Stourdens, and she began to feel more optimistic. The late June sun was shining, albeit weakly, the trees and meadows were flaunting their summer green glory, and rural calm seemed to prevail. From what Dora had told them, she reasoned that there would be enough diversions at this Gala not to become too heavily embroiled in emotional discussions with Elena. They might even escape the Clackingtons, once Peter had satisfied his interest in the Luckhurst murder.

Beyond them the ground rose gently to hill and woodland. The lane crossed the railway line and led on to the end of the tarmacked roadway and the beginning of Stourdens' drive. Georgia's optimism began to fade as they drove along it. The gravel needed weeding, and rhododendrons and undergrowth on both sides of the path blotted out what sun there was, which made the path in front of them look forbidding. As Luke turned into the field signposted for car parking the day ahead once more felt to Georgia like a very bad idea indeed.

The house looked less dilapidated than when she had last seen it, but that was perhaps because the sun had emerged once again, at least temporarily. Closer inspection revealed that the Georgian portico was roped off to prevent the unwary from walking under it, the roof was concave in places, and there were cracks in some of the stonework. Georgia decided that as a mere outsider she rather liked the air of decayed grandeur.

Arrows pointed Gala guests through a side gate to the rear lawns and on to an extended terrace, which gave Georgia a wide view of the gathering beneath. The landscaped gardens that she remembered were covered with marquees and stalls, peopled with a mob of visitors who from here looked to be clad in some approximation of Regency dress. Georgia was impressed. The TV and film productions of Jane Austen novels must have done a good job of raising awareness of costume; bonnets were bobbing, skirts were swishing, and men uncomfortably clad in boots (or Wellingtons, which would only just have squeezed into the time period) strolled up and down in a semblance of elegance. A grey-haired thin man in rather superior boots but a peasant costume glanced up at the new arrivals, swept off his low-brimmed hat and afforded them a deep bow, which she graciously acknowledged with a curtsy. Perhaps today would not be as bad as she had feared.

It was still only 11.30, thirty minutes after the Gala had opened, and yet it looked to be in full swing. Georgia had seen Peter's car in the car park, but so far no sign of anyone they knew. Two ladies sitting at a table at the foot of the steps down to the lawns eyed her meaningfully, flourishing what looked like raffle tickets in their hands. Were raffles invented by the 1790s? Could be, because gambling and lotteries were all the fashion then. In fact what these ladies were offering proved to be programmes in the form of a fan, with a map of the grounds and attractions. Georgia gratefully dropped a contribution into the box at the ladies' side for donations in aid of local charities.

She studied the map but could see no sign of the folly Dora had mentioned, only of something named Abbot's Retreat, which she assumed must be near to it. Both Retreat and Folly would probably have been part of the Humphrey Repton design for the gardens, to form points of interest to the overall effect of 'wild untrammelled nature' so popular in the eighteenth century when Stourdens was built. She remembered seeing an attractive small garden when she last came here and wondered whether this was Abbot's Retreat. If so, she would pay a return visit today.

'Georgia!'

Peter, looking rather grand in his hired costume of breeches, frilly shirt, waistcoat and topper, was wheeling himself rapidly towards her, with a somewhat frenetic look. Perhaps this was because Elena, in a pale blue low-cut silk number (which had no business to suit her years but somehow did) was doing her best to steer him – something Georgia knew he hated. Dora and Gerald were behind them, both trying to keep up with an increasingly faster wheelchair; coupled with their Regency costumes this gave the effect of a Caucus race out of *Alice in Wonderland*. Peter needed rescuing *now*.

'I'll deal with this, Luke,' Georgia offered. 'Unless you want to get involved, you can politely fade away.'

'Done,' Luke muttered, smiling warmly as he went over to make his apologies to Peter and Elena, with a friendly wave to the Clackingtons.

'Georgia,' Dora panted as she and Gerald reached them, 'is that your dear husband? Where is he off to?' Not waiting for an answer, she continued, 'You simply must come to meet Laura and Roy.'

'Roy?' Georgia asked.

'Laura's husband,' Gerald explained. 'A good chap. They've agreed to take us round Abbot's Folly. Officially it's off bounds today, but they'll open it for us.'

'There they are,' shrieked Dora, pointing to four people just emerging from the house.

If ever a group's body language was crying out not to be interrupted, this one's was, Georgia thought in dismay. There was an elegant woman in her fifties clad in a classical-style flimsy white dress with red spots, with a matching red handkerchief shawl round her neck, who seemed on the verge of tears; the red-cheeked man at her side in frock coat and hessian boots, presumably Roy, looked about to go off pop; and the younger couple in their twenties – a fair-haired girl who was clearly their daughter, and a dark saturnine-looking young man who held possessively on to her – looked respectively scared and furious. Nevertheless, Dora sailed blithely up to them in her flowing lilac muslin gown. Gerald at least had the decency to hang back on the grass with Georgia, Peter and Elena.

'Laura darling,' Dora cried. 'So good of you to agree to our little tour. Here we all are, ready for our treat. Marsh and Daughter are simply longing to see Abbot's Folly.' She turned round to beckon to them, but fortunately Peter's wheelchair gave them every excuse to remain where they were. 'They're simply fascinated by the murder,' Dora explained to her friend, 'and I told them you might show us your Jane collection as an extra special treat.' She beamed.

For a moment it seemed to Georgia as if someone had punched the Pause button and the screen had frozen. All four remained still, emotion raw on their faces. Reluctant they might be, but this seemed an extreme reaction.

Roy was the first to pull himself together. 'Glad to do so sometime. Very glad.'

Dora obviously wasn't good at reading subtext because she tapped Roy playfully on the shoulder. 'Now, you naughty man. Don't tease us. We know you're waiting until the announcement this afternoon to talk about it, but for old friends you can surely make an exception.'

Even Elena looked doubtful at this obviously unwelcome proposal, and Georgia would have quietly melted away into the crowd at this point if it wasn't for Peter. He, typically, backed Dora up. 'Just a quick peep,' he called out blandly. 'Can I get the wheelchair into this folly of yours?'

Georgia knew perfectly well that when he wanted to Peter could usually get in virtually anywhere and so had only raised the issue as a polite blackmail. Laura made what was clearly a supreme effort, as years of ingrained social politeness came to her aid.

'Of course you may see Abbot's Folly, and there's room for the wheelchair. There's a ramp somewhere,' she managed to say. 'Jennifer – Tim, I wonder if you'd do the honours and escort Dora's friends there?'

Georgia could read the dismay on their faces, and she blenched.

'I hope you'll excuse me,' Laura continued, 'but I have to see to the catering, so I can't take you myself. Roy . . .' She looked in appeal at her husband, and – reluctantly it seemed to Georgia – he followed Laura back into the house, leaving them with Tim and Jennifer.

Georgia was horrified at the way the issue had been forced, and she was also puzzled. Putting on an event of this size was a lot of work, and this one, with its Georgian buffet luncheon and its dancing and fencing displays, as well as other entertainments, was a massive undertaking. Even so, it seemed to her that Laura Fettis had shown more distress than overwork would explain, although her family did not seem to share the same emotion: they had looked angry and even fearful rather than upset. This was clearly a family at loggerheads, and whatever had happened had resulted in a heated discussion of some sort.

Whatever their problem, Tim took skilful command. 'Let's go.' He even managed to look enthusiastic about the prospect. 'You OK with that, Jen?'

'Yes, I'll just get the key.'

Jennifer seemed glad of the excuse to leave them while she dashed back into the house, and Tim jumped down to the lawn to join the folly party. Dora, apparently oblivious to the trouble they were causing, hurried down the steps and gaily chattered on. 'Of course, dear Jane Austen visited Stourdens frequently, and she must have known Abbot's Folly and the Retreat. That's the name of the garden that Laura has so beautifully restored. Stourdens, according to the records, was lying empty when

Edward Austen, later Knight – Jane Austen's brother, of course – first moved to Godmersham Park. The third baronet had just died, and the title went to a brother who disliked Stourdens – dear me, how *could* he? – but then he died, and his son, the fifth baronet, and widow left it some years before they moved here. That's why there are no references to Stourdens in Jane's surviving early correspondence. After the Great Tragedy, she might not have wished to visit it . . .'

Dora rattled on infuriatingly as they waited for Jennifer to return. Eventually she did so, looking more composed, and Tim led the party off with a distinct air of 'let's get it over with'. Grim determination had replaced his initial burst of social welcome.

Someone had to break the silence that fell as they followed in Jennifer and Tim's footsteps, however, and it might as well be her, Georgia thought. 'I notice Abbot's Folly doesn't seem to appear on the plan of the garden we've been given,' she said.

'It's closed to the general public, that's why. We can't afford the insurance,' Jennifer said, turning round to explain. 'We will in due course, once—'

'When all the excitement begins,' Dora finished for her mysteriously, 'but I can tell that—'

'Not till after four o'clock,' Tim reminded her pleasantly. He had one of those bland faces that could produce emotions smoothly as required, Georgia thought. He would make a good politician.

'Oh, of course,' Dora agreed hastily. 'My lips are sealed.' To prove the point she placed a forefinger over them.

'We do have plans for Stourdens.' Tim relented a little. 'You'll see in the programme that Laura will be making an announcement this afternoon. Press, TV, you name it.'

Georgia noticed that Jennifer remained silent, which reinforced her feeling that all was not well with the Fettis family.

Dora seemed about to let forth again, but Tim forestalled her. 'The folly is on the far side of Abbot's Retreat, which we're just coming to.'

Georgia recognized from her previous visit where she was now, as the path left the main lawns and she could see the garden on the right. As they reached its gateway in the red-brick wall she could glimpse the small sunken garden that she remembered. It had a mock cloister round three of its walls, mostly covered in roses, and a spectacular fountain in the midst of a central flower bed with roses and lupins. At the far end was an arbour watched over by stone angels. There had been a peace and delight about this garden, and she would certainly come back to it alone later today, when she didn't have her mind on either follies or Elena.

'Who was this Abbot?' Elena asked.

'The youngest brother of the third baronet,' Tim replied. 'He was eccentric to say the least. He never married, lived here with his brother's family and died in 1790 not long before the third baronet died. The story goes that he was too mad even to be given that sinecure for younger sons, becoming a parish priest. Result: he called himself an abbot, built his folly and holed himself up here.'

'It would be nice to think,' Jennifer chipped in, clearly with some effort, 'that Stourdens inspired the gothic Northanger Abbey in Jane Austen's novel, but we don't have evidence to that effect. So far as we know no priory or abbey has ever existed on the site.'

'If one did,' Tim joked, 'it surely wouldn't be a monstrosity like this, would it?'

Georgia could see his point as they reached the folly. She thought it more of a fantasy than a monstrosity though. It was a stone building, with a large tower on either side at the rear and a forest of smaller turrets shielding a central domed roof. Overall, the effect was gothic in the extreme. The centre of the building with its domed roof might on its own have been imposing, but with the army of protecting turrets it looked more like a child's witch house than one in which any self-respecting abbot would want to immerse himself. The gothic effect was made worse by the fact that the building was surrounded by tall trees looming so close that they seemed to form an aggressive guard of their own.

Tim managed to find the ramp and beckoned them inside the folly. Georgia assumed that Peter would be eager to shoot in first, but for some reason he was hesitating, letting Dora,

Elena and Gerald precede him. As he followed them, he turned his head to call out sharply: 'Georgia!'

There was a warning tone in his voice, but it was too late. As she went in, a wave of nausea and dizziness swept over her, which was all too familiar. 'Fingerprints on time' was the name she and Peter had given to the sixth sense they shared, which kicked in usually where violence or injustice had taken place, both of which were present here. Abbot's Folly reeked with them. The atmosphere felt dank and evil. It would be easy to claim that this was sheer imagination, she thought, or that these 'fingerprints' had no such cause, but for Marsh & Daughter they sparked off the cases they investigated. This initial instinctive reaction was an unwelcome pivot, although from then on facts would take over in their investigations.

There were fingerprints here. No doubt about that. Max Tanner had been convicted for Robert Luckhurst's murder, but he had maintained he was innocent. A miscarriage of justice? She'd talk it over with Peter later, when she had recovered from the nausea that still overwhelmed her.

'Darling, you don't look well. What's wrong?' Elena said anxiously, fluttering around her as they stood in the entrance hall to the folly.

'Nothing,' Georgia muttered. 'Hunger pains, I expect.' She forced a laugh, but Elena did not let it drop.

'You were always a nervous child. Come outside,' she urged.

'No,' Georgia replied. 'I'll be fine.' She wanted to see how badly Peter was affected, but he was following Tim and the Clackingtons into the room on their right.

'Did Jane Austen know this folly?' she managed to ask Jennifer. This would be safe ground, for the girl was still exhibiting all the signs of wanting to be a hundred miles away. Change the subject, get away from murder, she thought, and this feeling will pass. Think about Jane, talk about Jane, forget fingerprints. And yet she couldn't, because the dizziness was clogging her mind. To her horror she realized she was clinging to Elena's arm as they followed the others.

'Robert Luckhurst's study,' Tim told them.

Despite herself, Georgia was impressed. Mahogany bookcases lined the three straight walls of this oddly shaped room, and where the semicircular entrance hall arched into the study, there were tables, cupboards and office equipment. The central desk had a large computer on it, and yet nothing in this room struck a false note. She felt Jane Austen could stroll in at any moment and feel at home.

Dora clapped in enthusiasm. 'Oh *look*,' she said, 'the very place where Robert must have communed with dear Jane. Now where, oh where, is your Austen collection kept, Jennifer?'

Jennifer was clearly unwilling to talk on the subject, because she simply replied that she did not know. Georgia took on the task of chatting to Dora to prevent her pushing the question further – at least it was a distraction from the nausea.

'Are you sure you're all right?' Elena whispered.

'I'll be fine,' Georgia repeated shakily. 'I can't miss this.'

She could do so all too easily, and from what she could see of Peter's expression he was suffering the same reaction as she was, although he was better at hiding it.

'Is this the room where Luckhurst was killed?' he asked Tim.

'Yes, as far as I can gather,' Tim said. 'Robert did his duty in greeting the classic-car owners in front of the main house, then retreated back here, probably because he'd been fore-warned about the protest group being on its way. Max Tanner seized his chance and barged in here, where they talked – or argued – for ten minutes or so until they heard the protest group outside, sounding pretty threatening. Max went out into the entrance hall, but the protest group pushed past him, and there was a confrontation with Luckhurst in the doorway here. Eventually, Tom Miller agreed to leave, after Robert said he would give the matter more thought. Well, according to Miller he did leave. According to Tanner, he left as well. The jury decided otherwise – that Tanner stayed behind, shot Robert Luckhurst and then went back to the pub.'

'No doubt that it was Tanner's gun?'

'None. It was found back at the Edgar Arms.'

'Didn't he know the protest march was going to take place?'

'Yes, he did. He just mistimed it.'

'Would anyone in Dunham still remember it?' Georgia managed to ask through another wave of nausea.

'Of course they do,' Jennifer said uneasily. 'They've long memories, and they brood. Even when Mum bought Stourdens and told them about the path being OK for them to use, they went on foul-mouthing her.'

'But if Tanner was convicted, why did the issue remain?'

'I don't know. That happens in small communities. Which is why Tim and I have made a point of making sure Dunham is included in any plans, but—'

'Jen,' Tim said quietly.

She stopped abruptly. 'Sorry.'

Jennifer had clearly been on the point of disclosing something about this famous Stourdens plan, but why did she take the matter so seriously? Georgia wondered. Was she scared of Tim? He seemed to have identified himself with the family, but was that because of his relationship with Jennifer or because he was a consultant of some sort?

'Did Amelia Luckhurst believe Tanner guilty?' Peter asked Jennifer.

'I've no idea. You'd have to ask Mum or Dad.' Jennifer cast an uneasy look round the room and was clearly eager to leave.

Then Dora's voice rang out – but from behind them on the far side of the entrance hall. 'Oh, *look!*' she cried.

Taken by surprise when Tim realized Dora was no longer with them, he let out one furious expletive before hurrying to join her in the room opposite, leaving them to follow in his wake.

Elena sighed. 'Oh dear,' she whispered to Georgia. 'Dora really does go too far sometimes.'

This room was smaller than the study and different in style. It had less natural light, but was painted pale green to offset that disadvantage, and it was simply furnished with a sofa and three armchairs, together with several beautiful small tables.

'Not here, please,' Tim was saying to Dora, almost pleading. 'You really must leave.'

'But the door was open.' Dora looked hurt. 'I only had to push it a little way. I won't do any harm, will I?'

'No,' Peter said, before Tim could answer her.

Dora took this as encouragement. 'Just look at them, Peter,' she said innocently. 'Aren't they beautiful?' She was pointing at the wall to Georgia's right. Georgia caught her breath as she looked at the three paintings that hung there. There were two charming watercolours, one of a man, and the other of a young woman. Between them was an oil painting of a man in Nelsonian naval uniform in heroic pose against a background of a stormy sea. It was badly in need of cleaning, but it was still striking, although it was the watercolours that held Georgia's attention. Not, she thought, by the same artist, and yet the two seemed linked, partly through the fact that the young woman was gazing straight across to the companion piece, whose subject was returning the look with great tenderness. Looking at the oil painting carefully, she was almost sure it was the same young man in both.

'Aren't they gorgeous?' Dora trilled at Georgia's side. 'This one is Jane herself.' The young woman was clad in a long white dress with a blue shawl around her shoulders, and she was sitting in a garden, perhaps even Abbot's Retreat, judging by the cloister and roses around her. She was seated, but the book in her lap lay disregarded as she looked lovingly outwards. 'It's painted by her sister Cassandra,' Dora added.

Jennifer and Tim's faces were perfectly blank, and neither of them confirmed or denied it. That would only goad Peter onwards, Georgia thought. Sure enough he asked: 'Who's the naval captain in the middle, Tim?'

For a moment Georgia thought Tim would not reply, but at last he said, 'We think it's a John Opie portrait. It's of a Captain William Harker, and no, you won't have heard of him.'

'The watercolour is also of him,' Dora added eagerly, 'and it is by *Jane herself*. She was talented at drawing – her brother Henry testified to that.'

If this was correct, Georgia knew these watercolours were something remarkable indeed. Virtually nothing remained of Jane Austen's own artistic work, and there were hardly any drawings or other likenesses of the novelist, only one or two by her sister Cassandra. And here might be a third. If so, it was of major importance.

'You two lovebirds can tell us much more, I'm sure,' Dora said archly to Jennifer and Tim. 'You have the collection here – the room at the rear?'

Tim stiffened. 'I'm afraid there's no time for that now.'

'Just a peep,' Dora said, inching past him to the door.

This time she had gone too far. 'No,' Jennifer said flatly, visibly trembling with either fear or fury. 'The room is locked, and we have to go. Don't we, Tim?'

'Sorry, but yes.' Tim positioned himself in the entrance hall and in front of the third room, as if daring Dora to try the doorknob.

He and Jennifer then almost bundled the five of them out of the folly – to Georgia's relief, interesting though the portraits were. Thankfully, once she was outside in the fresh air the nausea began to pass, but as she turned to speak to Tim and Jennifer, she realized they had locked up and were already hurrying along the path back to the house.

THREE

G eorgia felt numb as she watched Tim and Jennifer disappearing and was momentarily unable to cope with both Elena and the after-effects of the fingerprints. She tackled the latter first. Dora was chattering avidly to Elena, as though nothing had happened, so Georgia took the opportunity to whisper to Peter: 'You felt it?'

'Yes.'

'Me too.'

She was not able to say anything more as she could see Elena had her eye on her and her intention was obvious. She would want to find out what was going on: why was Georgia feeling sick? Was she pregnant? No, she wasn't, and Georgia couldn't bear the thought of being questioned. It was time to find Luke, and quickly. 'Will you be OK?' she asked Peter.

'You mean OK with Elena?' he queried drily. 'Yes, Georgia, I will be. We were married for over twenty years. I can manage an hour or two more of her company.'

'If it's only that,' she replied without thinking. She could have kicked herself, as he looked at her steadily, almost reproachfully.

'I know there's something on her mind, Georgia. I suspect she wants to come home.'

Her mouth went dry as the shock bore into her. 'To Haden Shaw?'

'To Kent at least. How would you feel about that?'

'Numb.'

He sighed. 'Go and find Luke, Georgia.'

He was obviously gently reminding her that she had a partner and that he was a grown man with his own decisions to take. 'Damn, damn, damn,' she said softly to herself. All this and fingerprints as well. She brightly excused herself to Elena and hurried away back to the mass of people surging around book-stalls, Georgian flower stalls, stalls where one could sign up for everything under the sun.

But there was no Luke to be seen. With lunchtime fast approaching she made her way to the two catering tents. Still feeling somewhat sick, she decided that a cold drink would be a good idea. One tent was offering snacks, advertising Jane Austen's toasted cheese and other delicacies. The other one went further with a Jane Austen buffet. Both had bars, so she chose the latter. The Jane Austen wines she would leave until Luke appeared, but a barley water seemed a good idea. She remembered too late that Elena used to make her drink it when she was a child, but luckily it still proved comforting, and she found herself a seat near the entrance to watch the crowds go by. By now it seemed normal to see people wandering around in Regency dress – or near equivalent – and she felt more relaxed about her own modest contribution, even though many far more sophisticated outfits were whisking past her.

At last she spotted Luke, looking rather dashing in his outgrown tailcoat. He was not alone, however. To her surprise she could see Luke's son Mark together with his American wife, Jill, and baby Rosa. They had moved back from the States to a Victorian terraced house in Canterbury in March, three months after Rosa had been born. Georgia got on well with Mark, but Jill was harder to fathom out. After Washington DC she might be having a hard time adjusting to Kentish life, but if so she gave no sign of it, and she had brushed aside Georgia's well-intentioned efforts to help. Seven-month-old

Rosa was a delight, although Georgia was not sure she liked
the title step-grandmother – especially as she was still clinging
to her own thirties and certainly did not rank as highly in the
pecking order as Jill's own formidable all-singing, all-dancing,
infuriatingly capable mother, Pat. The Incomparable Pat had
only just flown back to the States after a month's stay.

Today, Jill could pass for one of Mr Bingley's haughty
sisters, Georgia decided, taking advantage of her as yet unnoticed position to cast a critical eye on her new family. Mark
was a younger edition of Luke, Jill was moving as gracefully
as if born into the Regency *ton*, and in her pushchair Rosa
seemed to be enjoying her brush with history. For a moment
Georgia thought of the child she would never have herself,
then firmly disciplined herself. That disappointment was in
the past. Think ahead.

'Hi!' she called, walking over to join them.

'Look who I ran into,' Luke said, obviously delighted.
'Serendipity, eh?'

In the crush Georgia saw that he was with a larger group
than she had realized. There were two youngish men with him
– one in his early thirties with black curly hair and lively eyes,
who introduced himself as Jake Halliday; the other, who looked
a year or two older and much more serious, announced himself
as Philip Faring. Neither of them looked as if they were enthusiastic about galas, however.

'I met Jill in the States,' Philip explained, 'and lo and behold
she turns up in Canterbury. Luke says that you've just been
to see Abbot's Folly. How did it go?'

'Weird building but interesting. My father and I wanted to
see where Robert Luckhurst was killed in 1985.'

Philip looked somewhat surprised, not unnaturally, Georgia
supposed.

'My step-ma is part of a crime investigating team, Marsh
& Daughter,' Mark explained. 'Dad publishes their books.'

The name Philip Faring had run a faint bell in Georgia's
mind, and she realized why. 'You write literary biographies,
don't you?' she asked Philip. 'I've read your book on
eighteenth-century novelists. Very good.'

He muttered a thank-you, and Jake laughed. 'Not much

good at self-publicity is Philip. He wouldn't last two minutes in the film world.'

'Is that your line?' Georgia asked, then made a mental leap. 'Is that the reason you're here?'

'Our lips are sealed—'

'Until four o'clock?' Georgia laughed. The great event was billed on the programme simply as 'Speech by Mrs Laura Fettis'.

'You got it.'

'So let me guess. You're working on a Jane Austen theme?'

Jake's glance at Philip confirmed this – and also that they were probably an item in their private lives as well. 'Ask Tim Wilson,' he answered lightly.

'Not the Fettises?' Georgia was surprised – or was she? Tim seemed to be nicely in control, even if Laura was actually the owner of Stourdens. Jake shrugged. 'Tim will be in the family soon enough, and he's got a PR background. He's getting things moving here to secure Stourdens' future.'

'You don't sound as though that's a good thing.' Georgia was curious.

'On the contrary. It's a very good thing, isn't it, Phil?'

'Yes.' Philip seemed so tense that Georgia became even more puzzled. Maybe it was just that they did not get on with Tim Wilson. Jake and Philip seemed straightforward enough, but Tim was someone with whom she would not want to fall out.

Philip ostentatiously looked at his watch. 'Time to see Laura, Jake? Details to discuss,' he added to them deprecatingly. 'Sorry, we'd better be off.'

'Was it something I said?' Georgia commented ruefully, watching them disappear with haste.

Jill took her seriously. 'I don't think so, Georgia,' she said kindly. 'Phil gets easily wound up. I've known him for years. He was in the States on a temporary assignment, but now he's back at Sandwich – the University,' she added in case Georgia had missed the point that Phil was an important academic.

'Jake and Phil seem remarkably reticent,' Luke said as Jill and Mark then moved away. 'Not usually the case with authors and film directors. I wonder if Phil's hunting for a new publisher?'

'You always wonder that.' Georgia laughed. 'They're prob-ably not very chatty simply because of this big announcement coming up. Perhaps Phil has a new book on Jane Austen to announce. I'm surprised he hasn't cashed in on her earlier. She's been high profile for donkey's years.'

'It's more likely to be the launch of this collection you told me about,' Luke said. 'The Fettises might not have had the know-how or the contacts, but Tim Wilson obviously has.'

'Especially as he's hooked up to Jennifer Fettis.'

'Engaged is the more usual word,' Luke observed. 'Don't you take to him?'

'Pleasant enough, but on a summer's day at a show like this Jack the Ripper might look an attractive proposition.'

'How about lunch? Food might make you less critical.'

She laughed. 'Good idea.'

There was a long queue at the main-course buffet table in the dinner tent. Georgia could see Jennifer Fettis keeping an overall eye on what was going on, but there was no sign of the Fettis party yet. Pity, they were missing something, Georgia thought. Interesting dishes bore tempting labels including pork frigasy, haricot mutton, rolled salmon, stewed cucumbers, salmagundi, hunting pudding and salmon pye. The queue was moving amazingly quickly, considering the mind-boggling choice. Several women were serving, but one was clearly in charge, a rough complexioned, determined-looking woman of about forty-five or fifty, whom she heard addressed as Barbara.

'Difficult to know what to try,' Georgia remarked lightly to the woman behind her in the queue. In her sixties, a Regency high-waisted clinging dress should not have been first choice for her short and rather dumpy figure. Her face was a strong one, however, which suggested that clothes were of little importance to her life.

'Have the potted shrimps,' she advised Georgia. 'Jane Austen must have gobbled them up, because the Medway estuary area was famous for its pink and brown shrimps in her time. To coin a phrase, people came from far and wide.'

'That was before they had to cope with the M25,' Georgia joked.

'I managed it today.'

That seemed to end the conversation. Georgia decided on the pork frigasy, Luke chose the haricot mutton and then they attempted to get near the bar for a brave attempt to buy two drinks. Jane Austen's orange wine was being so strongly pushed by the barman that she didn't have the heart to choose anything else, while Luke went for Mr Knightley's spruce beer. The barman was a young chap in his twenties, who – she worked out from the shouts across from the food counter – was called Craig and he was Barbara's son. The family was doing a good job, Georgia decided, because once she and Luke had found themselves somewhere to sit outside on the grass, the food proved to be as delicious as it looked, and the wine too was worthy of Miss Austen's name.

Perhaps with the help of the wine, the afternoon seemed to pass quickly, even though the magic hour of four o'clock loomed large in her mind. Nevertheless, she found herself playing an elegant game of shuttlecock with Luke, Mark and Jill, while Elena and Peter looked after Rosa. The men had a distinct advantage, owing to their wearing trousers as opposed to long skirts, but Jill turned out to be a superb player (naturally) and she and Georgia won comfortably. For the first time, Georgia felt at ease with her stepdaughter-in-law, and her hopes grew of welding the four of them into a contented family group – five with Peter, and if the worst happened six with Elena. She pushed that thought away. She couldn't cope with it yet.

Luke then swept her off into the Sir Roger de Coverley, the only country dance that Georgia knew. She enjoyed stripping the willow – or threading the needle as the Dancing Master termed it – followed by a cotillion, and she realized the day was turning out much better than she could have hoped . . . save, she thought uneasily, for the fingerprints. She had a moment of fear that the nausea would return, but it didn't, and she fixed her mind on what was going on around her. She noticed the woman who had been behind her in the food queue dancing nimbly with someone whose face, or rather costume, she recognized as the peasant who had bowed to her when they had first arrived.

'This is a very egalitarian cotillion,' she joked to Luke. 'Fancy letting peasants in.'

Joke over, the uneasiness returned as Luke pointed out that it was getting near to four o'clock. She had caught glimpses of Roy, Tim and Jennifer at intervals, but not of Laura. What was she worrying about? she asked herself. The anxiety that she had noticed in the Fettis family or the fingerprints? The latter had no relevance to the future of Stourdens, if that was to be the subject of the speech. They belonged to the past not to the future. She could see microphones and cameras installed on the terrace, and people were beginning to gather there.

She and Luke went over to join Peter and Elena just as the magic hour struck, but if she was expecting a simultaneous dramatic entrance by Laura and her family, she was disappointed. Instead Tim appeared, but went back into the house without making any public statement. Then nothing. As the minutes passed, it became clear that this was not merely a late arrival, and a ripple of restlessness spread through the crowd. Finally, the tall figure of Roy Fettis appeared from the door of the house, but there was no Laura, no Jennifer and no Tim. Just what was going on?

Roy looked confused and ill at ease, and he had to clear his throat several times before he managed to speak. Something was wrong, and the crowd realized it as the level of murmuring rose. At last he said simply, to Georgia's astonishment, 'My wife is not well enough to speak to you this afternoon. She begs that you will excuse her until a later date.' With that, before he could be questioned, he almost scuttled back into the house. The silence of surprise was followed by more murmurs and then by raised voices as people began drifting back towards the refreshment tents.

'I don't believe it,' Luke said crossly. 'What a way to do it. Why on earth couldn't he read her speech if she's ill?'

'Something must have happened.' Peter frowned. 'Interesting. How do we find out? The Clackingtons might know, but I can't see them. Or Philip and Jake. Jill might have heard something. I know it's nothing to do with Bob Luckhurst's death, but it's intriguing, since we know today is all about Jane Austen.'

'Tea,' Luke said firmly. 'The only solution.'

'Splendid,' Elena said. 'Peter?'

'Why not? Let's go.'

Georgia demurred. Now that she had stopped dancing, a headache was beginning to rage, and a stuffy tea tent was not the answer. She clutched at the excuse that there was still Abbot's Retreat to see. She would go nowhere near the folly, but the garden would be safe. No fingerprints there. In the Retreat she could be on her own, away from the Clackingtons, away from Elena – and away from any immediate obligation to talk. Just rest for a while.

Her hopes were dashed. Elena had either overheard her quiet few words of explanation to Luke, or had simply followed her. 'I'll come too, darling,' she said happily as she caught Georgia up.

Georgia's heart sank. She could hardly say no, although it was all too clear that Elena was aching for a mother-to-daughter chat. Was Georgia up to coping with one? No, especially if the question Elena wanted to ask was whether she was pregnant or not. Or maybe she was wrong. Perhaps Elena wouldn't be concentrating on Georgia's life but her own. She would be eager to discuss the matter of her returning to Kent to live.

Georgia braced herself. 'That would be nice,' she said.

Elena was shorter than she was, and slenderer, and years of living in France had given her a poise and sophistication that Georgia felt today at least she could not begin to match. And yet for all that elegance and for all her self-centredness, Elena had an inner fragility that Georgia knew she could no longer ignore. It was Elena who was the child now.

'Georgia, there's something I want—' Elena began as she walked beside her.

'To talk about your return to Kent? That's splendid. Where are you thinking of settling?' Georgia asked, with as much enthusiasm as she could muster.

Elena looked taken aback. 'Probably in Canterbury. I have friends there.'

How to interpret that? Did Elena mean male friends? If so, that would lift the burden from Peter. Or would it make it worse? Georgia wondered. She had a terrible suspicion that the answer to that was yes, but she could not battle with the implications. Think of Abbot's Retreat instead, Georgia told herself. After all, the 'abbot' must have gone there for its peace and quiet, to get away from his own problems.

'Of course,' Elena was saying, 'I'd have to have a garden.'

A garden. Georgia remembered Elena and her garden. Remembered herself as a child, sitting on the grass playing while Elena pruned roses, weeded, tended her sweet peas – they were her favourite flower. Could one recreate that peace? Did she want to help Elena do so? Did she seek it herself?

As they reached the gate into Abbot's Retreat, Georgia could hear the tinkling water of the fountain, even smell the roses blooming in their peaceful home.

'Isn't it lovely?' Elena whispered behind her.

'Lovely,' Georgia rejoined automatically as she drank in her first complete sight of the garden. The cloisters, the statues, the roses, the petals by the fountain – and what was that? Scattered rose petals? No, more. Someone was sprawled there, someone wearing a white dress with red spots, someone whose head was buried in the red petals that spilled out across the stone path.

Only, now she could see that they weren't rose petals. It was blood.

FOUR

This couldn't be happening. This must surely be some costume drama into which she had been unwillingly cast. Her role? Reluctant witness. The person who found the body. Georgia shuddered. Clad as she was, it felt wrong to be sitting silently on the terrace of Stourdens at a Regency event waiting for the all too real twenty-first century police to interview her for the second time. She tried to imagine what it must be like for the police with three or four hundred possible witnesses to record and interview, but gave up the attempt. She could only think of Abbot's Retreat, of Elena's screams and of herself, stricken to frozen horror.

Her automatic reaction had been to rush to the fountain to see

if what she dreaded was true. It was. There had been no doubt
that Laura Fettis was dead, probably shot in the head. Then the
screaming had begun, as Elena had unwisely followed her. People
would be gathering, and Georgia had braced herself for a supreme
effort. Ensure Laura was no longer alive – no doubt there, but
a ghastly task. Ring for the police. Keep everyone at bay to
maintain the scene as free of contamination as possible.
Fortunately, one of the early spectators to arrive had known what
was needed and taken that task on. Elena had been shepherded
away, and Georgia had waited for the police. The minutes had
dragged by as she tried to concentrate on anything other than
what she could see. Her mother – was someone looking after
her? But it was hopeless, for she could not drag her thoughts
away for more than a moment from Laura Fettis's terrible end.

Now it was gone six o'clock. Luke was with her, as were
Peter and Elena. Every so often on the lawns, or passing to
and fro from the house, Georgia glimpsed someone she recognized. Naturally, there was no sign of Roy Fettis or Jennifer,
but every so often she saw a haggard-looking Tim trying to
cope with the one PR job he could never have dreamed of
being his responsibility. Dora seemed to be in perpetual motion,
alternately coming to join Elena and trying to cope with Gerald,
who was sitting at the former entrance table and looking as
dazed as though he, not Roy, were the bereaved husband. Dora,
remarkably, was far from being hysterical herself and was
managing Elena's distress much better than Georgia could.
She could see Philip and Jake were still around, and she
recognized a few other faces as they flitted past her on the
lawns or moved in and out of her sight like characters in a
silent movie. Overall, however, the number of guests was
quickly diminishing as the police checked them off.

By the time Georgia had left Abbot's Retreat, the cordon tape
was already in place and incident vans had parked by the side
of the house. The SIO from Kent Police Stour Area was a DI
Diane Newton, whom she had not met before, but the good
news was that Chief Superintendent Mike Gilroy had arrived.
She had supposed that Peter had rung him, but it seemed not.

'Too much of a coincidence,' Mike had explained, when he
came over to speak to them. 'First you ring about the Luckhurst

murder, Peter, and twenty-four hours later there's another one in virtually the same place. Sure you haven't turned to murder in your old age?'

'The deaths are twenty-five years apart,' Peter pointed out.

'Linked, do you think?'

'I can't see how – not yet.'

'Which means you intend to look into it. Our job, Peter,' Mike said in warning.

'Of course,' Peter promptly agreed. 'However, the fact that this is a day devoted to Jane Austen and—'

'Thus useful to gain access for those intent on killing,' Mike cut him off. 'Just as Tanner took advantage of the protest march in 1985. But let me point out that Robert Luckhurst's murder was due to revenge plus possible personal reasons. Jane Austen never got a look-in.'

'Nevertheless, today she's upgraded to star status as far as Stourdens is concerned,' Peter commented. 'Laura Fettis was murdered before she could make her speech, which almost certainly would have involved Jane Austen's connections with Stourdens and the memorabilia held by the family. There seemed to be some family distress about the matter.'

Mike looked interested. 'Do you smell a motive?'

'I can't see how there could be, but it's easily settled. The husband and daughter are going to know what Laura intended to announce. I expect you've heard that she didn't appear as planned.' When Mike nodded, he added, 'There was certainly something troubling them all in a big way this morning.'

'I'll pass that on right away.' Mike frowned. 'This must have been a big shock for you, Georgia, and for Mrs Congreve.'

Who? Georgia wondered – then realized. Elena, of course, who was sitting on a garden chair with Peter's arm round her. She was very white, and her pale blue dress emphasized it. All the pretensions and artistry that her face usually presented had vanished.

'I'm told DI Newton has taken your statement, Georgia, but I'd like to know first-hand what made you walk over to the garden,' Mike continued. 'And you too, Mrs Congreve,' he added, turning to Elena.

Georgia answered him. 'It seemed a good idea – while

everyone else was rushing off to tea after the let-down over Mrs Fettis's speech. Abbot's Retreat isn't the sort of place to appreciate with a lot of other people around. I had some crazy idea about walking in a garden where Jane Austen must have walked, and my mother –' she was surprised to realize that the word was coming more naturally to her now – 'decided to come with me.'

'Yes,' Elena faltered. 'I'm only here for a short visit, and I thought it would be nice.' Tears welled up again, and Peter put his arm round her once more.

'Have you any idea why Laura Fettis should have gone there, Georgia?' Mike asked quickly. 'I'm told she was ill all day, so it seems odd to decide to go for a walk.'

'I didn't know her, Mike. I saw her this morning, and it's true she didn't look well, so I agree it was odd.'

'Her husband says she was lying down in the bedroom when he last saw her about three o'clock, and that she told him then she wouldn't make her appearance at four. But he went to double-check at about five to four only to find no one there. He and his daughter quickly checked the house, but there was no sign of her, so he went ahead shortly after four o'clock, while his daughter checked the house again. What did he actually say in this announcement, Peter?'

'That there wouldn't be one until a later date.'

'So the family might have already known she was dead?' Mike said.

'Your job, Mike,' Peter said mildly. 'I take it you don't know exactly when she died yet?'

'We do. Roughly, anyway.' Mike looked at his notes. 'A Mrs Dora Clackington seems to have been the last person to see Mrs Fettis alive when she looked in on her just before three thirty to wish her luck for the big speech. She was in a downstairs room by then and told Mrs Clackington that she was too ill to make the speech.'

'No more?'

'No. Probably wanted to get rid of the woman. Can't blame her. Have you talked to her?'

'I'm staying with her,' Elena put in somewhat reproachfully.

Mike grinned. 'Don't worry. I don't see Mrs Clackington wielding a gun, silencer or not. Do you?'

'No.' Elena managed a weak smile in response.

'Was the gun still around?' Peter asked. 'Georgia said she didn't see one.'

'No. And before you ask if it was the same one used in 1985, I can't say yet. The 1985 handgun was a Beretta, found, as I'm sure you know, at the Edgar Arms where Max Tanner was the landlord.'

'Thank you, yes,' Peter replied calmly. 'Of course,' he added, 'Luckhurst's murder was an open and shut case, so I suppose there wasn't a large-scale investigation.'

A steely glare from Mike. 'From what I read about it, that wasn't called for. It came down to Tanner or the leader of the protest march, one Tom Miller.'

'Any idea what happened to Tanner?'

Mike sighed. 'Knowing you, Peter, I had it checked out. I was going to ring you on Monday. Released in 2000, not re-offended. No record of him since, under that name or any other. We had no reason to keep tabs on him, and DNA was in its infancy. His prints were on the gun. So was his DNA.'

'As they both could well have been, quite innocently. So there's no clue as to whether he's still in this area?'

'None.'

'I gather Amelia Luckhurst—'

A look from Mike quelled even Peter, but all Mike said was, 'Luckhurst will have to wait. I have to get back to that poor woman's murder. Any detail you remember that you haven't yet told Newton, tell her right away. I have a feeling this one's going to be tricky.'

'The tea tent still seems to be operating,' Elena said timidly after Mike had left. 'Would anyone like something to drink?'

'Yes,' Georgia replied, hardly able to believe she had said that, even though from the look on her face and the quaver in her voice it was clear that Elena needed it. Nevertheless, it seemed bizarre that tea should go on as usual in the midst of a murder investigation. On the other hand, she supposed that keeping normal life going was a sensible idea.

'I'll bring some back here,' Luke offered.

Georgia decided to go with him. Action, any action, was better than sitting on this terrace with her mind full of that red spotted dress. Luke seemed about to suggest she remained, but he refrained. Once walking on the lawns and part of the general scene, Georgia felt it easier to cope, even though her costume began to seem even more incongruous with uniformed police everywhere, not to mention the scene-suited SOCOs.

'I'll get everyone some cake as well,' she suggested. 'Eating can take one's mind off things – if that's possible today.'

'Depends on the cake,' Luke observed. 'It will need to be a good one.'

The tea tent was acting as a refuge for all those not yet given permission to leave. Luke had told her that Mark and Jill had been allowed to go because of the baby, but there were still a few children running around in their restricting Regency clothes. Luke and Georgia's presence was immediately spotted by Dora, however, who came anxiously over as they joined the queue.

'How's Elena?' she asked, although it was barely ten minutes since she'd asked the same question of Elena herself. 'I've been so busy helping the police – what a terrible ordeal for the poor darling. I'll look after her, Georgia, you can count on me.'

Georgia knew she could. There was one field in which the Dora Clackingtons of this world excelled – they knew how to fuss and cosset, and thank heavens for them. And yet she remembered that Elena had chosen to sit with Peter and herself on the terrace, not join the Clackingtons. Was that significant? Georgia pushed the thought wearily away. She could not cope with everything at once, and her mother's future was too emotional a question to deal with at present. Instead she tried to concentrate on Dora, who still seemed to be in shock.

'If there were something I could do,' Dora mourned. 'But Roy is with Jennifer, and of course I cannot intrude. The police asked me all about seeing Laura. I was the last person, it seems, except the person who . . .' Her voice trailed off, and tears followed. 'Laura said she was feeling a little better when

I saw her. How can she suddenly have been murdered in that garden less than an hour or so later?'

'Perhaps her murderer timed it for when Roy would be speaking,' Luke commented. 'And if she was feeling stronger that would explain what she was doing outside the house.'

'But why Abbot's Retreat?' Dora wailed. 'As she was downstairs I thought she was going to make the speech after all, but she said she wasn't. She was too ill. So why go out? And the family was so upset.'

'Perhaps something had happened that morning?' Georgia ventured. 'Jennifer looked very worried when she took us to Abbot's Folly.' She longed to ask whether Dora could talk about what the intended announcement was about in case that had relevance to Laura's murder, but with Dora in her present state that would be a step too far.

Dora broke down. 'Oh, I can't bear it. I really can't . . .'

Seeing her tear-blotched face and heaving shoulders, Georgia immediately felt remorseful for questioning her, but Luke was made of sterner stuff.

'How long were you with her?' he asked.

'Only five or ten minutes,' Dora sobbed. 'I could see she wasn't well. She was in the Yellow Room at the front of the house, huddled in an upright armchair, not even lying down. "Go back to bed," I told her. "Perhaps I will," she said.'

'Did anyone else know where she was, or did you tell anyone?' Georgia asked, more sharply than she meant to.

Dora looked up, and for a moment it occurred to Georgia that Dora might not be as innocent and childlike as she had assumed. 'I'm not sure. I might have mentioned it to one or two people.'

Which meant she had, Georgia thought ruefully, and couldn't remember who. To be fair, with four o'clock fast approaching it would have been natural enough to chat to all and sundry about how Laura was. Luke was at the head of the catering queue now, and Georgia had to turn her attention to the matter of orange versus almond and rose-water cake, and try her best to push away images of Laura Fettis.

She and Luke were on their way back to the terrace when Dora wrong-footed her, having insisted on accompanying them. 'Georgia,' she said earnestly, 'I do hope that dear

Elena does come to live here. She needs caring for.'

Don't we all, Georgia thought mutinously. She murmured something in response, but it was inadequate and she knew it. Soon she would have to deal with the problem of Elena, but not now, not *now*. Fortunately, Dora was approached by one of the PCs, which enabled Georgia to escape.

Back on the terrace, Luke handed out tea and cake while she joined Peter and Elena who were deep in conversation with Philip and Jake. She thought this would mean nothing was expected of her, but Jake turned to her, and she was forced to say something to them both. 'I'm so sorry,' she said. 'Did you know Laura well?' It sounded trite, but at least she was trying, she thought ruefully.

Philip looked at her as though she were speaking a foreign language, but Jake replied readily. 'Yes, we both did. She was a good friend to us.' A quick look at Philip. 'It seems crass to mention it now, but it's got to be thought of. There's a TV documentary about Stourdens which is all signed up, and Laura was very keen on it. That meant we saw a lot of her, and of course she helped Phil enormously with his book.'

So there was a book. 'Is that what Laura's announcement was about?' she asked.

'Part of it.' Jake glanced at Philip apologetically. 'It was focused on general plans for Stourdens, though.'

'Based on the Jane Austen connection?'

Neither of them answered, which was an answer in itself. Georgia tried to rescue the situation. 'Perhaps the film can go ahead in due course, even if it's postponed.'

Jake shrugged. 'Postpone is a word one doesn't use in filming. It's all booked in for late August. Sorry,' he added, 'I shouldn't have mentioned it. Shock does odd things to you, and Phil and I still can't take in what's happened. Who would want to kill Laura of all people? She was one of the most popular people I've met in a long while.'

Not with everyone, it seemed. And what, Georgia wondered, was the family situation? This morning it had not been a happy one. This was hardly the time to raise the matter though, and anyway, that was Mike's territory, not Marsh & Daughter's.

*   *   *

How could a garden as peaceful as Abbot's Retreat be reconciled with anything as frightful as Laura Fettis's murder? Georgia remembered Laura's pale, troubled face earlier that day, with the fine lines of worry etched between the delicate features. She hadn't known Laura Fettis, and yet just that one indelible image of the morning now had to be set beside the one she could never eradicate.

She left Stourdens with relief at seven thirty when they were finally given permission to go. Peter assured her that he would be all right driving home alone. He confessed that he had hastily claimed one of his turns was coming on when Elena showed signs of coming with him, and she was returning to Edgar House with the Clackingtons. Georgia knew full well that what Peter was longing to do was to return to his own house, heat up the dinner left by his carer, Margaret, and withdraw to living room or bed, whichever took his fancy. His expression told her that for today he had had enough, and that hardly surprised her. He'd been interviewed, without being in a good position to interview – always a situation guaranteed to drive him to distraction. If this had been his case, he had muttered to her – but of course it wasn't. Not even Robert Luckhurst's murder was 'his' case yet, despite those fingerprints. By tacit consent that subject had been left until Monday.

On Monday morning, therefore, it had to be faced. Georgia arrived at Haden Shaw somewhat early and prepared to tread gingerly, but she was pleasantly surprised to find that wasn't necessary. Margaret greeted her from the kitchen, and Peter was already at the computer. There were signs that he had actually breakfasted, an impressive array of reference books was piled on the desk, and Marsh & Daughter's website was on the screen.

'I've been looking back over our case,' Peter announced without preamble. So that was that. Robert Luckhurst was 'our case'. Did she mind? No, she realized. So far it had not seized her imagination, but after Laura's murder, it began to seem inevitable that Marsh & Daughter should pursue the earlier tragedy.

'I've set Cath on to the problem of tracking Max Tanner down,' he continued.

'Good.' Georgia was pleased. Cath Bone was newly married to Charlie, Georgia's cousin. She was a journalist and shared Charlie's inquisitive nature into anything that took her fancy, not only the stories she was asked to cover for her newspaper. 'Useful income,' she said practically, and, put that way, Marsh & Daughter had had no hesitation in hiring her services when something suitable came up. This seemed an ideal opportunity.

'Isn't it premature though?' she asked.

'The fingerprints were shouting loud enough,' Peter pointed out.

She couldn't deny that they certainly suggested there was more to Robert Luckhurst's story than she and Peter had heard so far. 'Tanner claimed he was innocent, and if so are there any candidates for guilty?'

'Rather premature, but we can tentatively list a few. Mike offered his help over that.'

'Offered?' she queried ironically. Mike had looked too busy to be in an offering mood when they had last seen him on Saturday.

'Agreed, then. Apart from the toughie Tom Miller, Amelia Luckhurst is one obvious candidate. Mike also suggested we talk to Barbara Hastings, who was barmaid at the Edgar Arms at the time of the murder and in charge of the catering at Stourdens on Saturday – I think I remember her. She also does the teas there on open days. Her son Craig was at the bar. He's barman at the Dunham pub, plus part-time plumber. Remember him?'

She did. In his twenties, stocky, brown hair, rather fresh, round pleasant face. She remembered his mother too – and her remarkable cooking. 'I do. He can't be on the suspect list for 1985; he'd have been a babe in arms. Anyone else?'

'Not yet. We'd better start with Tom the toughie.'

'Toughies who lead protest marches don't usually carry guns with them.'

'They might if they were particularly eager to solve the issue quickly, which Miller did. He had a small struggling fruit farm which was heavily dependent on the track through

Stourdens' estate. Without it he was undoubtedly out of business.'

'Did that happen?'

'No. Because of strong local feeling, Amelia Luckhurst made it a condition in the sale of Stourdens that farm traffic could continue to drive through, and the Fettises were happy about that. It does no harm to the gardens, only to the fields let out to farmers, one of which unfortunately ran quite near Abbot's Folly – the field Miller rented. Luckhurst might have seen it as a threat to his beloved collection.'

'I bet Jane Austen didn't have this neighbour trouble.'

'Who knows? Her brothers, especially the one who owned Godmersham, must have done. Mud was a big problem in her day, so he was probably always being badgered to maintain the tracks better.'

So easy to have an image of Jane sitting on her own quietly scribbling away without a thought in her head save who was to marry whom, and the niceties of social life, but it must bear little relation to the truth, Georgia thought.

'You seem to be getting interested in Jane Austen,' she commented. 'You're getting as bad as the Clackingtons.'

'Mike says he dislikes coincidences, but I love them, because they're so often not coincidences. When you look at this one . . .'

She sighed. 'There's nothing to suggest that Robert Luckhurst's murder had anything to do with Austen. Nothing about Jane Austen changed at Stourdens when Luckhurst died, except that the collection went with the house and the Fettises inherited it. Nothing was stolen though, which is the important point.'

'You can't avoid the fact that Laura was murdered on the day when she might have been going to announce that Jane Austen was going to become big news at Stourdens.'

'Granted, but one could equally argue that since Jack the Ripper's cases were all committed in East London they must have links to East London history.'

'Far-fetched, isn't it? We need to find out what this big news will consist of, other than this TV documentary. And we don't even know the theme of that yet. My guess is that it's Jane Austen's secret love affair and the Stourdens collection.'

She agreed. 'But we've no idea whether Laura's death will change anything about whatever plans she had in mind. Even if we're really sure there was trouble at the family mill on Saturday, we can't barge into the Fettises' affairs.'

'Ah, but we can barge into the Clackingtons'. I'll ring them up.'

She was forced to laugh. 'I don't see any problem there.'

'Tomorrow OK?'

'Elena will still be there. She's not going till Thursday.'

'We can't let her rule our lives.'

She gave in. 'Agreed. Once we've seen Dora and Gerald though, who comes first? Still Tom Miller?'

'Depending on what we learn at Edgar House, yes. Then there's Barbara Hastings, who still lives locally. Pity Amelia Luckhurst's whereabouts aren't yet known. Dora thought she saw her at the Gala on Saturday, but she isn't on the police list of attendees. I asked.' Peter hesitated. 'About Elena, Georgia. She seems serious about returning to England for good. Are we going to be able to live with that?'

'Bless you for that "we".' Georgia grappled again with the myriad consequences that this might bring.

'We need to plan together.'

'Comforting words, but that might not be possible. Not when it's a reality.'

'I'll try. I can't pretend it will be easy. Nor for you?' he asked.

'No, but I'll try too. After all, if she lives in Canterbury—'

'Don't kid yourself, Georgia. Wherever she lives in England, she'll ensure that we fall over her left, right and centre. Could we take it?'

She tried to think carefully about this. 'Remove the centre, and I think I could take the left and right.'

Peter understood immediately. 'You mean if she leaves Marsh & Daughter alone?'

'Yes, but not just because it's work.'

'No interference between father and daughter?'

'It sounds hard put that way. Unreasonable – and, worse, impractical.'

'Will you take the risk?'

A watershed. Could she face it? She'd faced one – no, two – watersheds in the last year. But in future if she looked back after having said no, what then? Didn't that run the risk of driving a wedge between herself and Peter? There were still signs of a tie existing between Peter and Elena. If she tried to snap it artificially, wouldn't that be fatal? What way was there, but forward? Even if forward meant actively trying, not just accepting.

'Yes,' she said firmly. If she drowned in the Rubicon she was crossing, so be it.

Tentatively, she explored what reasons there might be for her to be shying away from contemplating a future with her mother close at hand. Resentment immediately occurred to her. She could deal with that. Regret was another matter. Regret for the childhood memories, both of laughter and tears, that would always now be blurred because of what had happened more recently, when the way Elena had treated Peter had made her realize that the fluttering butterfly who had brought such pleasure and excitement into their lives was in reality supremely self-centred, her love only superficial while it suited her. Was that fair? Perhaps not, but while the thought stayed in her mind no real relationship could be established. Did that matter? Could she manage with her mother living locally but without having close involvement with her? No. There was the possibility that in the not-distant future Elena too might need care. Would she give it? Of course she would. She knew that she could not turn her back as Elena herself had done fourteen years ago. Did she *want* to walk away? Agonizingly, amazingly, the answer was no.

'I feel the same, Georgia,' Peter told her. 'If our rock centre stays solid, we can help her without *needing* her – that's when the trouble starts.'

'It's a deal, guv,' she growled.

Peter laughed. 'You must admit it will make life interesting,' he said.

'So does a volcano.'

FIVE

'**D**arlings!' Dora threw her arms wide open in welcome at the door of Edgar House the next day, and then emerged to hug Georgia. Dora was still tearful, naturally enough. She had obviously been very fond of Laura, and the shock itself would take time to wear off, let alone the loss.

Gerald strode out purposefully towards Peter. 'Good to see you, old chap. Show you round, shall I?'

Peter grinned at this tactfulness. 'Thanks.' He had had only limited success. The Clackingtons were very happy to let them see the whole of Edgar House, but Gerald had awkwardly explained they felt they could not talk freely about Jane Austen without the Fettises' permission.

'We'll all go that way, Georgia,' Dora suggested. 'It will take us past the old kitchens – there are still traces of how they used to be.'

Dora was clad in serviceable trousers and top this morning, and wearing everyday clothes rather than the flowing tea-gown or Regency costume, Georgia found it much easier to talk to her. 'Where's Elena?' she asked.

'Making us coffee. She has already had the tour of Edgar House, so she'll join us later.'

'It's good of you to let us come, with so much on your minds.'

'Takes our minds off it,' Gerald replied, embarrassed. 'Sorry we have to hold back on too much talk about Jane Austen's love affair until the Fettises have declared open season.'

'We don't know when that will be now,' Dora said. 'We don't like to ask Roy and Jennifer what their plans are. Dear Jennifer says they've no idea when the funeral will be yet. I suppose that's inevitable. The police . . .' Her voice faltered, and she began again. 'Tim is so talented, though – he has just the right touch. He will know when it is proper to talk about Stourdens. As if it mattered now.'

'I take it that Edgar House is involved in their plans?' Georgia asked, as casually as she could.

Dora and Gerald exchanged a glance, halting at the side door. 'Well, yes,' Dora said. 'When you see the old Assembly Rooms you'll appreciate the potential. We've always hoped that they could be restored and used again, perhaps for recitals, but it would require a great deal of money. And now – who knows? All we can think of is Laura.'

'And the police,' Gerald added practically.

Georgia longed to ask if they knew how the investigation was going, but decided that it wasn't tactful to ask.

Peter had no such reservations, however. 'The Stourdens' plans might be relevant to Laura's murder,' he pointed out. 'And your involvement also. The police will naturally be following that up.'

'Ours?' Dora went white with terror. 'But we had nothing to do with her horrible death.'

Peter explained. 'I know how the police work. They have to consider every angle just in case. One possible avenue, unlikely though it seems, is the coincidence that Robert Luckhurst was a collector of Jane Austen memorabilia, and Laura Fettis was killed on the day of a Jane Austen gala. On the face of it, it might seem as though someone didn't want some facts about Jane Austen to come out. That's the reason,' he added, looking very innocent, 'that both we and the police need to hear the story about the plans for Stourdens – if only for your own security.'

Gerald understood immediately. 'You mean this murdering devil might have a potshot at us?'

It took Dora longer, but then the message came through loud and clear. '*Us?*' she shrieked. 'You mean someone might try to *murder* us just because of our modest contribution to the story?'

'It's not impossible,' Peter said gravely.

Oh, how unfair, Georgia fumed, to use this kind of pressure. Surely Peter did not really think Laura was killed for that reason? It wouldn't make sense, as other members of the family would carry on where she left off. Or was Peter in earnest? It was a sobering thought, if so.

'Gerald,' Dora announced firmly, 'we can explain more about the Assembly Rooms and their connection to *The Watsons*. Jennifer and Roy wouldn't mind that.'

'All right, Dollybird,' Gerald said affectionately, putting his arm round her. 'We'll do just that. And I'll have a word with Roy about the rest.'

The rest? Just what did it consist of? Peter did not comment, however, as they went into the corridor leading past the kitchens. The kitchens were on their left, although the one in use might be vastly changed from how it must have been in Jane Austen's time. The fireplace, however, was original, except that it now sported a fine array of copperware rather than a fire and spitjack.

Gerald ignored the passageway leading to the right, which would have taken them back to the drawing room, and continued straight ahead until he came to an old but quite narrow wooden staircase. 'This takes us up to the first floor and through to the Assembly Rooms on the other side of the house,' he explained.

She saw Peter's face drop. No way was his wheelchair going up there. Dora too had seen his expression. 'Don't worry,' she said. 'We have a lift. Gerald's mother lived here for some years and insisted on installing it. The staircase at the other end of this wing wasn't suitable for a stairlift, and nor was this one.'

'The lift creaks a bit,' Gerald said cheerfully, 'but it's regularly serviced.'

'Thank you,' Peter replied gravely.

The stairs brought Georgia and Dora up to the first-floor landing where Peter and Gerald joined them – and then to a passageway leading along the wing. It was enclosed now, but Gerald explained it was once open, looking down to the courtyard beneath. At the end of the wing, it turned right into a small room which would, Georgia worked out, clearly eventually link up with the east wing, at least at this level. Under it must be the archway at the rear of the courtyard.

'This is one of the former Assembly Rooms,' Dora announced with pride as they went into it. 'It was the tea room, hence the stairs to the kitchens.'

'It's been used for all sorts of things since then, although not in Tanner's time. Not much to look at,' Gerald said apologetically.

He was right. The room was empty, although the walls had once been wallpapered. Enough had been torn off to reveal a painted wall beneath, and old gas mantels indicated where oil lamps or candles must once have been. No spiders or even cobwebs though, Georgia noticed, so the rooms were still being cared for up to a point; they were merely barren of life.

But to Dora, they weren't, Georgia thought. It was clear from looking at her rapt expression that to her Jane Austen still walked these floors. It must have given Dora pleasure, because she was much brighter now that the subject of Laura's death had been temporarily put aside.

'Dear Jane describes this room so clearly in *The Watsons*,' Dora said. 'Remember? The tea room was a small room within the card room, and in passing through the latter, where the passage was narrowed by tables, Mrs Edwards and her party were hemmed in. And, Georgia,' Dora added, 'Mr Howard was nearby.'

Who? Georgia nearly asked, then remembered he was a character in *The Watsons* and probably the man that Emma Watson was destined to marry.

The room beyond the tea room was also empty. 'The card room,' Gerald explained gruffly. Georgia could see that this opened off the large Assembly Room itself, into which Dora led the way. Disappointingly – though Georgia didn't know quite what she had expected – this too was empty. She had hoped for candelabras, polished floors, and potted palms, but this had few hints of what it had been like in its heyday.

'Not like Bath, of course, or Tunbridge Wells,' Gerald admitted, 'but, after all, Harblehurst was only a village then, even though the Edgar Arms was well known locally.'

'Remember Emma Watson, Georgia?' Dora trilled. 'Can't you just see her dancing with Master Charles Blake? Remember Emma being told by her sister that the party would arrive early as Mrs Edwards might then get a good place by the fire? And there it is!'

It was an impressive – and atmospheric – Georgian fireplace

with two rather battered chimney-board figures flanking it. Somehow the hearth succeeded where the rooms themselves alone failed. Georgia could imagine the music of the violins, the dancing master calling the moves of the sociable country dances and the excitement of the cotillion.

'Oh, what fun it must have been,' Dora said wistfully.

Perhaps, Georgia thought, but now it was cold and smelled of disuse. It was a room in waiting – but waiting for what?

Peter echoed her thoughts. 'What are you planning to do with the rooms?' he asked politely.

Dora glanced at Gerald, who gave a warning cough, and she evaded the question. 'The potential is enormous,' she replied dutifully. 'You'll remember, Georgia, that *The Watsons* is set in Surrey, but clearly Jane is describing Kent and the Edgar Arms. The Edwards party enters the courtyard of the inn and takes a wide staircase up to the first floor where there is a short gallery, in which they pass a bedchamber out of which Tom Musgrave appears. We'll go down that way, for at the foot of the stairs is a very special room. While they are in these rooms they hear the sound of horses and a carriage entering the courtyard. The Osbornes are coming, the *Osbornes* are coming, everyone cries. Can't you see it happening, Georgia? Of course the novel was set here. Come, you shall see the staircase.'

She hurried them both out of the assembly room and into the gallery somewhat faster than necessary, it seemed to Georgia. Whatever lay in Tom Musgrave's bedchamber or the other rooms on this floor they were not to know, for Dora was intent on returning to the ground floor by the wooden staircase, while Gerald escorted Peter back to the lift. This staircase was much wider and more ornate than the kitchen stairs, and at its foot a door led back into the entrance hall of the house. To its left, however, was a room looking on to the street, which was the Clackingtons' dining room.

'A private room in Austen's time,' Dora explained while they waited for Gerald and Peter to arrive. 'We believe this is where lady passengers waited for their carriage or post-chaise so that they didn't have to mix with the hoi polloi.

'And where,' she added grandly as Gerald arrived with Peter,

'Jane and Cassandra were waiting for the Godmersham carriage when Captain William Harker walked into their lives.'

'Dora!' Gerald said warningly.

She hesitated. 'We should really leave it to dear Jennifer to tell you the full story, but I can't resist—'

'*Dora!*'

'Oh, listen,' Dora said hurriedly. 'I think Elena's ready for us.'

Georgia was both annoyed and irked. She wasn't deeply into Jane Austen, but if it was going to be relevant to Bob Luckhurst's death then the sooner she and Peter heard the story the better. Peter was already signalling that he couldn't see any future in pursuing the subject, and so she followed meekly when Gerald firmly led the way back to the living room.

Wasn't it suspicious, Georgia thought, that this great love affair had only just come to light? It was true that such treasure troves were still found nowadays, leading to new interpretations. Lost poems, music and plays were found, and unknown paintings by the masters discovered. Meanwhile she realized there was Elena to face. She was waiting for them in the living room and jumped up eagerly when she saw them, coming over to kiss them both.

'Are you feeling better now?' Georgia asked, tongue-tied over what to call her. Elena no longer seemed right, and yet any form of Mother wasn't right either. She'd stick with Elena, she decided.

'Darling, thank you. A little. And isn't it impressive?' she asked. 'Here I am serving coffee in a room where Jane Austen might have taken tea.'

She and Dora fussed with cups and plates of biscuits while keeping up a determined conversation about the rival merits of *Persuasion* and *Pride and Prejudice*. To Georgia's relief, it was clear that no personal topics need be broached. When she and Peter left, however, Elena followed them out to the car, Georgia presumed to talk about her future life in Kent. Once again she was wrong.

'I've been plucking up the courage to talk to you both,' Elena began hesitantly, 'but I can't wait any longer. I just *can't.*'

'About your moving back to Kent?' Georgia asked.

'No, about Rick.'

Georgia felt as if she'd been punched in the face. She could have stood Canterbury coming up for discussion, but this had come out of the blue. So this was what had really been worrying Elena. Of all things to happen, just as she and Peter had come to terms with the fact that there would never be any more information about Rick's death than they had already unearthed.

'What about him, Elena?' Peter asked.

His voice sounded quite normal, although he must have been as jolted by this as Georgia had been.

'I went to Austria,' Elena started nervously.

'As I did. So we both know,' Peter said, 'all that's ever going to be known about his death.'

'But I heard about one of the survivors from the boat.'

A terrible silence as old wounds began to seep their own kind of poison again. Rick's story had been finished, laid gently to rest, and now Elena threw this bombshell in their midst, which would stir up once more that insidious feeling that there might be more to know.

'Is this survivor alive?' Peter asked evenly.

'I think so.'

'Where does he or she live?'

'He, but I don't know,' Elena said helplessly. 'I can find out. I wasn't going to speak about it until I found him, but I couldn't bear it alone.' She burst into tears. 'I did right to tell you, didn't I?'

'Straight clean bowled,' Peter said ruefully when they had returned to the office. He hadn't referred to Elena or to Rick on the journey home, and Georgia wasn't going to raise the subject. She wondered whether she should do so in case he brooded once he was alone, but she had to struggle to sort out her own feelings first. Elena had put the cat amongst the pigeons, and so all Georgia could do was try to shoo them off. Don't attack the cat. Shooing away in this case would probably amount to giving Elena her head in trying to track this survivor down, but Georgia vowed to try not to get too emotionally involved. If Elena found this survivor, that would be the time for her and Peter to decide whether they wanted to meet him. If her mother failed, then she did not want to be disappointed.

'My tactics are to retire from the pitch until summoned to bat again,' Peter continued, to her relief.

'Agreed.'

'And meanwhile a good antidote might be Barbara Hastings, so that we can continue filling in the background to the Luckhurst murder while we're waiting to talk to the Fettises. So far as we know, Jane Austen's love life is unlikely to have anything to do with Luckhurst's death.'

'I like knowing all the background though, not just parts of it, and Austen is certainly part.'

'Patience, daughter, patience. Be like me.'

She laughed, as he had meant her to.

Georgia drove to Dunham on Thursday morning, without great expectations of its producing anything other than background colour. Barbara Hastings had been more curious than welcoming on the telephone, which was hardly surprising, Georgia supposed. She must have been shocked by Laura Fettis's death, as she had worked for her, and it must seem odd to her that Marsh & Daughter were enquiring about events twenty-five years earlier at a time when Laura's death was on everybody's mind and lips. She lived on the outskirts of Dunham, in a farmhouse set well back from the road. The house was old and detached, with a former garage-cum-barn which Barbara explained had been converted recently into a dedicated kitchen for professional cooking. Her own kitchen had been large enough for the days she cooked for open days at Stourdens, but now she wanted to *expand*, and the look she gave Georgia suggested that expansion could well have to do with Stourdens. The kitchen was state of the art, but didn't look to be greatly used as yet. Barbara did not comment but led her into the garden where coffee and biscuits were duly produced – both excellent, as was the garden itself. When she complimented Barbara on its blaze of colour and thriving looking vegetables Barbara grunted.

'Got time to do it now the farm's gone.'

'Farm?' Georgia asked.

'Farmed by my late husband, but when Bill passed on I sold it to Tom Miller, since it was next to his place.' A pause. 'You were at the Gala on Saturday,' she said almost accusingly. 'I remember you. You had the pork frigasy.'

'And it was delicious. I came back for tea later.'

Georgia was glad at least that Barbara remembered her for the pork and not for being the woman who had found the body. It had been a mistake to mention 'later' though, with its reminder of Laura's death, but if it struck a wrong note Barbara Hastings showed no signs of resenting it. 'The frigasy was one of Mrs Raffald's recipes,' she told her. 'Book handed down by my granny. Mrs Fettis was very fond of it.'

'I'm sorry about her death,' Georgia replied. 'You must have known her very well.'

'Worked for her for ten years or more. Nicer lady you couldn't hope to find.'

'And Roy Fettis?' Georgia hadn't seen enough of him to get any clear impression.

'Didn't deserve her is all I'll say. But,' she immediately added, 'he's a lazy lout. Her money, of course. Stourdens belongs to her, not him. He just wants to cash in. I've a lot of time for young Jennifer, though.'

'And Tim Wilson?'

'I wouldn't know about him.'

Georgia understood. Barbara did know about him, but end of subject. Did that mean there could be tensions in the Fettis family? If so, the police would presumably be hot on the trail. 'I haven't come to talk about Mrs Fettis,' Georgia said, 'if only because it must be very painful for you. It's Robert Luckhurst who interests my father and me.'

'So you said on the phone. Why's that?'

'We write a series of books about forgotten cases of the past. My father used to be in the police force before he was disabled, and the Robert Luckhurst case is one that interests him.'

Barbara said nothing, just waited and watched her.

'I understand you were working for the Tanners as barmaid at the Edgar Arms at the time of the murder, so I wondered if I could ask you what you remember.'

'About what?' was the stony reply. There was distinct hostility now.

Good, Georgia thought. Hostility is a defence, and the need for defence has a cause. 'Such as whether you think Max Tanner could have been innocent. He accused Tom Miller of being the killer.'

Barbara's answer was surprisingly sharp. 'He would. Blame anyone but himself, he would, and poor old Tom was the natural one to pick on. Mind you, Max was not the sort to go and blow a man's brains out over something that happened twelve month earlier like losing that licence. The trial said that was the reason he killed him. But he was a hothead. Is, rather. He's still going somewhere, I'm sure of that. A hothead,' she repeated. 'If he got an idea into his stupid head, it wouldn't go.'

'There was a rumour he was having an affair with Mrs Luckhurst.'

Barbara was eager to answer, and Georgia thought she seemed almost relieved at the question. 'Maybe that's right, maybe it's wrong. I'd no time for the woman myself. She was always nipping in and out. Poor Esther Tanner had a daughter and a baby son to look after, just like me, so I knew what it was like. Max was a womanizer, easy come, easy go, but that Mrs Luckhurst wouldn't let him go that easily. Had him by the short and curlies.'

'Did you like Robert Luckhurst?'

'Nothing to dislike. Mind you, I was only twenty-two so to me he was just the old chap to whom one had to be polite because he owned Stourdens. I preferred him to his wife, but I wouldn't go out of my way for him.'

'Did he often come into the pub?'

'Only when there was one of those car meetings on. He had this old car; Craig – that's my son – said it was a Lagonda. Mr Luckhurst liked showing it off.'

'Was he popular with the village?'

'Not when he got this bee in his bonnet about closing off the farm track. Then the sparks flew, obstinate old devil. Still, he didn't deserve what happened to him.'

'Did you believe Tanner was guilty at the time?'

'He had a fair trial. Seemed he'd done it. Who else could

have? That gun was his. He got back while I was still working there. I didn't see the gun, but it was found afterwards down in the cellars. I was in the pub between twelve and two for opening hours plus an hour or so either side. I'd have seen if anyone had nipped in to pinch it *and* replace it.'

'It could have been stolen from the pub the previous day and hidden there before the police came.'

A frosty look and a frosty reply. 'It could have been, Miss Marsh, but don't you go saying it was, because I wouldn't know one way or the other. Max said he didn't know how it got there.'

'Did you like him?'

'A great chap if you kept on his right side; if you didn't, there was hell to pay, especially if he was drunk.'

'Barmen don't usually drink much.'

'Max didn't. Not while the pub was open. But afterwards he went at it like a man possessed, effing and blinding about what great things he was going to do with the Edgar Arms. He had ideas above his station, did Max Tanner, and eyes bigger than his bank balance. He was going to convert the old Assembly Rooms for private hire, Jane Austen weekends, posh hotel restaurant and goodness knows what. Looking forward to that, I was, but it never happened. Never had the cash.'

'Was the drink problem the reason his licence was taken away?'

'Not really. After-hours drinking got him. He said he'd closed the bar, but someone – he reckoned it was a pal of Mr Robert's – grassed on him.'

'What about his family? Did he have children?'

'A couple, boy and a girl, and Mrs Tanner, she was devoted to him – until they fell out over Amelia Luckhurst. Then the trial came and that was that. Divorce.'

'Was it Mrs Tanner who was the Jane Austen fan?'

'No. She went along with it, but it was Max did the running. Doubt if he ever read the novels though. Just saw a path to fame there. Why do you want to know that?' Barbara looked suspicious.

'Only because the Clackingtons said they bought the pub for its Austen connections.'

'Mrs Clackington lives in cloud cuckoo land, unlike Mrs Fancy Herself Luckhurst, who made a pile when she sold Stourdens to the Fettises on the strength of Jane Austen even though the house was falling down.'

'Are you still in touch with Mrs Luckhurst?' Georgia asked hopefully.

A snort. 'What, her? No way.' A glimmer of humour. 'I don't reckon she'd bother to keep up with the likes of a barmaid.' A pause. 'But I know where she lives if that's what you're after.'

Amelia Luckhurst had agreed to see them on the following Monday, albeit reluctantly. Georgia supposed this was not surprising, as she had remarried and was living in Putney. The past must seem very far behind her.

'Shall we both go?' Peter had asked.

'Yes.' Amelia was so central to their case that it would be sensible for both to meet her.

As soon as Amelia opened the door, Georgia recognized her, despite the fact that she was now wearing jeans and a shirt-top and not Regency dress. 'We met,' she exclaimed. 'In the food queue at Stourdens.'

'Did we?' A split-second pause. 'Of course. I remember now. Though it's not the first thing I connect to that day.'

Polite put-down, Georgia thought ruefully. Bob Luckhurst had been a reclusive non-aggressive man who had stepped out of his normal pattern and ruffled feathers. But he'd been murdered, and there was a big gap between the two facts. She wasn't at all sure that his widow was going to be able to fill it for them. She must, after all, have been a suspect at the time of the murder, even if Mike had not mentioned that to them.

'I didn't see your name on the police list of Gala attendees,' Peter said as she led them round the side of the house into the garden. It was a small modern garden designed to within an inch of its life, as if waiting for the next Sunday magazine to spot it. 'But then I was looking for Luckhurst on the list, not Collier,' he added.

'Why look at all?' Amelia retorted. Not rudely, Georgia thought, merely cool. This lady would not suffer fools gladly.

'I thought you might be there because of your former asso-
ciation with Stourdens, and I wanted to meet you both for that
reason and because you must have known Laura Fettis,' Peter
replied mildly.

'I did, if you call selling someone a house a basis for
knowing them.' Then Amelia relented. 'Forgive me, I'm rather
prickly on the subject of Stourdens. I gave in to the temptation to see what was going on at the old place. Too many
recollections though. I was pretty shaken by what happened,
so I escaped from the horror as soon as I could. That must
have been before the police imprisoned everyone in the
grounds.'

'It must have brought back your former husband's murder,'
Peter said sympathetically.

'Believe me, it did. That seems foolish since that was a long
time ago, and I've been married to John for yonks. But I really
needed that quick getaway last Saturday. The last thing I
wanted to do was talk again to the police about Bob's murder,
if the subject came up. So if I sound unwelcoming that's for
the same reason. Question though: I can't see why on earth
you want to nose into Bob's death now.'

'I don't want to distress you—'

'Distress?' Amelia gave a bark of laughter. 'I couldn't stand
him by that time. That was why it was such a strain. We'd
have divorced if it hadn't been rendered unnecessary.'

'We got the impression he was usually a quiet, mild man.'

'He was. Didn't stick his neck out anywhere. That was the
trouble. Retired early, no pension, but wouldn't make use of
the one asset he had: Stourdens.'

'Max Tanner always protested his innocence. Rightly, do
you think?' Peter asked – deliberately naively, Georgia
suspected.

'Of course he'd say he didn't do it,' she replied briskly. 'He
was a dreamer. He'd do anything to link up with Stourdens
and live in the reflected glory of Jane Austen, and being a
murderer didn't fit that image. As far as I recall, Bob found
two or three letters concealed in a painting Max owned, and
Max got grand ideas about how to use them and how Bob
could help. No chance there.'

Letters? Georgia pricked up her ears. Were they part of the Clackingtons' 'modest contribution'?

'So you don't think there was *any* doubt that he'd killed your husband?' Peter asked again.

'I do not. Guilty as hell. He had threatened Bob on several occasions, but my husband chose to take no notice, and that was the result.'

'Threatened him over what? The licence?'

'Partly. Tanner was an ambitious man and hated playing second fiddle to his wife when she had to take it over. He resented it and blamed Bob. The other reason, as I said, was that Bob was reluctant to let the world know about the Stourdens Austen collection. Max was full of plans to upgrade the Edgar Arms, but they depended on our cooperation. They couldn't do it alone. Bob wouldn't budge. I think Max saw a kind of literary trail – lunch at the Edgar Arms, and tour and entertainment of some sort at Stourdens. He became fairly manic about it and wouldn't take no for an answer. Something must have tipped him over the edge that day. I saw him drive up that morning and fondly hoped that with the other classic car owners about to descend on us, he meant no harm. I was wrong. He knew about the planned protest march and decided to use that as a cover to kill Robert and cast the blame on Tom Miller who was leading the march.'

'What did he hope to achieve by Bob's death?'

'Knowing Max, I doubt if he thought that far. Or perhaps the idiot thought he could persuade me to help.'

'Were you at the Folly when all this was going on?'

'No way. I stayed with the classic cars and directed the march to the folly to present its petition. I thought that would scotch any plans Max had, but I was wrong.'

'Petition?'

'Yes, signed by virtually the whole of Dunham. It was meant to be a peaceful protest though. I stayed inside the main house seeing to the nibbles and drinks and so on – and if you're interested –' she grinned – 'I stayed there well after twelve fifteen. Bob was killed about twelve thirty, and I couldn't have sprinted along the path in time. Happy with that?'

'Thank you,' Peter said, on his best behaviour. 'Have you seen Tanner since his release?'

'No, and before you ask, I am perfectly well aware of the rumours of an affair between us. I can only say that it was another figment of that man's overactive imagination. He began the rumours himself. He saw himself as lord of the manor even if it wasn't true.'

'Were you as devoted to the Jane Austen collection as Bob was?' Georgia asked.

'No. I indulged him in it though. It seemed a harmless hobby.'

'Yet he never wanted to exploit it, with or without Max Tanner?'

'There you have it. Exploit. Bob liked the thrill of owner-ship, to know that he alone knew about Jane Austen's love life. You've been told about that, I'm sure.'

'Only a little, until the Fettises are willing to talk about it. Your husband seems to have been the sort of man to hug the collection to himself, not share it. Would you agree?'

Amelia looked at him quizzically. 'I imagine what you really want to know is what sort of man Bob was. I take it you never met him?'

'I remember hearing about him, and I think I saw him at community events once or twice, but our paths never crossed more specifically.'

'I don't remember you either, so that's fair enough.' Amelia considered. 'Difficult to describe a relationship so far in the past. It ought to give you a different perspective, but somehow it just seems to smooth things out and blur the pertinent points. But so far as I recall, here goes. Bob wasn't an extro-vert, he wasn't a mixer, although he liked talking about Jane Austen with enthusiasts, and he liked talking about cars with enthusiasts. He wasn't a womanizer – as far as I know, anyway.'

'Did you share any of his interests – cars for instance?' Georgia asked.

'None. I just let him lead his own life. I had my own car, and I ran a travel business for a long while, then opened an antiques shop.'

'From what you say you were in favour of developing Stourdens too,' Peter said.

'True enough, although developing tourism wasn't so much of a fashion then as it is now. The most I got Bob to agree on was to open the gardens for an annual fête – not a Jane Austen fête, incidentally.'

'The Fettises seem to be very enthusiastic about developing it.'

Amelia chuckled. 'I know. Laura got in touch with me some time ago about the Gala. I suppose I should confess that as a result I went to see Laura at Stourdens on the Wednesday before it took place.'

'At her request?' Georgia asked. Perhaps at last she and Peter might get some idea of what Laura had intended to announce.

'Yes. Laura was upset and said she'd asked to see me because of all people I would be able to understand. Naturally, that fed my ego. She said there were great plans ahead for Stourdens using the collection, but she was beginning to have cold feet. Would commercialization be the wrong thing to do in Jane Austen's interests? Jane Austen had plenty of exposure, anyway, with the wonderful societies and films and documentaries devoted to her, so it seemed wrong to exploit her for their own financial interests.'

Peter whistled. 'That must have thrown a spanner in the works.'

'Not at all. I think Laura just needed persuading that she was doing the right thing. She seemed happy enough when I left.'

'So why did she look so upset three days later?'

'I really don't know,' Amelia said blandly. 'A family matter, perhaps?'

SIX

'Any news from Dora and Gerald?' Georgia asked hopefully when she arrived at the office on Tuesday morning. She could tell from Peter's expression that there probably wasn't. The Clackingtons had promised to let them know if they had any information about the funeral or if the Fettises had contacted them over their future plans for Stourdens.

'Not a word, and nothing from Mike either. He said he'd tell me when the crime scene was lifted. It's been over a week now – it can't be taking that long. Meanwhile, the Bat and Trap awaits us.'

'The what?' Then she remembered passing it in the car. It was the Dunham pub, named after the old Kentish game played with a racquet and a ball lodged in a trap at one end of a see-saw. 'Why on earth are we going there?'

'Because a disagreeable-sounding gentleman by the name of Tom Miller declares that's the only place he can be found most of the time. Just as in 1985, it seems he's still a protester.'

'Or petition presenter.'

'According to one's point of view,' Peter conceded. 'I wonder how he sees himself nowadays?'

So did Georgia. He sounded an awkward cuss, and Peter might get more out of him than she would. 'Do you want me there or is it a man-only event?' she asked.

Peter considered for an untactful length of time. 'I need you there,' he finally said. 'I told him I'd go today, and I don't want to find myself surrounded by a group of Millerites all eyeing me to work out my evil intentions.'

'So my job is to fend off aggressive cronies,' she said resignedly.

'Plus pick up interesting crumbs.'

Georgia laughed. 'Understood. You're definitely seeing the Luckhurst case as one for us?'

Peter was cagey. 'Aren't you?'

Her turn to consider her answer carefully. 'Meeting Barbara and Amelia hasn't brought us a clear way forward – isn't that a worry, in case there might not be one? We've no lead at all on Max Tanner's current whereabouts – and even if we had, nobody so far seems to be convinced of his innocence except himself. The victim is squarely in our sights, but I don't feel I *know* Bob Luckhurst sufficiently for that alone to give us an incentive.'

'Explain, please.'

'His wife couldn't stand him, although Barbara thought he was nice enough. At least Amelia was honest, but it might have been a biased view, not least because he might have been blocking her plans rather more forcefully than she implied. On the other hand, if she hated him enough for murder, she wouldn't have admitted even dislike to us. He'd have changed into her favourite person.'

'Why?' Peter asked mildly. 'It was safe enough. Legally, the killer was found and put behind bars.'

As they drove to Dunham, the July countryside was looking its best with the wooded slopes of the hills providing a soft green background to the sleepy clusters of houses. It was hard to connect with the gruesome murder of Laura Fettis. As Peter turned into the pub car park, the Bat and Trap looked a dismal place. There was no attempt to attract passing traffic in the way of hanging baskets or a prettied-up forecourt.

There was a gate into the garden and Georgia walked over to peer into it. This was not a pub that offered customers parasol-shielded tables and chairs. There were only a couple of broken-down seats to be seen, lodged against the pub wall, and a gravelled area, now half weeds, roped off – where presumably the bat and trap game had been played, judging by the see-saw. The game was still very active in Kent, but this pitch looked unused and the wood of the see-saw was rotting.

A blackboard outside the pub unconvincingly claimed to provide good food, but to her the Bat and Trap looked to be one of those rare establishments, a pub that was still surviving on regular clientele – save that from the outside at least it looked only just alive. A lick of paint might help.

Inside, however, the pub presented an amazingly different image. It was spartan, but light, clean and welcoming, even cheerful. Georgia recognized Barbara's son Craig behind the bar and wondered what his take on his mother's catering projects was, and whether he was playing an active role in them. Barbara would need help.

Gathered round the bar was a group of regulars, judging by their body language, and there were no prizes for guessing which one was Tom Miller. The leader of the pack – in his fifties and red-faced – was centrally placed in the group, one elbow on the bar, and his shout to Peter of: 'Over here, mate,' left no doubt about his identity.

Peter wheeled himself up to the group, but Georgia received a less cordial welcome and decided to retire to a watching position from the sidelines. There were few other customers, although she was aware of an elderly man watching her from a table near the window. His face seemed vaguely familiar, but she could not place him, so she took a few moments to sip her drink and then strolled over to sit near him, but not too obviously near. At his age – maybe early seventies – he could well have been living in Dunham for a long time and known Robert Luckhurst.

Once she was seated the conversation at the bar held her attention for a while. Some of the group had dispersed, but two cohorts remained flanking Tom Miller. Peter must have established his position remarkably early or else Miller was uncommonly eager to talk, because the discussion certainly seemed animated, and with so few people in the pub, it was easily audible. Miller's voice was – like his ego, she suspected – loud.

'Just what was it like that day, Tom?' Peter was saying. 'Long time ago, I appreciate that, and it must have been a confusing situation with so many people crowding into the folly. Still, it seems odd that Tanner consistently claimed his innocence.'

'So would Jack the Ripper,' one of the cohorts snarled.

'I read that Tanner had a witness to support him,' Peter continued blithely.

'Yeah,' Tom drawled. 'Mick Rider swore blind he walked back with him.'

'But he didn't?'

'I never saw Tanner after we left that folly place. I was at the back of the crowd, so he'd have been in front of me and he weren't. And before you ask, Frank here can tell you we walked back to the house together, didn't we, Frank?'

Frank received a dig in the ribs, and nodded. 'Bloody Luckhurst.'

'Did you actually talk to him at the folly?' Peter persevered.

'Yeah. It was like this, weren't it? When we got inside, we could hear Tanner and Luckhurst going at it hammer and tongs in that study of his. Door was shut. So we stood there like chumps, not knowing what to do.'

'What you want to know for?' Craig put in from behind the bar. 'All this is old stuff.' He seemed a Miller partisan, which was natural enough, Georgia thought. He would have been a babe in arms at that time, though.

'I prefer it from the horse's mouth,' Peter replied blandly, which earned him a suspicious look. 'Could you hear what they were talking about, Tom?'

'Not a lot. There was a lot of shouting and yelling.'

'From inside the room or outside?' Peter asked.

Tom grinned. 'Both.'

'Tanner picked on you to blame for the murder. Was that only because of the footpath issue?'

Tom carefully replaced his glass on the counter and demanded a refill. 'What else?' he said casually. (Rather too casually, Georgia thought.) 'Anyway, like I said, I had this petition to hand over,' he continued, 'so I banged on the door to get some action going. But it was that bastard Tanner who came out, wouldn't let us in. The chaps behind me started to push, and we were in what you might call a warlike situation instead of the quiet chat I wanted. I'm a quiet sort of fellow, ain't I?'

The cohorts speedily agreed.

'But you did speak to Luckhurst himself?' Peter asked.

Tom Miller gave him a caustic look. 'He weren't dead then, if that's what you mean. Far from it. Yeah, he moved his fat bum from the desk and came out to talk gentleman to gentleman.'

'Any sign of a gun?'

'Weren't looking for one.' Tom chortled. 'And yes, unless he had a twin brother, it was Luckhurst, and Tanner wasn't having him waste time talking to the likes of me. Told us to get out. Some of my lads didn't like that, and a real shindig brewed up. I told Luckhurst that I'd see him another day with the petition, and I got my chaps out of there. It was turning ugly, and I don't like that sort of thing,' Tom said virtuously. 'That was the last I saw of Bob Luckhurst – and of Tanner too, except in the dock.'

'How many of you were there on the march?'

'About thirty, maybe.'

'Quite a lot. Would you have noticed where Tanner was while you were talking to Luckhurst?'

'He wasn't in the room if that's what you're after. Outside in the lobby place. Must have nipped back in once we were out of there.'

'But you didn't see him do so.'

Tom stared at him. 'Look, mate, we chewed it over afterwards. The Old Bill took all our names and talked to the lot of us one by one. Satisfied?'

'This witness of Tanner's – did you see him as you were on the way back?'

'Sure did. But not Tanner. Look, chum, if Tanner had been fool enough to walk back with us he'd have been torn limb from limb for mucking up our march. We were fired up about it at the time, I can tell you. It was only thanks to Mrs Fettis that we kept the right of way, and now someone's done her in.'

Peter steered clear of that topic – rightly, Georgia thought. 'Did you know Tanner well?'

Tom picked up his glass and drained a large portion of its contents with a flourish. 'Sure. Used to go over to the old Edgar every now and then. But we weren't what you might call mates.'

'News of the murder must have come as a shock.'

'Too right it did. We was all back in the pub here. Heard the

Old Bill's cars screaming by. "Summat's up," I said. Then the police came barging in and wanted to know what we knew about it. We told 'em. They already knew Tanner had been there. Mrs Luckhurst told 'em.'

'She wasn't at the folly though.'

Frank snorted. 'Some woman was. Heard her voice.'

This was a new angle, Georgia thought hopefully. There had been no suggestion of this before.

'Imagination, Frank,' Tom said unfazed. 'I never saw her, and I was in that study.'

'Heard it as we got there. It was some woman.'

Peter abandoned the mysterious female. 'Apart from the footpath issue, did you like Bob Luckhurst?'

Georgia saw a general shaking of heads.

'No,' Tom replied forcefully, 'and here's for why. If you're going to be a country squire and lord of the manor you got responsibilities. He never took 'em on. Never showed his face except to complain about something. There were too many tractors, and not on the path. Too close to his blooming folly. Why should he worry? He had enough in the bank to put food on the table. Even if he didn't, he owned all that land. Had a duty to look out for us, know what I mean?'

Peter nodded.

'He didn't have no love for the common man,' Tom continued viciously. 'We could starve in our beds and he wouldn't have noticed. Respect has to be earned, don't it, and he didn't.'

'He's wrong, you know.'

Georgia jumped at an unexpected voice and turned to look at the elderly man on her right. And now she remembered who he was. 'I know where I've seen you before,' she exclaimed. 'At the Gala.' It was the 'peasant' who had bowed to her.

'That's right,' he agreed. 'So come a bit closer, m'dear, and I'll tell you why he's wrong.'

Georgia promptly did so. 'Did you know Bob Luckhurst?' From his long lugubrious face she had put him down as a retired professional, but she was wrong.

'Delivered his milk for thirty years,' he told her. 'Very nice

gentleman was Mr Luckhurst. He liked his milk fresh from
the cow, or as fresh as the regulations let you. Quite a joke
we used to have. Is it Buttercup's or Daisy's? "Daisy's," I'd
say. "It's a bit on the frisky side." I had a herd myself once.'

'You must have liked him a lot,' Georgia encouraged him.

'Used to play chess with him most Monday evenings.'

Chess? 'Was he a serious player?'

The man grinned. 'Is there any other sort? But if you're
asking if he minded me winning, no. "Your turn, Alf, I'll get
my own back next week."'

'Did you play in Abbot's Folly or in the house?'

'That folly. He liked it. It was his space. He was a kind sort
of chap by nature. Not a good-deeder, but he kept his eyes
open.'

'One of the men standing at the bar was saying that he
heard a woman's voice at the folly on the day he died. Was
it usual for Mrs Luckhurst to go there with her husband? Could
it have been her?'

'I wouldn't know. I was on a campsite at Clacton when he
was murdered.'

End of that line. 'Did you know the Tanners?' she tried.

'Went to the pub once or twice.'

End of that line too. 'Did the Luckhursts have children?'

'No. That's why the house had to be sold. Mrs Luckhurst
was always too busy to have kids around. Pity. Bit of a tough
nut was that lady. She would only have been about forty then,
and she was a looker in her way. But what I'd call determined.
Always nagging him about developing Stourdens into one of
those tourist attractions.'

'She was pushing hard for it?' A different impression than
Amelia had given them.

'Oh yes. One time I heard them rowing about it. It was
winter so we set up the board in the house. They were in the
next room. She wanted to give up her job and put Stourdens
on the map with Jane Austen days and tours and so on. He
wouldn't have it.'

'Did he talk to you about Jane Austen?'

'Now do I look that sort of chap? Me and Mr Luckhurst
talked about sport. I'd a lot of time for him.'

'That's really helpful,' Georgia said gratefully. 'No one else we've talked to *liked* him. So I'm glad to know you did, Mr . . . er . . .'

'Alfred Wheeler at your service. Wouldn't hurt a fly would Mr L. Makes me mad the way that Tanner murdered him – just over a blinking licence.'

'You don't think he could have been innocent?'

'How would I know? The jury didn't think so. Glad I wasn't here. I'd put in a quiet word for Tom Miller the last time I was at Stourdens. Tell you one thing – whatever Tom's telling that chap in the wheelchair you came in with, take it with a pinch of salt.'

'I'll remember that. And the chap is my father.'

'Looks a decent sort of bloke.'

'He is.'

'The sort to buy a chap a pint?'

Georgia laughed. 'If not, his daughter is.'

'What did you get out of that?' Peter asked as they drove away. They'd had a very poor sandwich lunch, and between their curiosity value to the pub and battling with tough bacon they hadn't been able to talk freely.

'The words "good food" they boast about are misleading.' She'd been surprised that Craig hadn't enlisted his mother's services.

Peter laughed. 'We suffer for our art.' A pause. 'I wonder which woman's voice was heard in the folly that day?'

'*If* there was one. And *if* it was Amelia Luckhurst's why didn't anyone else report it? Or did they? If she was there, where did she disappear to without being noticed?'

'Unless it's a belated addition to the story, the police must have followed it up. She had good reason if, as Alfred Wheeler claims, Amelia and her husband were at loggerheads over Stourdens.'

'But if so why didn't she develop Stourdens afterwards?'

'She did in a way. She sold the house on the strength of the Austen connections. And thus,' he added triumphantly, 'Austen *could* have been a factor in both murders.'

Georgia objected. 'No, that's a bee in your bonnet. There's

a difference between them. You're arguing that Bob's death came about because he stood in the way of development but that Laura's was for the opposite reason. Doesn't work.'

Peter rounded on her. 'It does. Laura was having doubts about it. This Austen collection is beginning to loom large, isn't it? I wonder what it consists of, and how carefully the Luckhursts and Fettises went into the authentication question. Some of it at least seems to have been in the family for a long time, which is a good sign. And then there are the letters Tanner had, so don't forget the Clackingtons.'

'How could I?' Georgia murmured.

'Georgia? It's Jennifer Fettis.'

Of all the people to be calling her in the evening at Medlars, Jennifer was the least expected.

'Dora told me you're keen to know about the Jane Austen story and that she's holding back on telling you herself,' Jennifer continued. 'If that's so, would you like to come over to Stourdens? I'd be happy to talk to you, and Dora can feel she has a clear field too.'

'I'd love to,' Georgia said, 'if you feel up to it.' At last she and Peter could move on.

'Yes. We're rather pushed for the next few days. How about Friday afternoon? And bring your father too.' A pause. 'I should tell you that Tim thinks I'm crazy, because it's the Luckhurst murder that interests you, not Jane Austen, but I need to talk about something other than my mother.' It seemed to Georgia a cry for help.

It was raining on Friday when she drew up outside Stourdens with Peter, and the house looked an even sadder place. 'Perhaps bereavement has its own fingerprints,' she said as she got out of the car with a large umbrella to try to shield Peter. She was hoping against hope that only Jennifer would be present, but it was Tim who opened the door. He did his best to look as though he were pleased to see them, but she could see the set expression despite the welcoming words.

'Jennifer's in the living room,' he said. 'Go gently, will you?'

'Of course. Are you still swamped with the media on top of everything else?'

He shrugged. 'Yes, but it's inevitable. Ironic to think we wanted publicity for Stourdens and now we've got it, though hardly as we would have wished.'

'Are you still holding back on future plans?' Peter asked as Georgia and Tim dealt with wet coats and umbrella.

'It's a complicated business with wills and so on. We're thinking that the best way to deal with it may be to let it all happen gradually without any fanfares. Too many people besides us depend on us now. Laura wouldn't have wanted to let them down.'

'Jake Halliday mentioned a documentary about Stourdens, and I gather that Philip Faring has a book on the stocks about it too.'

'You're well informed,' Tim said pleasantly.

'Our job,' Peter said mildly. 'It all sounds interesting.'

'It is. Phil's a first-class scholar, and he's had a breathtaking subject to work on here. It would be a crying shame if we didn't support it; it's due out in December. And Philip and Jake aren't the only ones. There are commitments to Tom Miller, some of whose land Laura was planning to buy; Barbara Hastings has set up her company ready to expand the catering side, and Craig is coming in with her on that. The whole of Dunham is going to be affected – and for good, not bad.'

And so, it occurred to Georgia, quite a few people would have reason to wish Laura Fettis dead, if she was beginning to have doubts about commercializing Stourdens.

Jennifer came out to meet them, looking very wary. From the look she gave Tim she wasn't pleased when he followed them into the living room overlooking the terrace. 'We're only going to talk about the same old story, Tim,' she said pointedly.

The hint for him to leave failed, and he sat on the arm of her chair with his arm around her shoulder, until she made a direct appeal to him to ask if he could bring tea in and he unwillingly left.

'Sorry,' Jennifer said to them. 'It's just that I know how important the Austen collection was to my mother and I didn't want to be distracted.'

'You showed us some of it in Abbot's Folly,' Peter prompted her when she seemed uncertain how to begin.

'So we did. I'd forgotten – we showed you the portraits, didn't we, and I imagine Dora's already told you quite a bit.'

'No. We only got as far as its having something to do with a love affair beginning at Edgar House when Captain Harker came into a room where Jane Austen was waiting. Dora implied that in the end something nasty had happened in the relationship.'

Jennifer managed a smile. 'Dora must be longing to tell you more. She revels in it.'

'Until Gerald calls a halt,' Peter said.

Jennifer shrugged. 'It hardly matters now. In a nutshell: William Harker was paid off in 1802 from his ship HMS *Rhea* because the Treaty of Amiens called a halt to the hostilities between Napoleon and England. His brother owned the Edgar Arms, which was then an inn for changing post-chaises and stage coaches. William was staying there, and Jane and Cassandra were waiting for the carriage from Godmersham to pick them up. When they visited their brother Edward Austen, who then lived at Godmersham Park, they often hired post-chaises, stopping at coaching inns en route. Harker was a frequent guest at Stourdens because he was a friend of the fifth baronet and therefore knew his mother well, the widowed Lady Edgar. Stourdens is so close to Godmersham Park that Jane and Cassandra frequently visited it with their brother Edward and his family, and – as Dora would say – romance blossomed between Jane and William. Their stay was during September and October 1802, and on that occasion Jane's brother Charles was also present at Godmersham Park. It was during that time that Jane painted her watercolour of William and Cassandra drew Jane herself. We don't quite know how they came to be in the Luckhurst collection, but we suspect that Lady Edgar might have confiscated them.'

Georgia blinked. 'Why on earth should she do that?'

'Because she was the fly in the ointment. She seems to have mistaken the relationship she had with her son's best chum Harker for love, not just friendship. Unfortunately, he wasn't in love with her, but in Jane Austen's time there were rules about that sort of thing. He had been so constantly in Lady Edgar's company since he was paid off from his ship in May that gossip had them an affianced couple. So late in October poor old Jane went back with Charles and Cassandra to Steventon, by then her brother James' home, under the happy impression that William would be coming to visit her in a week or two's time. All she got was a letter saying that he was to marry Lady Edgar.'

'Tough on Jane,' Georgia commented.

'And Harker too. His marriage duly took place in March 1803, and two months later the Amiens treaty broke down and war broke out. He was recalled to his ship and died at Trafalgar two years later. He probably didn't see his blushing bride again, and maybe was glad not to do so. But it left Jane Austen so devastated that she accepted the first offer of marriage she received, which was at Manydown Park near Basingstoke in early December. The rebound, in fact.'

'Harris Bigg-Wither,' Georgia said. 'And then she immediately regretted it. But I thought there was a story about another man she was in love with earlier on – 1801?'

'Date in doubt, location of meeting in doubt, and name and profession in doubt,' Jennifer said. 'I talked this over with Mum time and time again. I don't see that it matters. Perhaps by the time Cassandra came to tell the story the passing years had confused the details with someone else and she was actually referring to Harker; if Harker wasn't the lucky man, then she had two beaux in addition to Bigg-Wither and not one. Not unlikely.'

'Did your mother believe in the Harker story?'

'Oh yes. After all, it fits so well with *The Watsons*. Stourdens is Osborne Castle where the widowed Lady Osborne lived with her son, the new fifth baronet. In the novel Emma Watson attended the local Assembly Rooms and danced with a Mr Howard. That's more or less the end of the action in *The Watsons* because Jane Austen abandoned it, but after her death it emerged – though it's disputed – that Jane Austen planned to have Lady Osborne make eyes at Mr Howard. In the novel, as distinct from Jane Austen's own love affair, Mr Howard was to disentangle himself and marry his true love Emma Watson. Wishful thinking on Jane's part.'

'Still at it?' Tim appeared with a tray piled with cups and saucers, and it seemed to throw Jennifer off her stride because she busied herself with laying them out ready for tea. When Tim had fetched the teapot and a plate of biscuits, he went over to kiss Jennifer, but it seemed to Georgia she flinched a little.

'Is the collection still in the folly?' Georgia asked brightly, to cover an awkward silence.

It was Tim who answered. 'Yes. I gather Laura wanted it kept there just as it was in Bob Luckhurst's time, because it was away from the main house. She wanted it to be accessible, but not to every Tom, Dick and Harry who might come into Stourdens. Ridiculous, really, because it costs a small fortune in insurance to have it out there, plus the heating bills to keep it from the damp and frost. We might move it back indoors now.'

Jennifer did not comment, but again Georgia sensed a withdrawal in her, as though putting distance between herself and Tim.

'Amelia Luckhurst told us that your mother was getting worried about the possible effects of your plans for Stourdens,' Peter said.

'Nonsense,' Tim replied immediately just as Jennifer spoke again.

'She was. It worries me too. Mum loved the peace and quiet and the atmosphere here. She was afraid Stourdens would be ruined.'

'You don't want this place to fall down, do you, sweetheart?' Tim said solicitously, but there was an edge to his voice. 'Your mother's worries would have passed; it was just nerves, leading up to the Gala, and you're not seeing things straight either at the moment. Naturally enough. You'll have to excuse her—'

'Nobody has to excuse me anything, Tim,' Jennifer said coldly. 'The Fettises hold the collection, and I propose to talk to Peter and Georgia about it.'

'If you wish,' was all he murmured. 'It's your inheritance, not mine.'

She ignored this, went over to a desk and brought back a sheet of paper. 'Mum made a list of the more important documents in the collection; she made it in preparation for Jake's TV documentary, since she didn't want the collection itself to be seen in case it drew attention to the vulnerability of Abbot's Folly. The list was partly for that and partly as an aide-memoire for herself when she was to be interviewed about the collection. And now she never will be . . .' Jennifer struggled to regain her composure.

'Anyway, I made these photocopies for you,' she said, handing them to Peter and Georgia. 'I'd better run through one or two because Mum's descriptions aren't exactly explicit. The first is a letter from Mrs Wildman in 1806, who lived at Chilham Castle, addressed to Lady Edgar and recalling the balls at Chilham where Lady Edgar's late husband, Captain William Harker, had danced with Miss Jane Austen. That letter's either bitchy or ingenuous, I always think. Lady Edgar seems to have reverted to her former married name, which suggests a certain degree of snobbishness. There's a pocket book – they preceded diaries for noting one's daily events and thoughts – from a Tabitha Kemble recording her father speaking of a ball at Chilham where he danced with Miss Austen (which would be Cassandra, since she was the elder of the two); for the following year 1802 he recalled a friend of his named William Harker dancing with her sister Jane. The pocket book was given to the Luckhursts in 1890. There's a letter to Lord Edgar from Edward Austen's chum at Eastwell Park, Richard Milles, who was an MP and who had just dined at Godmersham; he had had the pleasure of sitting next to Miss Jane Austen. That's supported by a letter from his wife Mary to Lady Elizabeth Hatton, relating some gossip about the same dinner and the obvious affection between Miss Jane Austen and Captain William Harker.

'There's also,' Jennifer continued, 'a letter from the Reverend Isaac Lefroy to Edward Austen mentioning his having met Jane at Ramsgate in 1803 to whom he had recalled the happy occasion the previous year when she had been with Captain Harker. And just to whet the media appetite, Mum has underlined one from Jane herself to Lady Edgar congratulating her on her marriage in March 1803 which has a delightful twist about William: "He is the best of men, and one who thinks least of self and most of those for whom he cares, capable of riding out the heaviest weather." That's a gem because no letters from Jane Austen have hitherto been known to exist during this whole period. Cassandra destroyed them – for whatever reason. Dora's sure it was because she was jealous of Jane's love affair, and who's to know she's not right?'

'Could we go to the folly to see the collection?' Georgia asked.

A glance at Tim, and Jennifer replied regretfully, 'Of course. Not today though. But tell Dora she can show you the letters she has. They're quite something, especially combined with ours.'

Tim had remained silent, but the way he rose unasked to show them to the door spoke volumes.

'It strikes me that the household is at odds with itself over and above the problems of bereavement,' Peter said reflectively as they drove away. 'Mike hasn't commented, but I wonder whether any of them are on the suspect list.'

'Surely—' Georgia broke off. Just because she liked Jennifer didn't mean that her father and fiancé were immune from suspicion, or even worse, Jennifer herself, although that was something she could not entertain. 'Tensions are bound to be high,' she said. 'Just think what it must be like not only grieving but also having the police and the press on your back all the time.'

'You would think that would draw them together, not put a wedge between them. Abbot's Folly seems to be a tension point in itself – any chance that Laura was going there, not the garden, when she was killed?'

'It's possible, but why? It would have to be something dramatic because only half an hour before she'd told Dora she was too ill to make the speech. Something made her dash out of the house when she wasn't well and when her presence outside would undoubtedly be noted.'

'And yet it wasn't, which is even stranger,' Peter said. 'Her natural route would be over the terrace to the path that we went along on the day of the Gala. So with people setting up cameras and whatnot on the terrace and gathering for the four o'clock announcement, why on earth didn't anyone see her?'

'I think there's another route,' Georgia said. 'I saw a path leading off through the stretch of woodland that bounds the gardens. I bet it leads back to join the front forecourt.'

'Could be. But why so anxious to avoid being seen?'

'For the very reasons you state. It would be thought odd for Roy to announce she was ill and for her then to be spotted.'

'So returning to where we began: why go at all?'

SEVEN

'Peter's here,' Luke announced. 'He's getting out of the car.'

Georgia's first reaction was to ask: What's wrong? Peter seldom arrived at Medlars without prior warning, and a sudden arrival on a Saturday morning was unprecedented. Alarm bells were ringing furiously. The washing machine promptly then added its own contribution by sounding the alert that it had finished its cycle, and simultaneously the phone rang. She left Luke to deal with these two demands, while she hurried out to meet Peter.

To her relief, far from looking as though he had a disaster to announce, he was obviously excited.

'What's up?' she asked cautiously.

'A cup of coffee and I might condescend to tell you.'

She gritted her teeth and followed his suggestion. It was quicker that way. Coffee was easy to fix, and Peter beamed his approval.

'Care to share the news?' she asked.

'The bad or the good?'

'Bad first.'

'Cath rang me about the Tanners. She thought she was doing rather well on Max. He was released in 1999 and went to live in London with his parents. Then he moved to Norwich and vanished from the records, and Tanner isn't an easy name to

track down. Too many of them. So the trail goes cold. Esther
Tanner, on the other hand, moved to north London and
remarried.'

'New name?'

'Wilson.'

It took a moment to sink in, and then: 'Are you saying . . .
but you can't be. Wilson's also a common name.'

'Agreed, but this Esther Wilson does have a son called
Timothy born in Canterbury in 1982.'

'That's extraordinary,' Georgia said. 'I wonder if Jennifer
knows? Or if Roy or Amelia does? Or come to that, does Tim?
It opens up a minefield of possibilities. Does Tim know where
his father is? Did he meet Jennifer by chance? What's Esther's
role in this? Does Tim's parentage have any relevance to Robert
Luckhurst's murder? All that remains to be seen, but what do
we do with the information?'

'Maddening though it be, I suggest we sit on it for a while.
The Tanners don't come into DI Newton's investigation, but
Tim does, so I'll tell Mike in case there turns out to be a link.
That's the problem with this case. We can't fight our way to
the truth about Luckhurst's death until we've cleared up whether
or not it's linked to Laura's. That is,' Peter amended crossly,
'if the trial story isn't the truth. It still could be. After all, it
isn't unknown for our "fingerprints" to be misleading. We've
assumed that they had a bearing on Luckhurst's murder, but
suppose some Neanderthal man was killed and buried beneath
what is now the folly? It could be him reaching out to us.'

'As the old song goes, smoke gets in your eyes,' she
remarked. 'But who lit this particular bonfire?'

By the time Georgia reached the office on Monday, Peter had
lost some of his ebullience. Suspicious, she thought and slipped
away to beard Margaret, his carer, in the kitchen. Margaret
simply raised a despairing eyebrow at her, which instantly
made Georgia think of trouble from Elena. She proved only
partly right.

'Elena?' Peter repeated when she asked if her mother was
on his mind. 'Could be.'

'Because you have or haven't heard from her?'

'The latter. That woman's like buttercups. Lovely to look at, but they creep along underground and spring up in unexpected places.'

He was right. Her mother could indeed coil her way round their hearts and minds, but, Georgia reasoned, only if they allowed her to. How to convince Peter of that, though? There was no way except to fix his mind on something else, she decided. The Clackingtons would do nicely, and she urged him to ring them.

'Oddly enough,' Peter told her, 'I've already done so. Dora didn't seem as keen as we expected, but I've fixed for us to go over tomorrow.'

When they arrived, however, the greeting they received was a warm one, although Georgia thought that Dora seemed subdued and her fussing over the delicate ruffles of her chiffon blouse indicated nervousness. Almost immediately she excused herself to return to the kitchen, leaving Gerald in charge.

'Busy morning here,' Gerald explained awkwardly. 'Only lacks Jane Austen dropping in to chair the meeting. You pop into the living room, Georgia, and introduce yourself, and I'll see you in, Peter.'

Something was certainly going on, but what? Georgia obediently opened the door and found not strangers but Philip and Jake perched on spindly chairs and talking quietly. There was something about the intimacy of the conversation that confirmed for her that they were partners. They seemed oddly matched, however: Jake extrovert and impulsive, Philip typecast as an academic with his long serious face.

Like Tweedledum and Tweedledee, they simultaneously rose to greet her, save that physically this pair bore no resemblance to Lewis Carroll's battling characters. As before, it was Jake who came across to kiss her.

'Great to have you with us, Georgia. Dora said you and Peter might be coming. Peter with you?'

'On his way round,' she said, curious about Jake's choice of words. 'Have you with us' sounded more like an event than a casual call.

'How are your plans for the documentary, Jake?' she asked as Peter and Gerald appeared through the far doorway.

'As far as I'm concerned, it's going ahead as planned. I can't see any reason that Roy and Tim would want to cancel it,' Jake said easily. 'We'll be tact itself, obviously, but we're far too much into it for Roy to want to cancel the contract.'

'And your book, Philip?' Peter asked.

Philip hesitated, but Jake nodded. 'We have to move on, Phil. The rules of the game have changed.'

'We were supposed,' Phil said awkwardly, 'to be keeping the subject matter of my book under wraps until Laura had made her announcement. It was a key point in the publicity plans for Stourdens' future.'

'Will it still be published in December?' Georgia asked.

'I'm discussing it with the publishers. It's almost as hard to change a book's publication date as it is a film, but I hope they don't see any problem.'

He didn't look happy though, Georgia thought, and she could see his point. Stourdens was still a volatile situation.

'He's fussing,' Jake assured them. 'We're still aiming to shoot in late August, and include a shot of Jennifer and Tim's wedding in September, so why not leave the book as it stands too?'

'Is the wedding still going ahead?' Georgia was staggered. There'd been no mention of such imminent wedding plans, and the relationship between Jennifer and Tim seemed wobbly for a romantic wedding in two months' time.

'We haven't heard that it won't be. Like my film, wedding arrangements tend to be set in stone. Rooms booked, staff booked, guests invited, catering booked.'

Unfortunately, Dora was coming in with a fresh pot of coffee to join them at that moment and must have overheard because she looked aghast. 'Whatever would Laura have said?' she moaned.

Jake hastened to reassure her. 'She loved Stourdens, Dora. She wouldn't have wanted it to be force-sold for a hotel or knocked down, and so she would have urged us on, and Tim and Jennifer as well, if that's what they wanted.'

Dora did not look convinced, and Georgia hastened to fill the silence that followed. 'Are you using Edgar House as well as Stourdens, Jake?'

'That's what we're here for this morning,' Jake said easily.

'We're doing a location walk-through. Phil's written a guideline script and a suggested continuity schedule. My production designer's joining us later. Phil and I have only come early so that we could have a squint at the famous letters. I gather that's what interests you two?' He looked enquiringly – challengingly? – at Peter and Georgia.

Dora still looked unhappy. 'I'd been looking forward to being on television,' she said helplessly, 'but so soon after Laura's death . . . my best friend . . .' She looked at Gerald for support.

'Jake isn't filming today, Dollybird. You'll see – it'll buck you up a bit,' he said encouragingly.

'But, Gerald, there's the *funeral*.'

'Is there news of that?' Georgia asked.

'Yes. Roy rang me. The police and coroner have given them the go-ahead. It will be a burial,' Gerald added awkwardly. 'I gather he's planning a public service in St Mary's at Chilham and then a strictly family burial and gathering afterwards. That's why poor Dolly's upset. Family only.'

Georgia could see tears on Dora's face and well understand why. It seemed a hurtful decision. Even if the burial itself remained private, surely the gathering afterwards could have been widened in scope.

'I know,' Dora said bravely, 'that family wishes have to come first, but I would so like to have been considered *part* of the family. And why not St Lawrence's at Godmersham, where Jane Austen herself attended services?'

Gerald cleared his throat. 'We should get going, Dollybird. We keep the letters upstairs. Face the lift again, can you, Peter?'

'Looking forward to it,' Peter said heartily.

He wasn't, as Georgia knew. He hated lifts, but they were preferable to missing out on something he wanted to see. And he most certainly wanted to see the letters. They had both been studying the lists that Jennifer had provided, and Peter had carried out further research to satisfy himself that from the brief headings they seemed a reasonable coverage of the Austen-Harker story.

'What are you planning to film here?' she asked Jake. 'Just the Assembly Rooms?'

'No. Phil's idea, and it's a good one, is to follow the course
of where Jane Austen might have trodden after her post-chaise
had deposited her here. So the camera would track her from
the point she steps down in the cobbled courtyard and goes
with Cassandra into what is now Dora and Gerald's dining
room. Then the door would open and Harker come in.'

This sounded ghastly to Georgia. 'You're hiring costumed
actors?' she asked doubtfully.

'Yes, but after we've all checked the location we'll decide
whether to film it straight or with depth staging or in-out focus
to distance the early nineteenth from the twenty-first-century
bits. We might even just see Jane Austen's feet descending
from the chaise.' He grinned. 'Sorry, that sounds a real mess,
but I need to get the feel of the place first before we fix how
to film it. Of course,' he added, 'what viewers are always dying
to see is where the ladies powdered their noses. Any idea,
Dora?' He put his arm round her and gave her a little hug.

Dora tried hard to enter into the spirit of the thing, but it
was clear her heart was not in it. 'We're not sure where that
was,' she faltered. 'She could have withdrawn to a bedroom
with a commode. It's possible it was the one above our dining
room where we now keep the letters.'

'Let's go, Dora,' Gerald said firmly and beckoned Peter to
follow him.

Georgia accompanied Dora, Jake and Philip up the stairs,
where Dora led them to the right, to the room they had bypassed
on Georgia's last visit.

'Shall we wait for Gerald?' Dora suggested timidly before
entering.

Jake nodded, and Georgia went to join him at the window
that overlooked the courtyard beneath. 'That's good,' he said,
peering down. 'We'll have to get the post-chaise in at the rear
but that looks possible.'

'Oh, here's Gerald,' Dora said with relief as he and Peter
appeared from the Assembly Rooms. It sounded as though the
trip by lift was a major achievement, Georgia thought in
amusement, but it was another sign of how upset Dora was.

Gerald opened the door into a small darkened room with
shutters over the windows, which he went over to open. Even

the light behind her was enough to make Georgia jump as three life-sized figures in the room fooled her into thinking for a moment that they were real. One, unsurprisingly, was of a man in naval costume, and the other two were young women in Regency dress standing either side of the window bay. The walls were full of pictures, but pride of place was given to an elegant antique table bearing a showcase, the glass of which was covered with a black cloth. Dora was back in her element now, standing proudly by it.

'Shall we, Gerald?'

'Go ahead, Dollybird.'

Peter eagerly propelled himself forward, but Jake beat him to it. Philip must have seen the letters before while writing his book and so he hung back, while Georgia pressed forward to see what was lying on the black velvet cushion. Two handwritten letters with typed transcripts beneath, plus part of a third letter.

The one on the left, written in heavy ink, was headed 10th November 1802. The paper had yellowed, it had been folded and the edges damaged. 'My dear Frank,' Georgia read with some difficulty, and then switched to the transcript for easier reading.

> News will no doubt have reached you that Lady Edgar has done me the honour of consenting to become my wife. Circumstances have prevented my conveying these tidings to you earlier. May I beg you to put from your mind, as I do from my own, all thought of Miss Jane Austen, of the precious weeks of autumn, and of the happiness that might have been mine. You will know how limited are my expectations – I have no ship or prospect of one. The great kindness that Lady Edgar has shown me these six months past has long been evident to me, to you and to all who have observed it. I am thus in honour bound to repay it, and to forget that happy day when my eyes fell upon Miss Jane Austen and her sister in your . . .

Whatever followed had been lost, perhaps a second page, but even what was there was quite something, Georgia thought. The writing was uneven, as if done in agitation – as it could well have been. Jake, to whom this must be new material, was giving whoops of delight at what he was reading and only reluctantly swapped places with Georgia.

'Hold on to your hat. This one's Jane herself speaking,' he told her.

The writing in this scrap of a letter was entirely different, smaller and lighter. It was dated 4th November 1802, just after Jane Austen would have reached Steventon from Kent.

> My dearest Captain Harker,
> The day is near. Pray acquaint me with how you shall arrive at Steventon. Shall you come in yellow stockings cross-gaitered like poor Malvolio? Shall you come with smoke made with the fume of sighs as did Romeo? How shall I greet you? As our dear Lady Disdain at Stourdens or . . .

A week later the mood had changed. The last letter read:

> My dear Captain Harker,
> I had anticipated your visit to Steventon with pleasure, and had little expected it to be replaced by the happy news of your betrothal to Lady Edgar. I offer you my felicitations. Lady Edgar will recieve [sic] a husband who is the most honourable and sensible of men, and yet I must confess I would wish that sensibility might have prevailed over sense.
> I am yours etc
> Jane Austen

A put-down indeed. Georgia had recalled reading somewhere that Jane Austen's spelling varied from today's norm in respect of 'ie' and 'ei'. She also remembered that Jane Austen's first novel to be published was an earlier work rewritten and renamed *Sense and Sensibility*. All too pat? She decided not. The difference between the two Austen letters was convincing enough.

Dora was watching them anxiously, and after Peter had finished reading them she said tentatively, 'They're so very moving, aren't they?'

'They are indeed,' Peter replied. 'I take it you've seen the full collection in the folly, Philip? Are the letters there in the same style as these? This –' he pointed to the incomplete one – 'is certainly unlike any in the published collections of her letters.'

'Of course it is,' Dora said simply before Philip could speak. 'Because Cassandra destroyed all her other letters between 1801 and 1804, which includes the autumn of 1802 and its aftermath. I believe she was jealous of the love that existed between Jane and William because she loved him herself.'

'I suspect,' Philip added, 'she also destroyed many of Jane's other letters, any that reflected Jane's own feelings. If you're worried, I can assure you that there is no doubt that Harker was Jane Austen's great love. It all checks out. The Kent Archives confirm that from 1800 to 1810 the inn was owned by a Francis Harker, and I found references both to him and to his brother in Mrs Warlington's diary.'

'Who was she?' Georgia asked.

'The wife of a local rector who recorded in her pocket day book that she and her husband had visited the Edgar Arms. They had had the pleasure of meeting Captain William Harker, brother of the landlord, and of hearing about the late war with Napoleon and HMS *Rhea*. Naval records show that both *Rhea* and Captain Harker existed.'

'I take it the letters themselves have been authenticated?' Peter asked.

'I can assure you,' Philip said stiffly, 'that they have. Everything here and at Stourdens has been authenticated over the years by experts both in Jane Austen and in other relevant aspects.'

'Of course it has,' Dora said indignantly. 'We had ours checked before we bought the house. The ink is correct for 1802; so are the paper and watermarks.'

'What about the writing and signatures?'

'Checked by a graphologist for the appearance and by computer for conformity of language,' Philip confirmed. 'And the paper is hand dipped with watermarks for 1802 as used in *The Watsons*. And, incidentally, could I point out that no one would have bothered to fake Jane Austen's hand *before*

1806, when resin size was introduced with machine-made paper. Jane Austen's first novel appeared in 1811. Anything faked thereafter would in all probability have used post-1806 paper.'

Dora regained some of her usual vigour. 'Why should the story not be genuine?' she asked querulously. 'People are all too eager today to favour the negative. Of course there is a need for truth, but there does seem to be a disposition, almost a hope, towards assuming that everything good and interesting about the past must be false. Why can't we rejoice that Jane had this love affair instead of trying so hard to disprove it?'

'You're right, Dora,' Jake said. 'Count me on your side. It's an A1 story and I wouldn't be putting all my time into it without being sure that Phil and I are on firm ground.'

'We have to be sure too,' Peter said mildly. 'That's our job.'

'Which is Robert Luckhurst's death from what I heard,' Philip rejoined.

'It is, but bear in mind that Bob Luckhurst was the owner of the Austen collection, save for these letters here, and now there has been a second death.'

A moan from Dora. 'Please . . .'

'Seems a rum do to me,' Gerald said vigorously. 'The police don't seem to have a clue about finding Laura's killer. My instinct is that some maniac crept in from the footpath behind the folly.'

'Why?' Peter asked.

'Don't have to have a reason nowadays,' Gerald grunted. 'Drugs. That's what's behind it.'

'But even a drug-crazed maniac usually has a grievance if he comes out armed with a gun, as this one did. Why did he choose Laura?'

'Must have picked on the wrong person,' Gerald mumbled.

'It was a killing at close quarters,' Georgia pointed out, 'so unless her killer didn't know his victim by sight that's unlikely to have been the explanation. More likely he knew very well whom he was killing, especially as it's almost certain she came from the house *with* her killer.'

'Oh, I can't bear it,' Dora cried. 'I really can't.'

Jake put a comforting arm round her shoulders but

nevertheless said gently, 'The police have to work out how she was persuaded to go there so quickly after you saw her, Dora. You're sure she had no plans to leave the house?'

Dora shook her head violently. 'She didn't.'

'Not even to listen to what Roy said in place of her announcement?'

'No, no, *no!*' she screamed. 'Can't you understand that?'

'Steady on, Dora,' Gerald said.

Jake still pursued the subject. 'Odd though. Half an hour or so later she was in the garden, so someone must have gone to see her or contacted her somehow immediately after you left.'

Despite Dora's anguish, Georgia knew she ought not to let the opportunity slip. 'It takes eight minutes to walk from the house to the folly along the usual path, but—'

Jake saw her point immediately. 'I was on the terrace and so were plenty of other people, which means Laura must have gone out of Stourdens' *front* door to reach the woods and Abbot's Retreat unnoticed. Why though? If someone suggested they walked that way she would surely have thought that weird.' A silence. 'I'm wrong. Laura wouldn't have done that,' Jake eventually continued. 'She had a will of iron under that sweet exterior, didn't she, Dora?'

'Yes,' Dora said weakly. 'Oh yes, she had.'

There was something here she could not grasp, but Georgia was determined not to let the subject drop. 'Her family were looking for her about four o'clock. You left her at what time, Dora?'

'About twenty to four,' she whispered.

'And roughly ten minutes later she must have gone with her killer to visit the garden for reasons unknown. The woodland path would take much longer, so she would have to have hurried to be in—'

'No,' Dora moaned. 'Not if she took the tunnel.'

A moment of horrified silence, and Dora flushed red.

'What tunnel?' Georgia asked flatly.

'Gerald . . .' Dora appealed to him, but in vain.

'What tunnel, Dora?' he barked.

Dora must have realized there was no escape. 'Laura told

me about it. There was a tunnel – is a tunnel – leading from the house right over to Abbot's Folly. I think it has two exits: one in the folly itself, the other just behind its adjoining wall in the Retreat. Laura said it was built by the Mad Abbot, so that he could disappear from the house any time he chose – and not get wet,' she ended pathetically.

'Is it still in use?' Peter demanded. 'Have you told the police?'

'I didn't think of it until now,' Dora wailed. 'Laura told me about it, but I never saw it.'

'Who told her about it?' Georgia asked abruptly. 'Amelia Luckhurst?' This could affect more than the death of Laura Fettis. It could be the answer to Robert Luckhurst's murder too.

'I don't know.' Dora looked confused. 'Laura only found out about it not too long ago. Tim had something to do with it.'

'Is it still open?'

'I don't know,' Dora wailed again. 'I *really* don't.'

'I think,' Jake murmured, 'that I see a whole new scenario for my documentary. Secret assignations in the grotto for Jane and William. I thought the tunnel was just a legend, didn't you, Phil?'

'I knew there used to be one,' Philip said. 'I never dreamed it still existed.' He looked very white – and no wonder, Georgia thought.

'Does it affect your book?' she asked.

'I doubt it, luckily. Sorry, Jake, but there was no evidence about the tunnel or mention of Jane and Harker being down there, so how could I have known?'

'Eighteenth-century tunnels usually had grottos,' Jake ruminated. 'Look at West Wycombe.'

'What *I'm* looking at,' Georgia said firmly, 'is the need to call DI Newton right now.'

EIGHT

'That tunnel.' Peter was still fuming two days later. 'It has to be the answer, and we're forbidden to see it until after Her Majesty has finished there.'

'By "Her Majesty" I assume you mean DI Newton,' Georgia said.

'I do,' he replied sourly. 'Out of bounds until her team's finished. Understandable, but it's frustrating not knowing more about it – or what Tim had to do with the matter. That young man seems to have established himself very nicely under the Stourdens' table. Mike told me yesterday that the tunnel is stable, so presumably the Luckhursts must have looked after it, and depending on how recently Laura Fettis was told of its existence, she too. Which means Roy and Jennifer must have been in the picture. Workmen or even surveyors couldn't have worked down there without their knowledge.'

'So why didn't they tell the police about it? Did Mike comment on that?'

Peter did not reply for a moment or two. Georgia knew how keen he was to see the tunnel but also that it was unlikely to accommodate a wheelchair. It would be her job to explore the tunnel, and it was not one to which she would look forward. Little as she had had to do with Tim and Roy, and much as she liked Jennifer, a long tunnel, presumably only lit by hand-held torches, was not the best of places to get to know them better. If it was built in the late eighteenth century, it was likely to be creepy, if only because 'delicious horror' had been the objective of such tunnels. Grottos, temples, follies, all contributed to the shivers that ran up and down the eighteenth-century spine. She had walked through several such tunnels in her life, and if one needed evidence that violence and injustice could leave their indelible mark behind it was to be found there.

'According to Mike,' Peter replied at last, 'the Fettis family, including Laura, knew about it because there were mentions

of it in the archives, but they assumed it had fallen in long
ago – and they didn't know where it was, anyway.'

'So how come it's in good condition now?'

'Only Tim might be able to supply the answer to that – and
so far we don't know what it is.'

'It's interesting that Amelia apparently didn't tell Laura of
its existence.'

'And also significant if she'd used it on the day of Bob
Luckhurst's murder.' Peter beamed. It was a small step forward,
but one they had needed. 'You'd think the local tongues would
wag though if they had maintained the tunnel well. Amelia
must have had domestic help at Stourdens – cleaners, gardeners,
handymen, and so on.'

'Even the trial reports don't mention any evidence that
Amelia was involved. Which suggests the police investigation
had more or less cleared both her and Tom Miller, if they ever
did look on them seriously as suspects.'

'They would have done,' Peter said simply, and she could
not disagree.

'I suppose there was no mention of tunnels in the police
reports?'

'If so, I would have picked up on it,' Peter replied with
dignity. 'Mind you, tunnels wouldn't have been likely to pop
into Hamlyn's mind.'

'Whose?'

'Vic Hamlyn's. It was his case. Funny chap.'

'Still alive?'

Peter looked horrified. 'Georgia, I've been asleep at the
switch. I don't know. Anybody else I've overlooked? What
about Barbara Hastings as villain as well as witness?'

'She doesn't seem to have a motive, and she told me she
was on duty at the pub that day. Just because she was alive
at the time of both murders doesn't mean she's the missing
link.'

'But she could be,' Peter muttered in exasperation.

'Rubbish,' she retorted. 'Even supposing she had a yen for
Tanner or vice versa, sex as a motive for one murder and greed
for another isn't a likely combination. One stems from passion,
the other demands calculation.'

'Don't generalize,' Peter snarled.

Georgia was tempted to shout back, 'Why not? You do,' but restrained herself just in time. Childishness would get them nowhere, which, she reflected, seemed to be where they were heading, anyway.

Every parking space in Chilham Square, including the disabled ones, had already been taken when Luke drove up into the village for Laura's funeral the following week. Fortunately, Georgia and Luke had brought Peter in their car, which meant he could disembark here and make his own way along the path to St Mary's church, which lay back from the square itself. Luke then parked at the foot of the hill, and they walked back up to the square past Chilham's glorious medieval houses.

At least Jane Austen had known Chilham well, and it was still a lovely village. It was compact, perched at the top of a hill, with its shops, ancient houses, church, castle and pub huddled together around the small central square. Cottages sprawled down the hillside in every direction. It was so unchanged that it was easy to imagine Jane Austen arriving here in the Godmersham carriage perhaps to shop or to visit Chilham Castle.

By the time they had returned, Peter had already taken up a position at the rear of the church where he said he could best keep a discreet eye on the congregation. 'You never know who might be here,' he told them.

The church was nearly full. To Georgia, it seemed that the entire population of Dunham had turned out together with everyone who had attended the Gala. The press were heavily but discreetly represented, and she had seen TV cameras outside, which made her realize that there might be some sense as to why the burial and gathering afterwards were to be private. Even so, she felt sorry for Dora for being excluded, and it did indeed seem a pity that the service was taking place here and not St Lawrence's, which had such strong Austen connections.

Luke still maintained that families were entitled to plan funerals as they wished, but Peter agreed with Georgia. If Stourdens was to trade on its links to Jane Austen it would seem right for the funeral to take place in St Lawrence's, although she wondered if that were the very reason that Jennifer and Roy wanted it further afield. But who *was* family in this case? Would Esther Wilson, formerly Tanner, count?

She saw Peter's point about his position at the rear. When the funeral procession entered the church, it was hard for her to see through the sea of faces as she was squeezed in with Luke into the far end of a pew and up against the church wall. All that was visible were the large black hats of the women in the funeral party and a few faces she recognized here and there. She spotted Barbara Hastings next to Craig and thought she glimpsed Amelia Luckhurst, now Collier, but could not be sure. She also spotted another familiar face, Alfred Wheeler, and Georgia wondered what his connection with the Fettises was.

The service was a long one, during which Jennifer made a moving tribute to her mother, ending with the wording on Jane Austen's tomb, which she read with a trembling voice, saying that they could easily refer to Laura: 'The benevolence of her heart, the sweetness of her temperament, and the extraordinary endowments of her mind obtained the regard of all who knew her, and the warmest love of her intimate connections.' Georgia wished she had known Laura Fettis, and the tribute added to her determination to do all she could to help Jennifer.

By the time she and Luke had waited their turn to leave the church and rejoin Peter, she saw that the funeral party was about to depart. Most of the cars ready to follow the coffin looked full, and only Tim and Roy remained to greet the rest of the congregation. As she and Luke waited their turn, she noticed with surprise that Philip Faring and Jake Halliday were getting into one of the cars. Not solely family then, she thought wryly.

Other people had clearly noticed that too. She could see Barbara Hastings staring at the cars with a grim face, and more poignantly Dora and Gerald. Dora's face was puffed and red from crying, and it must be doubly hard for her to see that the family-only rule had been relaxed – but not for them. Funerals roused strong emotions, and not just in the family concerned.

Gerald took Dora's arm, and Georgia heard him say, 'Let's go to the White Horse, darling. We need a stiff drink.'

Many of the congregation seemed to have the same idea, for the pub, which was on the square and next door to the church, had a steady stream of customers making their way along the path towards it.

'Shall we go?' Luke suggested.

'Why don't we try the Bat and Trap?' Peter said, apparently casually.

Remembering that bacon sandwich, Georgia could not believe he was serious. She had assumed he would follow Dora and Gerald to the White Horse because they had agreed it hadn't only been the tunnel preying on Dora's mind. There was something else, but perhaps Peter thought this was unlikely to emerge in pub surroundings. When they reached the Bat and Trap, there were familiar faces here too, including Tom Miller's, whom she didn't at first recognize clad in his Sunday best.

She half expected that the buzz of conversation would abruptly halt as they entered, but she was wrong. Not only Peter, but she and Luke were positively welcomed. Perhaps Peter's liberal offer of drinks had played a part in that. While Peter joined Tom Miller, she and Luke were surprisingly beckoned over to a table with Barbara and Craig, who must be off-duty today.

Georgia trotted out the relevant conversational gambit. 'I'd expected the funeral to be in St Lawrence's,' she observed to Barbara.

'So did we all,' was the grim reply.

'I reckon the family didn't want us yobs there,' Craig growled. 'That sort likes to keep themselves to themselves.'

'Don't you go blabbing, Craig,' Barbara said quietly. 'You know where our bread's buttered.'

'Don't stop us thinking though, do it?' Craig said.

'Think all you like, but say nothing,' Barbara told him firmly. 'We need this catering deal. Just a shame we aren't working for Mrs Laura.'

'There's Jennifer,' Georgia said. 'Won't she be involved?'

'Yeah, but that Tim will steamroller over her. Not got her mother's guts.'

'But her father wouldn't allow that?'

Once on the subject of Tim, Barbara seemed to have forgotten her own edict. 'Wouldn't he just. Tim's got him where he wants him. Butters him up so he slips through whatever Tim wants.'

'It's the wedding soon too, isn't it?' Georgia asked as casually as she could manage.

'September the seventeenth. Surprised he hasn't rushed it forward,' Barbara replied. 'Can't wait to get his snout in the trough. There's a way to go yet though. Seven weeks is seven weeks.'

'I take it you don't like him,' Georgia said.

'Liking don't come into it with that sort. He's pleasant enough, if you do what he wants. So as long as he doesn't interfere with my job, I'll go along with it,' Barbara generously declared. 'There's Tom's land to think of too. Wouldn't be surprised if they don't try to wriggle out of that.'

'Could that happen legally?'

'Tom says it was agreed, nothing actually signed.'

That sounded bad. 'And you, Craig?' Georgia asked. 'Will you be joining the new company?'

'Give it my best. Build up the drinks side and run the bar at Stourdens. Spruce beer should be a winner.'

The bar? Georgia wondered where that fitted in, but decided not to stop the conversational flow by querying it.

Barbara's face lost its usual impassivity and her eyes brightened. 'As soon as the word comes we'll get going. The company's all legal now. It'll be good to have my own business at last. All down to Jane Austen, eh? Poor old Max. If only he could have foreseen this. I could have done it for the Edgar Arms, easy.'

A fleeting thought crossed Georgia's mind. Could Craig possibly be Tanner's son? He'd be about the right age. 'We haven't been able to trace Max Tanner yet. I suppose you haven't had any more ideas as to where he might be?'

Barbara opened her mouth to speak, but turned excitedly to Craig. '*That's* who it was. I said I knew that woman walking up the aisle. Her with the big hat. Didn't I, Craig? It was Esther Tanner. I'd swear to it.'

'The news will have spread,' Peter remarked as they drove him home. 'The time has come for us to have a word with the power behind Stourdens, Tim. Perhaps he might enlighten us as to where his father is now.'

'Visitors,' Luke remarked early that evening as she heard a car draw up outside. He went over to peer through the window. 'Good grief, it's Dora Clackington.'

'And Gerald, I presume,' Georgia said, leaping to her feet.

'No. On her own. Why's she driven over here?' Luke took a second look. 'She seems pretty agitated, Georgia. This is going to be girls' own talk so I'll leave you to it, and vanish.'

'Thanks a bunch,' Georgia said crossly, although conceding that Luke was right. Dora was more likely to need her than Luke, although she could have done without her company this evening.

Georgia waited until Luke had beaten a discreet retreat through the back door, from which he could reach the safety of his office, and then she went to the front door. Luke's 'pretty agitated' was an understatement. Dora was white and trembling, her face ashen against the pale brown of her dress and jacket.

'What's wrong?' Georgia asked in alarm.

'I need to tell you something, Georgia. Please. I know I can speak freely to you.'

Only so far, Georgia thought. She might be obliged to tell Mike, and of course Peter, but there was no point in scaring Dora still further by telling her so.

'I can't talk to Gerald,' Dora said, following Georgia into the Medlars living room. She looked around at its comfortable chairs and old sofa, and remarked pathetically, 'I like this room. So comforting. You are so lucky.'

'I know,' Georgia murmured awkwardly. 'Can I get you some coffee?'

This was waved aside. 'No thank you. I mustn't be long because Gerald doesn't know I've come. I have something to confess, and I know you'll understand. It's how we women work. But you see I should have told the police . . .'

'About the tunnel?' Georgia asked gently. 'We've already passed that on to them.'

Words came tumbling out. 'No, it was telling you about
that and realizing how I should have spoken before that meant
I simply didn't have the courage to tell you or the police. But
today at the funeral Laura spoke to me and I knew I must. So
I'm here.'

'So what is it?' Mad scenarios rushed through Georgia's
mind and were dismissed.

'That day . . . that awful day. The Gala. What I told the
police wasn't quite true, though I meant it to be. But somehow
it didn't come out as I intended. When I saw Laura that afternoon she was so upset. She hoped I wouldn't mind too much.'
Dora stopped and looked at Georgia in appeal.

'About what?' Georgia prompted her.

'She'd definitely decided that she wasn't going to let Stourdens
be commercialized. She said she'd agreed with the plans because
Roy and Tim were so enthusiastic and Jennifer too was in favour,
and she too could see the advantages, but she no longer did so.
There – I've told you.' Dora looked piteously at her. 'She said
that at four o'clock Roy was going to make her apologies for
her non-appearance, but her decision was final.'

The enormity of this disclosure made Georgia forget about
discretion. Roy had implied that Laura would make the
announcement when she felt she was well enough. In other
words, no change to the expected news of great things afoot
for Stourdens. 'But why on earth didn't you tell the police at
the time?'

'Well,' Dora faltered, 'I talked to Tim after Roy had spoken,
and he said Laura was always changing her mind and had
swung to and fro for ages on the question of how to save
Stourdens. And so I wasn't to worry about it. And then we
heard that she'd been killed and I forgot all about it.'

'Then why are you so worried now?'

'Because it isn't true,' Dora said miserably. 'She *had* been
unsure about it, that's true enough, but once she had made the
decision that would be the end of it. Laura would *never* go
back on something as definite as that. Not Laura.'

NINE

Georgia hadn't envied Dora her meeting with DI Newton the next morning. She had hoped Mike might have intervened, but there was no sign of him at Charing HQ. Dora had made Georgia promise to come with her, which showed a pathetic faith in the Marshes' powers, and Georgia was waiting with Gerald for her to be released from Newton's tender mercies. At last she emerged, and Georgia's heart sank when she saw her white face. She had clearly not been given an easy ride. Dora rushed straight into Gerald's arms.

'I said it all, just as you said I should,' she assured Georgia.

Not that that would have done her much good with Newton on her case, Georgia thought, but she soothingly replied, 'You did the right thing.' She saw Diane Newton leaving the interview room and her expression confirmed her fears, although even Newton could surely not seriously be thinking of Dora as a suspect. She wouldn't have the courage to take a gun in her hands, let alone fire one. Gerald might be a different matter, however, although Georgia could think of no possible motive for his wanting to murder Laura. Because she'd said she was going to abandon the plans for Stourdens? That seemed unlikely, even if Dora and Gerald hankered after Edgar House being included in them. Certainly, the Clackingtons seemed all for promoting Jane Austen, but murdering opponents who got in their way would hardly be their style. Not in a million years.

Dora's confession would be relevant to the police investigation, however, and the victim's family would surely be Newton's first port of call. Assuming it to be true, had they all known about Laura's change of heart or only Tim? The likelihood was that they all had, but they could well deny it, or claim, as Tim apparently had, that Laura was always swinging back and forth through indecision. Nevertheless, it could explain the family's being so obviously at odds with each other at the Gala, as well as the uneasiness between Tim and Jennifer. Georgia steeled herself to face the unwelcome fact that Jennifer might have been fully in the picture, and yet somehow she could not believe it.

Dora insisted to Georgia that she and Gerald offer her lunch, which she could hardly refuse although it entailed a long account of the houses that Elena might or might not buy. It was late afternoon by the time Georgia reached the office, and Peter was impatient to see her.

'Beware the Greeks bearing gifts,' he cried immediately she came in.

'Depends what the gift is.' Judging by his face it was good news though.

'Tim Wilson rang me before I could get on the blower to him. Anxious, would you say? A little call from the police?'

Peter still looked suspiciously happy.

'What was the gift?' she asked again.

'Tim suggested we might like to see the tunnel, now the police have finished with it. You, that is; I won't be able to make it.'

She braced herself now that the moment had come – in the worst possible way. Tim would be in charge. 'Will just walking along it add much though? We already know Amelia could have used it and possibly Tanner too.'

Peter glared at her. 'Don't you want to see it?'

'I suppose I should.'

'Then *enjoy* it. You're booked in for Saturday morning. Our Mr Wilson says they need a day or two to recover from the funeral.'

'And no doubt from the police visit they'll have had today. Are you coming?'

'Not necessary now.' Peter looked smug. 'I've had my few words with Mr Wilson about his interesting parentage.'

'On the phone?' That was unusual. Anything important and Peter liked to see the whites of their eyes.

'No. Amazing thing. The one word "mother" made him decide he needed to dash right over here.'

'Was that wise?' She frowned. Peter was physically vulnerable, and there was a murderer at large.

'No risk. You knew about it too.'

'He admits to being Max Tanner's son then?'

'Yes. Never met his father – not since he was two years old, anyway. No idea what's happened to him. His mother's happily remarried to David Wilson, who is a loving stepfather. A happy-ever-after story.'

'Especially as Tim's wound up engaged to the heir of Stourdens.'

'A poisoned chalice, don't you think, in its present state of health?'

'Chance or design?'

'You mean his meeting Jennifer? A bit of both, I'm told. His background is PR in London; he met her, dated her, fell in love with her, then heard about Stourdens. Name rang a faint bell. Mentioned it to Mum – and found out the story about his father. Got him curious.'

'Odd that he hadn't looked it up before.'

'He had. Just forgot the name Stourdens. Only Abbot's Folly rang a bell.'

'If Stourdens was in a healthy financial state, I'd say that was a fantasy, but as it isn't, the story's credible. And the tunnel?' she asked. 'Did Laura tell him about it?'

'That, dear daughter, is for you to discover.'

Georgia arrived at Stourdens with a sense of anticipation, even though the anorak and jeans donned ready for tunnel exploration did not exactly make her feel like Jane Austen arriving for a morning call.

'Hi.' It was Jennifer who opened the door. 'Welcome to Dissension City.' She pulled a face. 'Sorry, it's not the happiest place in the world at present.'

The house seemed to reflect that. As Jennifer led her through, Georgia was more aware on this occasion of the cracks in the walls, the pail that stood significantly under an ornate ceiling and the smell of damp that met her nostrils from a corridor to their left.

Jennifer led her to the same comfortable, shabby living room where they had talked before. This time Roy and Tim were both present, rising like a formal reception party to greet her.

Georgia decided to treat it as such. 'It's very good of you to let me see the tunnel.'

'Better you should see it, rather than have garbled stories getting into print,' Roy remarked ungraciously.

'Daddy!' Jennifer looked at him reproachfully, but Georgia was used to this attitude.

'They won't,' was all she said.

'So you're going ahead with this book of yours on Bob Luckhurst?'

'Still looking into it,' she replied steadily. 'Even though we realize it must be painful for you.'

'Before our time,' he said dismissively. 'It's old history to us, so investigate all you like, provided you're not poking around on Jennifer and Tim's wedding day, or barging into the film shoot.'

Georgia saw Jennifer flinch. Avoid the direct answer. 'I gather the wedding's on the seventeenth of September. Is the filming still the last week of August?'

'Begins on the twenty-third at Edgar House for a couple of days, then moves here.'

Jennifer did not comment, and Georgia saw Tim glance anxiously at her.

Roy cleared his throat. 'It's been a hard decision whether to go ahead with the film but we've decided to do it. And so –' a touch of defiance – 'we shall with the plans for Stourdens. Nothing too showy though, and we'll do it gradually instead of making the great announcement to the world.'

Georgia decided to plunge right in. 'Even though there's new evidence that your wife changed her mind about it?'

Roy's face darkened, and Tim quickly stepped in. 'Dora Clackington is hardly the most reliable witness in the world, Georgia. You were quite right that she should tell the police about it, but it's made things difficult for us, as only we know what the true position was.'

'The police have to follow it up just in case, but it's hard on you,' Georgia replied.

'Why do they have to?' Roy said sourly. 'Do they think we were all so shocked to hear my wife had changed her mind *again* that we rushed out and murdered her? A somewhat overdramatic reaction to a family argument, wouldn't you agree?'

Diffuse this quickly, Georgia thought, especially as he was implying that there had indeed been such an argument. 'A tough decision for you over going ahead with your plans, especially where other people's financial futures might depend on it.'

Tim shot her a shrewd look, as if reassessing some earlier conclusion, but it was Roy who replied. 'None of your business. It doesn't affect the Luckhurst investigation. Or who killed my wife.' Having made his point, he continued, 'We can't vet every maniac who attends the Gala and takes it into their head to kill someone at random.'

'Having brought a gun with them?'

'That is possible, Georgia,' Tim said gently.

He was right, but only partly. 'This particular maniac would have a problem first in finding Laura in the house, then in persuading her to walk to Abbot's Retreat, possibly by a tunnel which hardly anyone knew existed.' She had nearly added, 'Except you, Tim,' but held it back. She was in the enemy camp and preferred neutral ground. She was aware she'd already gone too far.

'There are references to the tunnel in the archives,' Roy said icily. 'And I believe you're here to see it for yourself.'

Tim took his cue. 'Shall we go, Georgia?'

So the tour was to be just with him. *Just* with him? A stab of irrational fear hit her, but common sense reasserted itself. Too many people knew where she was and who was with her, so if Tim had any intention of harming her it would not be by physical means but by intimidation. There she could hold her own.

Georgia had imagined the tunnel leading off from perhaps a library, with its entrance disguised as books and bookshelves. Instead, Tim led her to the far end of the house along the corridor from which the damp smell had emanated.

'The old kitchens were in a separate single-storey wing at this end,' Tim explained. 'In the eighteenth century when that was built there would have been an open corridor to link it to the house, but that was filled in when the Luckhursts took

over from the Edgars a century later. Here's the tunnel opening.'
He stopped by a doorway that looked identical to several
others. 'The door used to fasten back to disguise the tunnel
beyond it.'

When he opened it, however, Georgia could see nothing but
a solid wall.

'False,' Tim said.

Georgia was fascinated – and somewhat scared – when Tim
fiddled with a catch of some sort and the plain 'wall' opened
towards them revealing to her surprise not a tunnel but another
wall or door with a naked Venus painted in oils on it. Whatever
portion of her anatomy was misused as a catch, the goddess
obligingly swung herself open at Tim's touch.

'I'll go first, shall I?' Tim said, handing her one of the two
heavy torches he carried. Then he began to descend the steps.

There must be substantial cellars under Stourdens, and in
the direction they would be heading Georgia guessed they
would soon be at the old kitchens themselves. Any self-
respecting tunnel would therefore have been dug much deeper
than that level, or else it would wind amongst the various
kitchen storerooms and cellars. The latter, she decided, as the
steps ended sooner than she had expected, and a narrow curving
passageway lay ahead, judging by the uncertain light of her
torch.

'As you can guess, the police gave this a thorough going
over,' Tim's voice echoed in front of her.

A stupid question, but relevant: 'Is the tunnel safe?'

He laughed, as though this gave him some kind of victory.
'Yes, but not insured. Too expensive. We'll wait until we open
it up for the tourists.'

That struck an unpleasantly overconfident note. 'Surely
Laura learned of its existence in time to get it checked out?'

A pause. 'Yes. She was a nervous woman, and it hadn't
been opened in a quarter of a century at least.'

'Why not, if you and the Fettises knew about it?'

'As I'm sure you know through your police contacts, she
– we – assumed it had fallen in long ago and that in any case
it could have been just an unfounded story.'

'And what changed Laura's mind?'

He was ready for that. 'I did. Through my mother, who, as you doubtless know, was Esther Tanner. Amelia Luckhurst said nothing about it to Laura, but my mother knew it was in good condition at the time the house was sold. It sounded fun to me so Laura and I had a hunt for it, not long after I met Jenny. We found the opening, and Laura said that some day she would get it surveyed and restored. I never dreamed she had done so. Just shows how keen she was on keeping Stourdens going as a tourist attraction.'

Checkmate, Georgia thought ruefully. Tim was clever. No doubt about that. But if the tunnel was now safe, work had been done – and the whole family must have noticed. She shivered. Now was not the time to take this further.

She changed the subject brightly. 'Was it used as a smugglers' tunnel?'

'I doubt it. From what I've been told about the Mad Abbot, I don't see him as a village benefactor distributing smuggled goods to the needy. Careful,' he added as she stumbled behind him.

The arching roof of the tunnel seemed solid enough but was so close to her head that she kept wanting to duck. The floor was gravelled but concreted in parts, which suggested some kind of maintenance had been carried out, but the damp mustiness made her long for fresh air.

'Does it just continue like this?' she asked. If so, it was uninteresting compared with other tunnels. No gruesome or erotic figures were painted on the walls, and there was no sign of temples or grottoes.

'No. There's a turn ahead,' Tim shouted back to her.

She calculated they must be beyond the cellar area now, because the tunnel turned sharply to the right and, to her relief, widened. She felt tension draining away, perhaps because there seemed to be more air now.

Relief was short-lived. 'Tell me,' Tim said, his voice echoing in the dark because he had drawn ahead of the range of her torchlight, 'doesn't it get you down, investigating murders all the time?'

What was his game? If he was deliberately winding her up, he was succeeding all too easily.

'Sometimes it does,' she said steadily – or so she thought, but she could hear the tremble in her voice. 'But any job gets one down sometimes. Doesn't yours?'

'No man is an island, is that it?'

'It is,' she whipped back. 'What about Robert Luckhurst's murder, for instance? Didn't the fact that it took place at Stourdens affect you? And now Laura's too?'

'Only Laura's. Luckhurst's death is just a story like the Mad Abbot's. Gone. Past. Why should it be otherwise?'

She braced herself, remembering that Tim was a control freak. 'Because your father claimed he was innocent.'

'He was.' Tim stopped so suddenly that she cannoned into him.

'What makes you think so?' She could hear his breathing at her side. If she stepped back too far, she yielded power in any battle of wits, but he was blocking the way forward. He laughed, but there was no humour in his voice.

'Because you wouldn't be investigating it otherwise, would you?'

Damn. 'You're a good fencer,' she said. Play to his vanity. She could fence too. 'Have you ever met your father again, either in prison or after his release? We need to find him.'

'My only father is David Wilson. No one else, and my mother would tell you the same.' Before she could reply, he added, 'Look to your left.'

She'd been so intent on Tim that she hadn't noticed that the passageway had widened yet further, and the torch now revealed a semicircular cave arched out on the left. It seemed lighter than it had in the passageway, and she could see a domed roof high up above them. It couldn't be at ground level, she guessed, because she could see no light, but it must be near to it.

'Air holes,' Tim said briefly.

Now her eyes were adjusting, she could see something distinctive about the walls. They were covered in shells, some plain and some coloured, with designs on them. It was not nearly as large as the famous Margate shell grotto, about which people still argued whether it was a nineteenth-century creation or ancient Phoenician work. Whichever it was, it was still spectacular. There was no doubt that the Mad Abbot's hand was behind this one, however. The designs were not ancient trees of life but Bacchanalian revels.

'It's beautiful,' she said, 'from what I can see of it.' Then she changed her mind. Not beautiful at all. There was a feeling of decay here that even the rest of the tunnel did not reflect. 'Why hasn't it become better known?'

'No idea. Maybe Bob Luckhurst wanted it to be kept secret.'

A quick shine of the torch revealed a floor where falling shells had collected and a stone table to one side of the grotto.

'What did the Mad Abbot use this for?' she asked, stupidly playing into his hands.

'Nameless orgies, Georgia,' Tim taunted her. 'He probably came down here for nasty ceremonies to deflower virgins. Or maybe read a good book. Or perhaps he just wanted to keep out of the rain, as the legend says.'

'I think we should move on,' Georgia said coolly. 'Do you know who did the maintenance work on the tunnel?'

'As I told you, I didn't know any had been done. There would have been a health and safety issue when the police wanted to search it, but I managed to find some bills amongst Laura's papers showing that work had been done and there was some insurance of a sort. Can't remember the firm. Does it matter?'

'I suppose not, except that I wonder why she had it carried out.'

'Because, dear Georgia, she wanted to put Stourdens on the map. Please do forget this nonsense about her changing her mind. She'd begun some years ago to restore Abbot's Retreat and to catalogue the collection and so forth. It was she who first launched the Gala years ago. These ideas for Stourdens' future that everyone's making such a fuss about are only taking the improvements a stage further. The house is falling down – that much must be obvious – but Laura never moved quickly on anything. She was still wavering about what to do when she died. There's no great drama about it, whatever Dora told you.'

Put that way, it sounded reasonable, but was that the way it had actually happened? The behaviour of Laura and Jennifer on that fatal morning, and even Roy's, suggested not. Georgia heard in her mind that heartfelt cry of Dora's: '*Laura would never go back on something as definite as that. Not Laura.*'

'And now it's Roy's and my job to shoulder the task of restoring Stourdens,' Tim concluded.

'Isn't Jennifer involved?'

A silence. Then, 'Tell me what you would do with this grotto, Georgia,' came Tim's whisper. His face moved near to hers in the torchlight, and involuntarily she stepped back. 'Put on some nice orgies for tourists? Charge them five hundred quid to have dinner here and stay overnight in Jane Austen's bed? And what about Jane and William having sex down here on the Abbot's table? I grant you Laura might have baulked at that.'

Georgia's dislike of Tim Wilson increased several notches. The sooner she was out of here the better, but Tim was still blocking her way, seemingly transfixed by the grotto. He was staring into it as if he could see its builder sitting there enjoying a goblet of wine.

'How did the Mad Abbot die?' she asked. If she could keep Tim talking she might be able to push past him to continue through the tunnel herself, which would be better than retreat.

'Percival, youngest son of the third Lord Edgar, died peacefully in his bed at the age of thirty-four, so the records state. I must say I'm looking forward to merry trips along here when we develop Stourdens.' He must have realized he was too far out of tune. 'Let's move on,' he suggested.

That suited her. 'How much further is it?' she asked. Perhaps this was playing into his hands again, but she didn't care.

'Not far. This place does get to one, doesn't it? Laura must have wanted to get to Abbot's Retreat in a hurry if she did come this way at the Gala.'

'It could have been used for Bob Luckhurst's murder too.'

'I never met him, but you want my take on him? He was as mad as the Abbot.' The taunting tone had gone, and Tim sounded quite serious.

'In what way?' she asked.

'Abbot's Folly was his favourite place, which tells you something. He seems a shadowy sort of person. Some liked him, some hated him, and some thought him crazy. Perhaps that's all you'll ever know about him, Georgia.'

Perhaps it was imagination, the oppression of the tunnel getting to her, but his voice held threat. When he stopped suddenly, her heart jumped in fright. 'What's the matter?' She tried to keep the squeak out of her voice.

'This is the garden exit.' He sounded mildly surprised. 'The police were very interested in that. But I know it's Luckhurst you're concerned with, so we won't take this route but go on to the folly. I'll let you have the fun of going first. Flash the torch and shortly you'll see a door ahead. Just push.'

For one moment she had a panic that he intended to disappear through the garden exit and leave her in here with the darkness and the rats. But he stayed behind her, and she saw a short flight of steps ahead of her. Please, please, please, she thought. No more of this. Let me out of here *quickly*.

She reached the door, which was reassuring. Taking a deep breath she pushed harder than she had meant to. The door flew open, wrenched from the other side, and she jumped. She was face to face with an angry Philip Faring.

'What the hell are you doing here?' he asked. 'You gave me the fright of my life.'

'Thought the Mad Abbot was coming for you, Phil? Sorry,' Tim said from behind. 'Forgot you might be working here.'

Sorry, my foot, Georgia thought in annoyance. He had known full well Philip was here, and that was why he had urged her to go first.

Philip had clearly been working at the desk, which was piled high with papers. A laptop with an Excel sheet on the screen was open at the far end.

'Are you working on another book?' she asked fatuously, trying to get her breathing steady again.

She deserved the put-down she received. 'Of course,' he said coolly. 'Aren't you? We're both writers.'

'Another on Jane Austen?'

'No.'

'Georgia and I have had a jolly chat about Stourdens,' Tim said as Philip looked daggers at her. Was she imagining it, or was there some kind of warning in Tim's voice? And if so, was it for her or for Philip?

'I'm compiling a guidebook if you must know,' Philip said stiffly. 'Jake needs some stuff to hand out as background for his film.'

No one seemed ever to have doubted that the film was going ahead, least of all Jake, but was that really the case? Georgia wondered. 'If Dora was right and Laura did change her mind about developing tourism,' she asked, 'wouldn't she have cancelled the film too?'

A quick glance between Tim and Phil. 'No way,' Tim answered. 'Whatever she felt about this house, Laura wouldn't have let Jake down – or Phil. There's his book to consider. Plenty of houses have documentaries made about them. It was the other facets of commercialization, such as the residential courses and so on, that she must have been doubtful about. They would have involved Roy and Laura moving out of Stourdens and into the former Dower House – quite nice, but not exactly Austenesque.'

'Dora always makes a drama of everything,' Philip said sulkily. 'I'm surprised she doesn't want to turn the ballroom at Edgar House over to tourism irrespective of Stourdens. I can just see her dressed up in a frilly frock as Jane Austen and opening the ball with Gerald in full sea-captain rig. Isn't that what Max Tanner planned, Tim?'

'As I said,' Tim said firmly, 'David Wilson is my father. Max Tanner is long past. Except, of course, to dear Georgia.'

Her hackles rose. 'What "dear Georgia" and particularly "dear Peter" would like is to talk to your mother. Could you arrange that?'

A long pause. 'Why not?' Tim said at last.

TEN

'Interesting that young Master Tim did not think to mention his parentage earlier, although he knew we were looking into Luckhurst's murder,' Peter remarked on the drive to Burwash where Esther Wilson lived.

'Diffidence, perhaps,' Georgia suggested. 'It could have been a taboo subject as he grew up.'

'Does Tim Wilson strike you as diffident?'

'No.'

'And he wasn't pleased when I tactfully turned down his offer to drive us to Sussex.'

'Tactfully' wouldn't have been Georgia's description. Tim had raised no objections when Peter had rung him to arrange a date, which had been agreed for Tuesday, 27th July. On the other hand, she was sure Tim had expected to accompany them. He was quite capable of putting obstacles in their path, yet he had not chosen to do so – yet.

Esther lived on a modern estate not far from Burwash, a Sussex village that Georgia knew reasonably well because of its associations with Bateman's, Rudyard Kipling's home. She remembered seeing his beloved Rolls-Royce on display there and wondering how he managed to drive it along the narrow lanes. There wouldn't have been so much traffic before the Second World War, but tractors and hay wagons would be more numerous. On the other hand, the pace of life was slower then – or was that a myth?

When she pulled up in front of the Wilsons' bungalow, a tall, bearded, sturdily built man in his late fifties, presumably Tim's stepfather, was mowing the lawn of the neat front garden. He stopped to watch Georgia park, then came across to see if Peter needed help emerging from the car. He didn't, but for once amiably pretended he did. David Wilson introduced himself.

'Come inside.' He led the way. 'Esther's waiting for you.

I've cleared a path for the chair, and I've been appointed coffee-maker. I wasn't around in Luckhurst's day so I can't help much otherwise, but I do have my uses.'

Esther came to the door to meet them, and Georgia was surprised. The press photographs of the trial had suggested a steely quality that twenty-five years later was no longer evident. She was slim, dark and full of nervous energy in a way that reminded Georgia of Tim, but first impressions suggested she lacked the push that Tim possessed in spades. Perhaps she was happier now. She'd achieved what looked like a secure and contented way of life, which was a million miles away from the roles of, first, publican's wife and then publican at the Edgar Arms. They were difficult enough in themselves, let alone when her then-husband was enthused over ambitious but unrealizable schemes.

She led them to a comfortable living room with chairs, sofa and television, unadorned with memorabilia of the past. No knick-knacks, no photos – and perhaps understandably so.

'Is it going to be painful for you to talk about Stourdens and the Edgar Arms, Mrs Wilson?' Georgia asked. Tim had made it clear that his mother purposely kept away from the area, although the funeral and his wedding obviously had to be exceptions.

She frowned as she considered the question. 'I don't think so,' she replied. 'I've drawn a line underneath those days and prefer not to think of them, but it's not painful. They're just over. I don't seek out anyone I knew then – especially my former husband.'

'So you can't have been very happy when Tim met Jennifer and is presumably now going to live at Stourdens.'

Esther shrugged. 'I wasn't, but coincidences happen. Tim worked in London, and now Canterbury, and has clients all over the place. I couldn't stop him going to Kent. He knew about his father's connections with the Edgar Arms and – ' her voice trembled – 'the murder, but as he was only two when it all happened, and he's had no contact with Max since, he was intrigued rather than disturbed by it. I told him the bare minimum, of course, but no doubt he looked up the records.'

'Does Jennifer know who you are?' Georgia asked. It was a question she had not put to Tim, but she should have done so.

'I've no doubt she does, but you'll have to ask Tim.' A certain amount of ice had entered her voice, and Georgia now saw how this Esther could have survived at the Edgar Arms. She did have a tough side to her, a side that Tim had inherited.

'Do you mind talking about Max Tanner?' Peter asked, just as David arrived with the coffee.

He laughed. 'Shoot away,' he said. 'Don't mind me.'

Esther took her cue from him. 'I don't mind either. I haven't heard a word from Max since the divorce went through, so it's well behind me. Off with one of his other women, I suppose. He always had a way of getting round women.'

'Would that include your former barmaid, Barbara Hastings?' Georgia asked.

'She was Barbara Merryworth in those days. I was afraid she might recognize me at the funeral,' Esther said dispassionately. 'As for her being one of his floozies, Max usually had the good sense to keep them off his home patch.'

So Barbara could well have been unmarried at the time of the murder, Georgia realized, stowing the information carefully away in her mind – together with her recollection of Barbara's saying he was a womanizer. 'A difficult question I know, but did you think Max was guilty?'

'No.'

The answer was too quick, Georgia thought. Esther would have been expecting this question, and so it was reasonable to assume she'd considered it in advance.

'He told me he was innocent,' Esther continued, 'and that was enough for me. Max never lied. The licence motive was rubbish. He minded about it, but not that much. We were going along nicely.' Her words were coming rapidly now. 'So why would he muck it up by suddenly losing his cool? He was annoyed that morning and said he was going to see Bob about something, but whatever it was he wouldn't have shot Bob for it.'

'The gun was his though,' Peter pointed out.

Esther brushed this aside. 'Back in 1985 the rules about

where they were kept weren't quite so strict. Max kept it in
a drawer of the dresser in the hallway. Our part of the house,
but easy for anybody to get to. Anyone could have taken it
and put it back in the cellar where it was found. We were
running a pub not Fort Knox.' She was flushed with annoyance, and Georgia hastened to switch subjects.

'Did you know Amelia Luckhurst well?'

'Naturally. We didn't get on. She was Max's department,
not mine. She was always pestering him, but she wasn't his
type.'

'Tim said you knew about the tunnel at Stourdens.'

A split-second pause, but Esther recovered well. 'I don't
remember telling him, but I could well have done so when he
told me about Stourdens. I suppose I knew about it from Max.
Does it matter?'

Peter quickly cut in. 'We heard that Max had great plans
for the Edgar Arms. Were you a Jane Austen fan too?'

'Not me. I was all for expansion if it made us some cash,
but it was Max who was so keen on this Austen story. Amelia
was up for our having a joint approach to the development of
Stourdens and the Edgar Arms together, and he liked that idea.
Once Bob was dead, though, she dropped the plans and dumped
Max in the firing line.'

'Are you suggesting she might have killed her husband?'

'Why not? Tough as old nails is Amelia, and nothing gets
in her way. Poor Bob was wet putty in her hands. The only
time I knew him dig his heels in was over the Austen collection. Refused to go along with her plans.'

'That must have upset Max too, if his ideas for the pub
depended on Stourdens?' Peter asked mildly.

Esther wasn't fooled. 'If you mean, did it give him a motive
for killing Bob, no it didn't. Max was ambitious but not an
idiot. He knew there were plenty of Jane Austen connections
in Kent and other organizations and houses, and that he might
be able to link up with them. Or go it alone.'

'Was Max a Jane Austen fan irrespective of the pub and the
letters?' Georgia asked.

'Good grief no. She was part of his plans for the pub, so
he got interested in this love affair story. He walked into those

rotten floor-boarded, sad old Assembly Rooms and saw them through rose-coloured specs, all romantic candlelight, fires, violins playing and pretty ladies dancing the cotillion.'

'Do you by any chance have a photo of Max?' Peter asked casually.

David chuckled. 'Do me a favour. Think I'd want to see his face everywhere I went?'

'Nor me,' Esther chimed in. 'I threw them all out.'

'Wouldn't Max feature on photos of Tim as a baby?' Georgia pushed.

'I only kept the ones of Tim alone.' Esther looked apologetic. 'There are times in life when you need a clean break and this was one of them.' A pause. 'Give my regards to Barbara. She went through a rough patch when Craig was born, but Tim tells me they're both on to a good thing when Stourdens pulls its socks up.'

On Thursday morning, Georgia found Peter sitting with a mug of coffee staring into space, and there were no signs that he had done anything else for some while.

'What's wrong?' Georgia asked guardedly. She had not been to the office the previous day, but there seemed a big change from his confidence when they had left Esther Wilson's home. He'd been sure then that they were getting to grips with this case.

'Almost too eager to talk, wouldn't you think?' he had commented.

She had not been sure. 'Something odd certainly,' she agreed. She had put that down to the Tim factor, although that had not satisfied her either.

When Peter did not answer her, she asked again, 'What *is* wrong?'

A shrug. 'Nothing much.'

His tone of voice said enquire no further, so Georgia busied herself at the computer, then slipped away to the kitchen to consult her usual oracle. Margaret was preparing Peter's lunch. 'What's up?' she asked her.

'Not for me to say, Georgia.'

'Which means you want to.'

'Elena's been on the phone.'

Margaret had been Peter's carer ever since Elena had left, and as she lived in Haden Shaw herself she had known them both for a very long time before that.

'About her moving back to Kent?'

'That I don't know. But I can tell you she's up to her old tricks again now. Stirring.'

This sounded worse than she had thought, and Georgia returned to the office with foreboding.

'I suppose she told you,' Peter grunted, without even looking up.

'Only that Elena called. Has she found a house?'

'No. She's found that survivor.'

Georgia's heart dropped. She'd been counting on that issue quietly vanishing. 'Who is it?'

'A Frenchman called Lucien Marques. He lives in Turkey.'

That sounded a safe distance away, Georgia thought with relief. Then Peter added, 'He comes to London frequently for business reasons,' and the problem moved a whole lot closer. 'We can't have that hanging over us, Georgia,' he continued. 'What do you want to do?'

'If he's in London, I suppose we can't not see him.' She wished she had the strength to say they could, but it seemed unavoidable. There would always be a question mark if they did nothing. 'Is he going to add anything to what we already know?'

'Probably not, but if we don't see him, we never *will* know.'

'Has Elena met him?' Georgia asked.

'No. She says we should all go together.'

'Then to paraphrase Macbeth, if it has to be done, let's do it quickly. We'll tell Elena – I'll ring her if you like – that as soon as he announces his arrival we'll make a date.'

'I'll ring her myself,' her father said.

'Visitor,' Georgia called to Luke. She could see an unfamiliar blue Toyota drawing up, and being a Monday and thus a working day whoever its driver was must probably want to see him and not her. True it was late afternoon, which was why Luke was in the house and not in his office, but even so the likelihood was that Luke was in the firing line.

Luke obediently went to greet the new arrival but was quickly back. 'For you,' he said, popping his head round the door and then holding it open.

It was Jennifer Fettis, and Georgia rose in alarm at how distraught she looked. Luke must have deemed this something that Georgia would cope with better alone.

'I thought I'd come on the off-chance . . . hope you don't mind.' Jennifer's words stumbled out. 'I just want to talk, and my friends would think I was mad.'

'Talk away,' Georgia said. 'Shall I get you some tea? Cake? That can help a bit when one's upset.'

Jennifer nodded gratefully, and when Georgia returned she looked more composed.

'Basically, it's about Tim,' she began. 'Dad thinks he's the best thing since buttered toast.'

This sounded serious to Georgia. 'And you no longer do?' Tread carefully, she thought. Don't leap right in with 'drop him immediately'.

'I don't know, Georgia.'

'It's the second of August. It's only six weeks to the wedding. Don't you think doubts are to be expected the nearer it gets?' She watched Jennifer pace round the room, and then stop to look out at their garden.

'Did *you* have doubts?' Jennifer asked.

'Not at this stage,' Georgia answered, 'but only because I got over mine earlier. I was lucky.'

'I wish I was you,' Jennifer said abruptly. 'You don't know how much I long for everything to be settled and to be content with no decisions to be made.'

Georgia took the bull by the horns. 'Marriage often looks easy from the other side of the fence,' she pointed out, 'and some people find out too late that it isn't.'

'That's what I'm afraid of.' Jennifer threw herself down on the sofa.

'Only you can decide whether they're radical doubts or pre-wedding nerves. You've had a terrible time, dealing with your mother's death, so it's hardly surprising either way.'

'How can I decide *now*?'

How far should she go in her reply? Georgia wondered. If she passed on her own opinion of Tim, would that be fair or unfair? Undoubtedly the latter. 'For a start, did your mother like Tim?' she began.

'I think so. No help there.'

'You're sure about that? Parents can be quite good at hiding their personal views in such circumstances. Are you sure your father thinks he's right for you?'

Jennifer grimaced. 'Oh, he does. Dad's so blinded by the image of Stourdens being great and glorious again and of himself as its gracious host that he'd like Machiavelli if he was in charge of making it happen.'

An interesting choice for a comparison, Georgia thought, where Tim was concerned. 'All right, let's get basic: do you love Tim?'

'Yes. That's the trouble,' Jennifer said forlornly.

'Understand him?'

'No.'

Problem, Georgia thought. No one in the throes of love could fully understand the beloved, but for Jennifer to admit she didn't was significant. She would have to tread carefully.

'Is sex a problem?'

'No way.' Jennifer managed a grin. 'And if you're thinking that's the only reason I love Tim, it's not true. You can't define what makes love, but it's more than that.'

'Charm?' Georgia prompted.

'No,' Jennifer said dismissively. 'It's more a sense that without me he'd be a bit lost. I know that sounds daft, because he seems the one who's in charge. It's true, but he needs direction.'

Time to step in further, Georgia decided. 'Peter and I met his mother and stepfather last week. Have you ever met his real father?'

Jennifer sat bolt upright. 'Max Tanner? No, but I knew about him. Tim told me when Mum died. He said he'd been nervous about doing so earlier, but goodness knows why. I don't believe in the sins of the fathers and all that. I can't believe we're programmed to be exactly what our parents were without an X-factor included.'

Georgia's heart sank. Wouldn't the natural thing be for Tim to have told her when he first knew she lived at Stourdens? Perhaps not. She wrestled with her impulse to tell Jennifer what had happened in the tunnel: the menace, the implied threat, and Tim's obvious need for complete control. But she restrained herself.

'You sound still very committed to him,' she said. 'So what do you want from me?'

'Advice.'

Georgia blenched. 'I can't give it, Jennifer. I'd love to, but it's not fair to ask me. All I can suggest is that you postpone the wedding until you're more confident than you are now.'

'But I might never be. I've already decided to postpone, in fact. I'll probably call it off altogether in due course.'

Georgia stared in amazement at her. 'Then what on earth do you need advice on?'

'Tim's part in Stourdens.'

Georgia whistled. 'That's quite a tall order. Does Tim know the wedding's off for September?'

'I told him yesterday. I thought he was going to explode at first, and then he – and Dad, when he found out – told me that I wasn't in my right mind because of Mum. All I needed was time so it was agreed the wedding be postponed until the spring.'

'Are you happy with that?'

'For the time being, though I don't think it will change anything. Tim will still be the same man, and the same circumstances will still apply.'

'Which are?'

'Complicated. You probably know Mum owned Stourdens. In her will my mother set up a trust to look after its future and put most of what money she had into it. The beneficiaries are Dad and myself, and a trustee to see fair play and make decisions.'

'Your solicitor?'

'No, and not Tim either. It's an old friend of Dad's and Mum's, Douglas Watts.'

'And the trust includes the Jane Austen collection?'

Jennifer managed a smile. 'You've hit the nail on the head. For some reason she left that to me personally. Mum was in quite a state before the Gala and told me she was going to see her solicitors about her will, but I don't know what she intended to do about it. I didn't even know what was in it until after she died, and Dad was in too much of a daze to take it in.'

'So the complication is?'

'Tim.'

'What's his formal position at Stourdens? Is he working as a future family member or does he have a contract?'

'No contract as far as I know. He's still running his own PR business in Canterbury.'

That was one relief then, Georgia thought. 'Jennifer, what would you do if there were no Tim to direct the Stourdens' development? Would you follow what we've been told were your mother's wishes not to commercialize Stourdens or would you carry on?'

Jennifer stared at her. 'I'm not really sure. How stupid of me. I'm so used to the idea of Tim being in charge of everything.'

'Think about it now.'

'I suppose I'd have to consult Douglas Watts, the trustee, but my instinct would be to go ahead but much less fiercely, avoid commercialization on a big scale.' She flushed with sudden excitement. 'I wouldn't go down any avenue that Mum wouldn't have wanted. The development plans included turning the whole house over to Jane Austen, with fencing, dancing classes, cooking classes, that sort of thing. Maybe tourist accommodation too. But Stourdens needs to be lived in by a family, not a business. I'd definitely live in the house myself, but we could do the Jane Austen tours and talks, and perhaps the odd concert.'

'Would you build on the Jane Austen-Harker love affair?'

'Why not? And . . .' Her lips briefly trembled. 'There are the gardens, of course. Mum loved Abbot's Retreat, and I couldn't face that for a while, but eventually I may. But there's the folly and even the tunnel that we could use in the tours. We could link up with the other Jane Austen houses, perhaps.

Godmersham, Goodnestone and Godinton, all opening at the same time with transport between them. And there would still be plenty of ways to use Barbara's services. I couldn't let her down.' Her face fell. 'But there's still Tim to consider.'

'Discuss it with him. Does he get on well with this Douglas Watts?'

'As far as I know. Neither of them knows about the will leaving the collection to me, and I'm going to keep the situation to myself for a while longer. I can't help wondering why Mum changed her mind so adamantly over the whole idea of development. She'd gone along with Tim and Dad quite happily, although they disagreed initially over the role of Stourdens itself. She gave way eventually when Dad said they could live in the Dower House – it's rented out at present. Mum liked that house so we thought all was settled. So why, according to Dora, did it all change so suddenly?'

'What did she tell you about that?' Georgia asked cautiously.

Jennifer flushed. 'Tim would be furious if he knew I was talking about this. She told me that morning that she wouldn't be making the announcement about Stourdens' future, but not that she had changed her mind about the plans. She said she'd explain later in the day when we had more time. Because she wasn't feeling too good she asked me to take supervision of the catering tents in her place. She was going to stay indoors and would tell Tim and Dad about the announcement, and I think she said Phil and Jake too, since they might be affected if she didn't appear at four o'clock. As would Barbara and Craig. I returned from the catering tents just as she'd finished telling them, I think, because everyone seemed in a bit of a state. Then, of course, Dora turned up with you and Tim and I took you all to the folly. After that I was back in the tents and I only saw her at brief intervals if I had to dash back into the house for something. Now I know, thanks to Dora, that it was more than just not appearing at four and that Dora was right. Mum *had* changed her mind. Tim and Dad convinced themselves that she was simply blowing hot and cold, but it was much more than that.'

'Something must have sparked off such a complete volte face. You've no idea what?'

'I've been going over it and over it in my mind, but all that was unusual that week was that Amelia Luckhurst had come over on the Wednesday. I work in Canterbury so I didn't see her, but when I got home that night Mum seemed preoccupied. When I returned on the Friday though, she really did look ill, just as she did on Saturday. It was then she mentioned her will. I asked her what was wrong, and she said she was just tired. She had been in Canterbury herself and had some thinking to do. I asked her whereabouts in Canterbury, but she just said nowhere special.'

'Did she keep an appointment book?' Georgia tried not to sound too eager, an image of Mike Gilroy's frowning face before her. This was his case, she tutored herself, not Marsh and Daughter's.

'Only the computer, and the police have that.'

Georgia tried another tack. 'You said she talked to you briefly on the Saturday morning. Was it about Stourdens or the Austen collection?'

'No,' Jennifer replied. 'I asked her if Dad or Tim could make the announcement for her as she was ill, but she suddenly turned on me, looking almost manic. Then just as quickly she relaxed again. "No," she said. "They can't." I was too stunned to ask questions.'

'Is that why you were looking scared when you were all talking on the terrace on the morning of the Gala?'

'Scared?' Jennifer looked at her with startled eyes. 'I suppose it must have been . . . *no*. It was Tim. He was acting so strangely. I was scared of *Tim*.'

Amelia Luckhurst – everything seemed to come back to her, Georgia reflected. She had visited Laura before the Gala, and shortly afterwards Laura had changed her mind about the future of the house. Twenty-four years earlier Amelia had reason to kill her husband because he was standing in the way of her developing Stourdens. She had not mentioned the tunnel to Laura or to Marsh & Daughter. She had been at the Gala and made a speedy escape after Laura's death. What did it all add up to? Coincidence?

Georgia reached the office the next morning eager to tell

Peter the relevant parts of her conversation with Jennifer, but this was brushed aside.

'Bad news,' he said without preamble. 'I've had a call from Mike. He thought we should know.'

'Know what?' Her mouth felt dry.

'Amelia Luckhurst has been found dead. Murdered.'

ELEVEN

'**A**melia's husband John had been out yesterday and came back to find her dead,' Peter told Georgia gravely. 'Shot. It wasn't suicide, no gun, but no news on whether it could be the same one that killed Laura.'

A wave of nausea welled up inside Georgia as Peter's news became graphically real. She had not taken to Amelia, but her unexpected and terrible death was ominous as well as horrifying. 'One coincidence too far,' she managed to say.

'Mike agrees and so do I. The Met is handling Amelia's death of course, but Diane Newton is in touch with them. On the face of it Mike doesn't see how this could link with Laura's murder or with Bob Luckhurst's. But he agreed that there's "no harm", as he put it, in our poking our noses in if we don't tread on any toes. Ignore the mixed metaphor. We might add a few unconsidered trifles to their case. I have a feeling that there are a few left lying around that are beginning to stink. Agree?'

'I do, but how do we poke tactfully?'

'It's possible John Collier would talk to us.'

'He'll be overwhelmed at present,' she said doubtfully. 'Besides, how could he help? There's never been any suggestion he was around at the time of Bob's death.'

'He might know something about her visit to Laura.'

'Any chance that Amelia's death was coincidence though?' Georgia asked. 'Were there any signs of a break-in?'

'None, which means she was either killed by someone who forced themselves in when she opened the door, or she knew her killer. Probably the latter, as the coffee table was set with two places. So far no takers for the guest.'

'No one seen calling? Strange cars, delivery vans, and so on?'

'Give me a chance,' Peter said. 'Mike's only just heard the news himself. Time of death is estimated at between ten and twelve o'clock yesterday. The time when people have gone to work, taken the children to school, popped into the supermarket and are busy about their own affairs.'

'And not peeping through the lace curtains. Pity,' Georgia remarked.

'Any peeping is more likely at TV now rather than through windows. Anyway, Diane Newton rang later to say she's willing for him to talk to you and he's agreed to see you next week. It's fixed for eleven on Tuesday morning. Does that suit you?'

'It does.'

'Good, because in return for any snippets you might turn up, Newton might get more interested in Bob Luckhurst.'

By agreement with Peter, Georgia had come without him to see John Collier in order not to overwhelm him at a bad time. The door was opened by a woman in her thirties, who introduced herself as Julia, John's daughter by his first marriage. Georgia did her best to look non-threatening, and Julia must have been convinced because to her relief she made no suggestion that she should sit in on the conversation. John Collier rose to meet her, looking somewhat dazed, but he seemed eager to talk. He must be in his seventies, she guessed, and probably extremely sharp in normal circumstances.

'Sorry, I can't take it in,' he kept apologizing. 'I keep forgetting why you're here.'

He managed a sort of grin, and the haunted look on his thin face lifted slightly. Georgia wondered what his past had been and whether marriage to Amelia had been bliss or blight.

'Let me see,' he continued, 'you're from the police, aren't you? How's the search going? Found anything yet?'

She judged this was more a plaintive attempt to seem 'normal' than a request for information, but did her best. 'I came to visit Amelia one day when you were out. No, I'm not from the police, just working with them, together with my father. We're actually studying the death of your wife's first husband, and there might be something either in that or in Laura Fettis's death at Stourdens that could link with the tragic death of your wife. It's unlikely, but the police have to be sure.'

He suddenly looked much more alert. 'It's more likely in the case of Laura Fettis than that business with Amelia's husband.'

'Could we first go back—'

'To that scoundrel Tanner, I suppose.'

'Did she talk to you about what happened in 1985?'

'Rarely. She'd made up her mind to put it behind her. She went through a bad time, what with Bob and the malicious rumours flying around.'

'Do you know if she saw or heard from Max Tanner after his release from prison?'

He looked surprised. 'She wouldn't have told me, even if she had – which I doubt. What she did say was that he had ideas above his station, and everyone else suffered for them. The fool even suggested he divorced his wife, married her and moved into Stourdens. That would have suited him nicely. The man was crazed with ambition, and he was more than a touch below her class – and she told him so.'

'Was she sure he was guilty?'

He snorted. 'No one in their right mind would doubt it.'

But, Georgia wondered, suppose Amelia herself was involved in her husband's murder, what then lay behind her own death? Had Tanner reappeared to kill her? That seemed highly unlikely, especially coming so soon after the death of Laura, with whom Tanner could have had no quarrel.

She decided to tackle a surer line. 'Amelia told me that she went to see Laura at Stourdens a few days before the Gala she attended, and Laura's daughter told me her mother seemed disturbed afterwards.'

'Yes.' A frown came over his face. 'Odd that.'

'Did she tell you the reason she went there?'

'What's this got to do with Bob Luckhurst's death?' he demanded.

'I don't know yet,' she said honestly. 'Nor do the police. That's one reason they wanted me to talk to you about Bob Luckhurst – to clear any possible link out of the way.'

'Load of balderdash,' he muttered. 'Wish I'd never agreed to it.'

'I'm sorry,' Georgia said sincerely, 'especially at a time like this.'

'I suppose the quicker I tell you, the sooner you'll go.'

'You could put it like that,' she agreed. 'But I'll leave right now if you don't feel like talking – I wouldn't, in your place.'

He grunted. 'I'm going to disappoint you over that visit. Amelia didn't tell me why she went there to see the Fettis woman. Or why she went back on the Saturday, dressed in that absurd costume. I could see she was bent on going though. She said next year we'd be able to see the world in style, and I got the idea it was linked to Stourdens. We've lived rather too well these last years, but things were getting a bit tight financially, so I assumed it was one of Amelia's jokes.'

Where might this be leading? Georgia tried not to race ahead too fast. 'Was she still excited when she returned from Stourdens on the Wednesday?'

'Quite the contrary. She was in one of her moods. I couldn't say anything to please her. I asked if everything was all right. She said no, but there were other avenues.'

'What did she mean by that?'

'No idea. She shut up quick afterwards.'

Georgia frowned. 'Did you tell the police about that?'

'When they came storming round to the house, I told them she'd been to see Laura Fettis. They said something about Laura having second thoughts over what to do with the old heap. Did that nugget come from you?'

'No. The police had evidence for that.'

'When she got back from the Gala, she was full of Laura's death, as you can imagine, and jabbering about someone called Halliday and a few other names. She was in a foul mood that last week. Pity. I'd have liked . . .'

His eyes moistened, and Georgia asked hastily: 'Did Laura Fettis come here or did you have any other unusual visitors during the period?'

'There were one or two, but I wasn't here and she didn't tell me who – I just used to see dirty coffee cups or glasses around. I did ask her once who'd been over, but all she replied was, "The world in style, John. Style."' His voice broke.

On her return to Medlars Georgia found an email from Jennifer, which took her hotfoot over to Stourdens on the Wednesday morning. Jennifer had found some phone numbers jotted down that might be of interest if she wanted to look at them. She said that the police had already seen them, but a double-check would do no harm, Georgia thought.

When she arrived, however, she was taken aback to see that the world and his wife seemed to be visiting Stourdens. She recognized one car immediately, although as it was completely out of context it took a moment or two to convince herself she hadn't made a mistake. She was sure it belonged to Jill, Luke's daughter-in-law. Others were also easily identifiable, including Barbara Hastings' van.

Jennifer answered the door and immediately apologized. 'Sorry, Georgia, I couldn't stop you coming in time. Everything's gone pear-shaped.'

'What's happened?' Georgia asked in alarm. 'Shall I disappear?'

'No way. I'm glad you're here. It's getting a bit heavy.'

'Because of Amelia Luckhurst's death?'

'That hasn't helped, but it's not that. Tim laid on a big planning meeting for Jake's film shoot today, and neither told me about it nor wants me present. I'm pretty annoyed. Philip and Jake are with him.'

'And I saw Jill Frost's car.'

'The girl with the baby? Oh yes, she's one of the experts Jake's interviewing during the film.'

'Really?' On reflection Georgia wasn't so surprised. Jill had lectured in English literature in the States and could well have a soft spot for Jane Austen.

'It was Phil's idea to rope in Jill,' Jennifer added as she ushered her inside. 'Do you know her?'

'My stepdaughter-in-law. Tell me, what's so pear-shaped?' Georgia asked.

'Chiefly Tim. He's behaving like a petty Hitler, running rings round Dad. And me,' she added ruefully. 'He'd been living here, but we've agreed he should move into the Dower House now, as the previous rental ended early. I'm relieved because it makes Stourdens seem more like mine and Dad's again. What's not so good is that Tim's throwing his weight around even more.'

'Can't you and your father sidetrack him? Who's formally running Stourdens?'

'Dad and me with the back-up of the trustee, but with Tim buzzing around like a mad wasp it's in theory only. Tim's in his office two days a week, but the other five he'll still be around here.' She pulled a face. 'I suppose it's weak of me to let him – the reason is that I still want him around. Crazy, isn't it? Anyway, once I knew about the meeting this morning, I rang the Clackingtons and Jill. Tim went berserk. The meeting was not for every Tom, Dick and Harry it seems, but only for those involved in the actual planning of the documentary, which does not include Dora, Gerald, Jill – or me,' she added crossly.

'But—' Georgia broke off as Tim hurried past them in the entrance hall on his way upstairs, presumably to rejoin his meeting.

'Quite a regular, aren't you, Georgia?' The charm was growing thinner now, Georgia noted.

'Jennifer asked me to come over,' she said.

Tim gave his fiancée a cool look. 'Right. I'll leave you ladies to chat then.'

'Sorry,' Jennifer said, after he had left. 'He and Dad seem really shaken by Amelia's death. I find it all a bit odd. The circle seems to be closing in on me. Amelia, Esther, Barbara and Craig, solicitors, Douglas Watts—'

'And Tim,' Georgia supplied.

'I know everything must have a rational explanation, but sometimes I wish I could turn the tap off.'

'And can't you? You could always be brave and tell Tim to leave Stourdens completely, if only for a while.'

'It would mean two major battles, one with him and one with Dad. I'm not up to it at present. And there's Barbara,

going around so grim-faced because of the wedding postpone-
ment. She was doing the catering.'

'She must be very disappointed. Is that why she's here?'

'No, solely because of the documentary. She's doing the
catering for it. I persuaded Jake to call her in as a compensa-
tion for not doing the wedding. He wasn't best pleased, but
he gave way.'

'Is the filming still taking place in the week of the
twenty-third?'

'Yes. Two days at Edgar House, then it begins here on
the twenty-fifth.'

As if on cue, Jake came down the stairs. 'We're knocking
off for the day, Jen. We've tidied up the loose ends.'

'So pleased to hear it,' Jennifer said ironically.

Jake looked somewhat abashed. 'Amelia was going to feature
in the documentary to talk about the Luckhurst inheritance,
but it looks as if my humble film seems to have an evil star
over it. Jen, are you sure you're still happy about going ahead
with this film? I know Tim is dead set on it but—'

'One hundred per cent,' she cut in. 'Mum would never have
forgiven me after all the work she put into it.'

'Good. What about you, Georgia? Still on the trail of Bob
Luckhurst's murderer? Tanner or otherwise?'

The question seemed more casual than loaded, and so Georgia
answered it lightly. 'Another one hundred per cent. Amelia—'

'She was a troublemaker,' Jake cut in unexpectedly. 'Ask
Philip.'

'Her husband said she spoke about meeting you at the Gala.'

'Did she? I don't recall.'

'Maybe it was Phil she talked to,' Georgia said. 'Is Jill up
there? I'll pop up and have a word with her before I leave.'

'Take care. Tim says no outsiders,' Jake said awkwardly.

Georgia was taken aback. 'What on earth do you mean? I
only want a brief word, and it's semi-police business.'

'They're still talking in there, and you know what Tim's
like. Strictly *his* business.'

'*My* business too, I might point out, Jake,' Jennifer said
icily. 'If I damn well want to talk to Jill and take Georgia with
me, then I will.'

He groaned. 'Look, I'm sorry, both of you. Let's cool it. It'll only be another twenty minutes or so.'

Jennifer said nothing, but her face was very white, and after Jake had left she told Georgia, 'That's it. I'm going to talk to the solicitor and trustee in the morning. I'm going to run this damned development proposal myself. Including Jake's film.'

When Georgia reached Haden Shaw later that day she found Peter in his garden, to which there was a ramp from his office. It was clear that his mind was not on his work, although there was a file or two strategically placed on a table at his side. She had left Laura Fettis's notebook with him yesterday evening, so that he could study the scribbled phone numbers, and was eager to find out whether there was anything useful amongst them.

'Bad time?' she asked.

He roused himself and looked pleased to see her. 'On the contrary, bullseye. Most of the numbers had already been contacted by the police and had either never heard of Laura Fettis or lived nowhere near Canterbury. But one of them was a Howard Osborne, who said he had been away for some days and probably missed the police call. Yes, he'd arranged to meet Laura, and, yes, she had duly arrived, and, yes, he would talk to us about her if we cared to drive over there tomorrow morning. He lives in Sturry, not Canterbury itself.'

'It all seems too straightforward,' she said. So what was wrong about that? she wondered.

'Sometimes life is obliging in one way and then annoyingly reclaims its generosity,' Peter commented. Then a pause. 'Elena rang. Lucien Marques is coming to London next week and would be pleased to welcome us at his hotel.'

'All of us?' she asked doubtfully, knowing that even if driven there by car Peter was not fond of visiting the capital.

'Yes, all. Wheelchairs are no problem at the hotel. I checked. The only problem we have is the way the meeting is going to hang over our heads until it happens.'

'Which it will only do if we let it,' she said firmly. 'After all, we know that nothing he says will alter the truth about

Rick. We just have to nerve ourselves up to hearing about it in detail from a horse's mouth.'

'And what then? Have you considered the nightmares might grow *worse* when we have a graphic image in our heads? That it might be better not to know?'

'Yes, I have.' And she had been dreading the possibility. 'But we're so far in now that the images will come anyway if we allow them to.'

'How do you propose to stop them?'

'Throw ourselves into the future. Work, Rosa, even Elena's move here. How do you think she'll react to hearing about Rick?'

'Badly. At the moment it's not real to her, but as soon as it becomes so – if for instance he describes Rick's last moments – I'm afraid she'll collapse again.'

And so may we, she thought. So may we.

She struggled with her feelings. Her mother had brought this on them, albeit with the best of intentions, but now they had to see it through together – not only for Rick's sake, but for Elena's. What would Rick have done in the same position? Georgia struggled to think. Rick was tolerant and kind. He had inherited Peter's quick flashing temper, but also his essential humanity. From Elena he had received his whimsical and artistic side. Do it and survive, he would surely say, only survive. Last year she and Peter had met the girl Rick had loved, and she had survived. Married, flourished in her career, had children – but never forgotten Rick. Peter and she had to carry on too, if only to keep alive that hidden place inside them in which Rick still lived.

'Why, even though it's about Laura Fettis and not Bob Luckhurst, do I have the feeling that meeting Mr Osborne is going to be a watershed in this case?' Peter asked.

'Don't know, but I share it.' Georgia had negotiated the Canterbury road system, and they were rapidly approaching Sturry Hill, behind which was Roberts Street, home to Howard Osborne. The level crossing brought the car to a halt, and Peter began to strain at the leash with impatience. Finally, she was across but then had to face Peter's own style of navigation.

'Right here, *here*.'

Easier said than done in this racing traffic, and Georgia was forced to turn higher up the hill than she'd intended and weave her way back through the mass of small roads until she found Roberts Street. She turned into it with a sigh of relief.

Not for long.

'This can't be it.' Georgia frowned. Roberts Street looked far too short to accommodate a Number 82. She stopped the car and walked down the street to find out whether she was right, and then returned to Peter. 'It ends at Number Eighteen, and there's no sign of any continuation road after that. Are you sure you took down the number correctly?'

'Positive.' Peter was looking apprehensive.

'I'll try Numbers Two and Eight,' Georgia said.

Number 2 produced a harassed young mother and child, but no Howard Osborne. Number 8 produced an old lady and no Mr Osborne living there with her. Moreover she claimed to know everybody in the street and not only was there no Mr Osborne here but there never *had* been a Mr Osborne in the thirty years she'd been living here.

Peter must have been watching Georgia's progress and diagnosed it correctly, because when she returned to the car, he said without preamble: 'He deliberately gave us a false address.' All Georgia's fears resurfaced. A fine watershed this was. The niggle at the back of her mind then took tangible form.

'And a false name too,' she added.

'How do you know that?' Peter asked.

'He was having a joke at our expense. Mr Howard and Lord Osborne are two of the main characters in Jane Austen's *The Watsons*.'

A pause before Peter replied, 'Not, I think, a joke.'

TWELVE

'Voicemail again,' Peter reported gloomily. 'The final
frustration.' The fictitious Mr Osborne's number had
failed to produce its owner for the last twenty-four
hours. '*And* it's Friday the thirteenth,' he added.

Georgia sighed. 'At least it's still a live line. He can't merely
have chucked his mobile away.'

'Why not? I could ask Diane Newton to get a fix on it.'

'No.'

'It's part of a police investigation, and at least we'd know
the area where the damn thing was ringing.'

'We can't risk notching up a black mark with her until we're
sure there's no other way.'

'And what other ways would you propose?'

She tried to speak calmly and reasonably. 'Consider the
possibility that Mr Osborne might not have chucked his phone
away. Consider the possibility that he might assume we would
try his number again in the circumstances. Consider the possibility he would keep it on voicemail.'

'I follow,' Peter said grumpily. 'How long do we wait?'

'Two days?'

'Twenty-four hours?'

'Done.'

Twenty-four hours, Georgia reflected, can be a long haul when
one's champing at the bit. She decided to take up a suggestion
made by Barbara Hastings after she had finally emerged (or
been thrown out of) the Stourdens' meeting that she should
come to see her product range. Georgia wasn't that interested
in the products, but she was in Barbara Hastings herself, so
this seemed a good opening to follow up. When she turned
up later that afternoon, however, she found Barbara in gloomy
mood.

'I talked to His Nibs,' she said darkly. 'That being Mr Tim

Wilson. Thinks it a good joke that he had us all fooled not knowing he was Max's son. Thinks it gives him a special relationship to me. Even hinted Craig might be his half-brother. The nerve of the man. As if I would do it with Max when—' She broke off.

'You seem very low,' Georgia said sympathetically, frustrated that Barbara had halted so abruptly.

'I am. I asked His Nibs what I was to do over the Austen jams and jellies now nothing's happening on the Stourdens front. Answer? Carry on as planned. He don't realize what's involved, or doesn't care. There's something wrong at that place, something going on that's not to do with the police,' she declared. 'He booted me out of the meeting early the other day, so he could talk secrets – wouldn't even let Jennifer in. What's up that's so secret? It's my money involved *and* hers.'

'Perhaps he's embarrassed at not being able to tell you more about the future because he doesn't know it.' The reply sounded weak, even to her own ears. 'Jennifer said you have the contract for catering for the film shoot.'

'Five days' work if I'm lucky,' Barbara pointed out grudgingly. 'It's not that I'm not grateful, but I've gone and had this extension built and the company set up. Craig's as mad as hell.'

'Was he going to work full-time for you?'

She snorted. 'That was the plan. He was seeing it as a step towards having his own licence. Now what?'

'Could you market your produce locally – at farmers' markets and so on?'

Barbara dismissed this. 'You can cook or you can sell. You can't do both, and there's not enough money in it for both Craig and me full-time.'

Georgia tried again. 'Until the murder's solved, I doubt if anyone is clear about the future.'

A short laugh. 'Too true. And what if one of *them* did Mrs Fettis in, eh? Going to be a fine mess. What with her telling me that morning she might be calling it off—'

'She told you *herself*?'

'As good as. She said whatever happened she'd always do her best for me. More than that lot will.'

But would that 'best' have been good enough, Georgia wondered as she drove back to Haden Shaw? Barbara had shown her the plans for increasing the product range, and it went far beyond the occasional event at Stourdens. Moreover, bearing in mind Tim's joke, Barbara had had second thoughts about hinting at Craig's paternity – and if the father had been the late Mr Hastings she would have had no reason to.

When she returned, Peter had been busy in her absence. 'I managed to get hold of Vic Hamlyn at last,' he told her. 'The SIO of the Luckhurst case. He's been away on a long trip,' he added in tones of disgust. 'Lucky for some.'

'You never want to go,' Georgia pointed out mildly, but Peter brushed this aside.

'Want to come?'

'You bet.'

'You'll have to give up part of your weekend, because it's tomorrow. And after that, *then* we can try Mr Osborne again.'

When Vic Hamlyn opened the door, Georgia vaguely remembered his face and that she had met him when she was a teenager. A hearty man, hearty talker, hearty eater, and a mind like a razor. The first three were still in evidence now. The fourth remained to be proven. He lived with his wife (currently out shopping), in a flat with a view of the sea at Tankerton near Whitstable. On an August day such as this it seemed idyllic, she thought, but in winter when the winds would blow and the storms rage it must be a bleak place.

'Max Tanner – do I think he dunnit? That's what you want to know, isn't it?' Hearty laugh. 'The answer's yes.'

'Even though Bob Luckhurst's wife has now been murdered?'

'That's you all over, Peter. Nosing around in the past over what's self-explanatory in the present. Don't make waves is my advice.'

Which Peter ignored. 'What did you think of Amelia Luckhurst?'

'From what I remember, which isn't a lot, a first-class bitch. Her husband seems to have been OK, but Madam Amelia was a different kettle of fish.'

'Any chance that she could have been in collusion with

Tanner? There's a suggestion that a woman was in the folly
at the same time as Tanner and Bob Luckhurst. If it was his
wife, she could have reached it without being seen via a secret
tunnel from the house.'

'Tunnels?' Vic chortled. 'Been reading too many whodun-
nits, Peter. I don't remember any fancy stuff in the case.'

'That's because you might not have been told about the
tunnel,' Georgia said.

Hamlyn was unfazed. 'Too late now – if it was ever
relevant.'

'What about Tom Miller?' Peter asked. 'The chap who led
the protest march. Tanner accused him of having killed
Luckhurst. Remember him?'

Vic thought for a moment. 'With effort. Bit of a slippery
fish, that one. He had a good alibi. We followed him up, of
course, but I couldn't see him as a killer even if he did have
the motive for it. Am I right about that?'

'Yes. The motive could have been that his livelihood could
have been ruined by Luckhurst's decision to close the footpath.
He might have had the same sort of motive for killing Laura
Fettis, because she would have backed out of a deal to buy
his land.'

Vic was getting interested. 'How do you get round the fact
that Tom Miller left that folly place with Bob Luckhurst still
alive, while Tanner stayed?'

'Can't do it yet,' Peter admitted, 'unless Tanner went back
along the tunnel and Amelia did the deed herself.'

Hamlyn looked amused. 'If so, why didn't Tanner spill the
beans? Too much of a gentleman? No way. What's happened
to him, incidentally?'

'Disappeared, but his son is on the scene.'

'Typical Tanner to keep a stake in the game.'

'The son's doing nicely on his own. He is or was engaged
to Laura Fettis's daughter. Did you follow up the rumours that
Amelia Luckhurst was having an affair with Tanner?'

Hamlyn had to think about this. 'Now you're asking. Not
seriously. Tanner thrived on his fantasies, and she was at the
top of his list.'

'And fantasists don't give up,' Peter remarked to Georgia

after they had left. He had decided he wanted some sea air and ice-cream, and she stopped the car by the seafront to fulfil both requests. 'On the contrary, the fantasy can grow until it becomes a real world, alternate or otherwise, only inhabited by self.'

'Are you thinking Tanner might have paid a call on Amelia, or that he liked keeping a stake in things and Tim was it?'

'Fantasists prefer solo performances. He might well have seen Amelia, but he would have been recognized if he had come anywhere near Canterbury.'

'Prison life could have altered Max's physical appearance considerably.'

'So where is he now?'

'Perhaps he's our mystery man who likes playing jokes. Now you see him, now you don't. Now you hear him on the phone, now you don't.'

Peter finished his ice-cream with great satisfaction. 'Good point, so let's go. The twenty-four hours are up.'

As soon as they reached Haden Shaw, Peter insisted Georgia came inside for the great moment, and she waited in suspense as he picked up the phone.

'It's ringing and *here we go*,' he said triumphantly. 'Ah. Mr Osborne,' he purred. 'Peter Marsh here. We were wondering –' he switched to hands-free mode so that Georgia could hear – 'what went wrong. My daughter Georgia and I had a most interesting visit to Sturry yesterday.'

'My apologies. I quite forgot my address.'

Mr Osborne's voice rang a faint bell in Georgia's mind.

'Care to tell us why?'

The reply sounded remarkably cheerful. 'I've been considering that option for some time. You'll be pleased to hear that I would. Could I suggest we meet at the Dryden Arms near Warmden on Monday? I'd be honoured if you would be my guests for lunch.'

'I'd prefer—'

'The venue is not open for discussion. I assure you the wheelchair will prove no problem.'

'Most interesting,' Peter said as he put down the phone. 'How does he know I am wheelchair-bound?'

The Dryden Arms was between two small villages buried in the countryside between Canterbury and the south coast. This was no Bat and Trap, however, and to Georgia it had all the appearance of being a thriving gastropub at any other time than Monday lunchtime. There were only three other customers, two at the bar, the other sitting in a window seat at a table. She recognized him instantly.

'Alfred Wheeler!' Georgia exclaimed. 'I met you at the Bat and Trap.' It was the elderly man with whom she'd been talking there, the 'peasant' from the Gala. No wonder the voice on the phone had struck a chord. This surely could be no coincidence; this was the so-called Mr Howard Osborne. So what was going on here? Whatever it was, she had a deep sense of foreboding.

'I should have paid more attention to your story, Georgia,' Peter said grimly as he drove himself over to the table. 'Mr Osborne,' he queried, 'or Mr Wheeler?'

Their host rose to greet them. 'In fact, neither. Nor am I a milkman, Miss Marsh. I regret that I might have misled you there.'

'Then is there any point to our being here?' Peter enquired politely.

Their host laughed. 'They do an excellent lunch.'

'So does my carer,' Peter said tartly.

'I apologize. Yes, there is a great deal of point to your being here, although my real name need not concern you yet. Pray join me.'

He was a most studious host, and fastidious. Drinks and the selection of food from an interesting menu took some time, and it was only twenty minutes later that Peter lost patience.

'Your real name might not immediately concern us, but it does concern the Fettis family and the police.'

'You are right. My real name – which I'd decided to tell you – is Douglas Watts.'

Georgia's mind whirled as she struggled to grapple with suspicion turning into nightmare. 'You're the trustee chosen by Laura Fettis to look after the Stourdens trust – her and Roy's friend. What's going on? I presume that you arranged our earlier meeting at the Bat and Trap? How did you know we would be there?'

'You do me too much credit. I was present for much the same reason as I suspect you were. I felt the groundswell of village opinion about Laura's death might better be gleaned there than in a more distant pub. I knew of Marsh & Daughter – who doesn't? – and I heard from Tom that you were coming to chat to him at the pub. He was rather proud of the fact.'

'But we were there to talk about Bob Luckhurst's murder.'

'Come now, Miss Marsh. I'm the trustee of Stourdens. Anything concerning it concerns me. Which brings me to an interesting moral question.'

He has charm, Georgia conceded, even if she wouldn't trust him an inch. Peter did not seem to be succumbing to it, luckily.

'I need to understand this situation,' he said firmly. 'If you're the trustee of Stourdens, why was your mobile number so hastily scrawled in Laura Fettis's diary? She must have rung you many times before.'

'Because, like you, she did not know it was me whom she was calling. Amelia Luckhurst had given her the number on which I prefer to be called.'

'So that you can choose not to answer it?' Georgia enquired mildly. The lunch was superb, which was annoying when she needed to have all her wits focused on the conversation.

He held up his hands in surrender. 'I can only apologize again, but if you wish to know about Laura's visit to me, then I suggest we put other matters behind us. I'm afraid Laura believed she would be meeting an Alfred Wheeler until she arrived at our meeting place in Canterbury. Another pub. So useful when one shifts addresses. She was, I fear, somewhat shocked to find Douglas Watts awaiting her.'

'Why the need for such a charade?' Peter asked patiently.

'I use the number you rang for one of my alter ego businesses, in this case Jane Austen.'

Despite its infuriating her, Georgia admired his calm. Douglas Watts was in control, and that's what Peter didn't like. He liked to be in control himself and was ill at ease when this was not

the case. Nevertheless, he was obviously as keen as she was
not to interfere with whatever Watts seemed about to tell them.
Whether that would be the truth or not was another matter.

'I am a retired antiquarian book dealer,' Douglas explained,
'and one of my specialities is Jane Austen, a fact that has
helped me to give great assistance to Dr Faring over his book
as well as to Jake Halliday. I play golf with Roy Fettis and
was at Laura's side throughout her involvement with the Jane
Austen galas and plans. Before them I knew Amelia and Bob,
the latter much better than his wife.'

'Of course. As his milkman, you played chess with him,'
Georgia could not resist saying.

Douglas Watts laughed. 'The chess games were real enough,
although the milkman was a conceit of my own. In fact Bob
employed me on other matters.'

'Which were?' Peter enquired.

'To make his Jane Austen collection.'

The lunch suddenly looked unappealing to Georgia, and
from the instant stillness she knew that Peter too had been
taken unawares.

'*Make* it?' he asked carefully. 'You mean buy and sell on
his behalf?'

'I am as careful with words as with ink and pen, Mr Marsh.
I meant *make* it.'

'You mean . . .' Even now Georgia thought she must be
misunderstanding him.

'I do,' Watts replied gently. 'Ninety-five per cent of the Jane
Austen collection is fake.'

She wanted to laugh, she wanted to cry. The truth should
have been plain from the beginning for anybody who poked
far enough below the surface to see, and yet she and Peter
had not followed that line up. And why? The bigger the lie
the easier it is for people to believe it. She thought of the
numerous financial scams of the twentieth century. She thought
of the South Sea Bubble, and of the many brilliant art fakers
and forgers over the centuries, but *still* she found it hard to
believe the truth of what this gently smiling man was telling
them. The psychology was, she supposed, that she, as so many
hoodwinked people in the past, had *wanted* it to be true.

'Let me explain,' Douglas said blithely. 'When I say the collection is fake, there is as in all the best scams a strong element of truth. It began with the portraits. I had no need to fake the large oil painting of William Harker, which you have probably seen in Abbot's Folly. It is undoubtedly of a Captain William Harker of the *Rhea* who died at Trafalgar. It is by John Opie, and you will find it listed in his *catalogue raisonné*. The sitter's brother did indeed own the Edgar Arms. The painting belonged to the Harker family and was found by Max Tanner in one of the pub's attics. That does happen, you know. There is unfortunately no known connection between Harker and Jane Austen, although with the help of that portrait it was easy for me to convince Bob Luckhurst that there was. The Luckhursts had collected Austen memorabilia for some years, although it was of little value, consisting of occasional references to her in letters of the time and some early editions of the novels and so forth. Bob had longed to add his own contributions. With my help he was able to find so much more. I naturally allowed him to make some of his own discoveries to purchase, prearranged and faked by myself.'

'And the two watercolours?' Even now Georgia could not bear to think of those delicate paintings being part of a fraud.

'They are true eighteenth-century watercolours. All that is fake about them are the sitters attributed to them and the signatures they bear, thanks to my handiwork. My motives are altruistic. I believe in illusion, Mr Marsh, Miss Marsh. Illusion is a force for good in this world – not always, it is true, but often. Illusion can inspire hope, create art and ease troubles. It was in order to make dreams come true that I began my trade. So I did with Jane Austen. I made Bob's dreams come true over a period of ten years or so.'

'But at the expense of deluding those who value truth.'

'You are wrong. What did Bob do with the collection I found for him? He kept it, he loved it. He did not force it on the world.'

'But Amelia employed you in order to exploit it.'

'Wrong again. Amelia did not employ me. Bob did. Not Amelia and not Tanner either. I never met Tanner – I deemed it expedient not to – but it was only when he and Amelia entered the story that a darker side began which I was powerless to prevent. I am giving you the wrong impression, however. There was no wish on Bob's part to deceive anyone except himself. The illusion just grew, as so often it does. For Bob it began with those two watercolours, which he found amongst the family archives and showed to me. There had always been a family legend, he said, that Jane Austen had known Stourdens well and loved the folly, just as she had the Temple in the gardens of Godmersham Park; family papers mentioned her visits, and one indicated she had attended a dance at the Edgar Arms Assembly Rooms. Without doubt she knew the Edgar family well from her visits to her brother Edward at Godmersham, who, as you know, had married into the Knight family. That was a solid basis for me to work on.

'Then,' he continued, 'Tanner showed Bob the oil painting he had found at the Edgar Arms. Bob fancied he saw a resemblance between the captain and the subject of the watercolour. He contacted me as a Jane Austen specialist, and I agreed with him. There was a likeness, if not a conclusive one, as there was between Cassandra's known drawings of her sister and this watercolour. Bob was so enthusiastic that it would have been a crime to disappoint him, especially as I had skills at my command to help him. In my profession as antiquarian bookseller I had access to numerous old books or parts of them that were valueless in themselves but which often afford blank flyleaves. Provided they were published before 1806, when resin size was introduced with machine-made paper, I had the perfect base for my work. I even managed a few watermarks – an extremely difficult process and hence most satisfying. The ink was right, the paper was right – and the handwriting was not difficult as I chose letters and diaries of people whose writing would be little known if at all.'

'But the signatures are very well known,' Peter said.

'How often are your own signatures identical, Peter? Seldom, I suspect. So the art lies in controlling the pressure, stroke quality, the loops and angles of the characters, the way the signature is concluded and begun, making the spacing uneven as would normally happen and so on. Too exact a copy of a signature is suspect. It is the overall impression of the true signature that is required.'

'They were authenticated, however.'

'I flatter myself that my work is so good that it would pass the keenest eye. Fortunately, there was no need for that, as I myself was asked to authenticate the original small collection, together with Bob's acquisitions, and to re-authenticate them for the Fettises and Clackingtons. As regards the Austen script and signatures, I composed a letter from a fictitious friend who was a graphologist who had submitted the letters to computer analysis as well as his own considered opinion.'

Amidst this avalanche of mind-boggling claims, Georgia managed to seize on one point. 'Those watercolours had been in the family for a long time, though, and they had signatures on them.'

Douglas nodded his head approvingly. 'Forged, I'm afraid, by me. When Bob first found them in the Stourdens' attics or wherever, they had no signatures on them. I therefore had to pretend I had exposed the watercolours to a microscopic examination with a jeweller's loupe, which had revealed signatures that had vanished with age. I pretended my skills stretched to restoring their visibility. Bob was a simple man at heart, and with my help the idea grew that there must be some story behind these watercolours. I must confess that the challenge began to appeal to me. I began to believe in this great love affair myself. I discovered that Captain Harker had indeed married Lady Edgar of Stourdens, a widow considerably older than himself, but that he died two years later at Trafalgar and that after her brief marriage Her Ladyship had reverted to her previous name. When I thought of *The Watsons*, well, it quickly became apparent to me what had happened. While morally if not legally bound to Lady Edgar, William Harker had met someone younger, the delightful witty Jane Austen, who had a meddlesome sister, Cassandra. And so the collection sprang into being. It was an intriguing puzzle to fit fictitious dates, houses, and people with the known facts. Many of the people actually existed, of course: the Wildmans at Chilham, the Kemble family and so on.

'It is a strange phenomenon,' he observed, 'that after a while fact comes to the illusionist's aid. I explained to Bob that, as is true, very little is known of Jane Austen's life between the years of mid 1801 to 1804 and no letters were known to exist. All I did was to fit clues together from established facts. Not *all* the facts, I admit, but Bob was happy. I explained to him that Cassandra was always vague about the gentleman with whom Jane had fallen in love for reasons of her own. It was Cassandra who wove the fiction, not us. We were just filling gaps in order that the truth might come to light.'

Georgia struggled to tread a tightrope between wanting to hurl contradictions at him and succumbing to his persuasive tongue.

'So how did Amelia and Tanner affect this harmonious arrangement?' Peter asked drily.

'Tanner was desperate to realize his own dreams.' Watts smiled. 'As desperate as his son is now. I'm sure you're aware of that. Stourdens and Jane Austen are their own personal property. Ideally, Max wanted to live in Stourdens, but if that were not possible then he wished to restore the Edgar Arms to run as a tourist attraction side by side with Stourdens. Unfortunately, Bob threatened his plans. Bob did not want to exploit Stourdens and Jane Austen. He wanted to treasure his collection alone.'

'He knew it was mostly fake then?'

'Not at all. He believed in the basic truth of it and understood that gaps had to be filled.'

'The moral issue didn't affect him?' Georgia found that hard to believe.

'It disappeared. Bob did not want to share his dream with anyone, even me. He reached the point where he could blank out the fact that I had faked documents to link to the true ones. The gap between what was fact – the original watercolours and oil painting and the few letters that had long been in the Luckhurst collection – and what I had produced in my studio grew narrower and narrower, until it began to vanish altogether, like the Cheshire Cat's smile.'

'But then Bob died,' Peter said bluntly. 'Murdered by Amelia?'

'I would not know.'

'You heard that man in the Bat and Trap say there was a woman's voice in the folly just before Bob was murdered.'

'I so enjoyed our chat in the pub, Miss Marsh, but I don't recall that.'

Georgia glared at him. Never had she felt so impotent in the face of brazen nerve.

'How long have you lived in this area, Mr Watts?' Peter asked abruptly.

'I was wondering if that would occur to you. Ten years. Before that I lived and worked in south London. Are you by any chance wondering whether I might be Max Tanner? After all, I am a declared illusionist.'

'I'll consider that possibility,' Peter said evenly. 'Could you tell us why Laura Fettis visited you?'

'Of course,' Watts said agreeably. 'Amelia guessed long ago, as did Tanner, that the collection was fake, but she scented money. On the strength of the Jane Austen story, she sold Stourdens at an inflated price to the Fettises, leaving Tanner in prison. Recently, she must have read about the increased visibility of Stourdens and decided to raise a little more cash. I can't be sure, but I suspect her visit to Laura was therefore less altruistic in nature and more for reasons of blackmail. She had long known who had worked with Bob on the faked collection and tried to put a little pressure on me a week or two before the Gala, hence her telling Laura that she knew the collection was fake but not mentioning my real name. I told dear Amelia to publish and be damned, knowing nothing could be proved against me, and gave her my Jane Austen business number in case other interested victims wished to speak to me. Laura Fettis was not a woman to be easily blackmailed, however. She had a warped sense of morality, whereby everything had to be judged by the law of the land. It is a point of view, but not one I share.'

'After Laura knew the collection was faked,' Douglas continued, 'she decided to call all the plans for Stourdens off, having refused to be blackmailed. But first, as Amelia had predicted, she had to confirm this extraordinary story with me on the number Amelia provided. Not under the name of Douglas Watts, naturally, whom she knew as a retired antiquarian, golfing friend of Roy's, Jane Austen expert and her proposed trustee if she died young.'

'How could you accept that position?' Georgia asked. 'Trustee means just that – trust.'

'Correct. I am trustee to ensure the good of Stourdens. What would you judge to be in Stourdens' best interests?'

'Making money to keep it going,' Georgia groaned, seeing the trap ahead.

'And the best way to achieve that?'

'Follow the original plans and ignore the faking aspect, but—'

'Quite. However, Laura's death put a spoke in that wheel. Once I had confirmed that the collection was fake, she was all for stopping the exploitation, as she called it, in its tracks, no matter what harm was caused to innocent people. She would rewrite her will, she told me, cancelling the trust, or at least removing me as trustee, although that naturally only came into effect after her death.'

'And what was your reaction?' Georgia asked.

'I tried to make her see sense, that there was more good in going ahead than in calling it off. She would not have it. She was going to tell all those most closely concerned before the Gala, which was the next day. I suggested she keep my name at least temporarily out of it, and she reluctantly agreed when I pointed out she had no proof and that libel and slander are powerful weapons of offence as well as defence. I gather she slept on the problem and the next morning told Tim, Roy, Jennifer – and probably Philip, Jake and Barbara too – that she had changed her mind about developing Stourdens commercially.'

Not Jennifer, Georgia remembered, because Laura asked her to take her own place supervising the catering tents. She had been going to talk to her later, obviously about the commercialization issue and perhaps even about the fakes – if, of course, Douglas Watts was telling the truth about them.

Peter picked on the same point. 'How do we know that what you're telling us isn't just another game for your amusement?'

'I am still Laura's trustee,' he said complacently. 'I have the future of Stourdens to consider.'

'Even though you know the collection is faked and that Laura had changed her mind over developing Stourdens?' Georgia asked in amazement. 'I presume that's why Jennifer was kept away from the meeting yesterday.'

'Possibly. I would not know. I did not attend as I understood it was focused on the planning of the film.'

'Which as trustee you would allow to go ahead.'

Any sarcasm fell on deaf ears. He simply replied: 'As trustee, yes.'

'Even though it's based on a lie?' This was unbelievable.

'I dislike the word lie. That too is an illusion. It depends which world one is living in at the time. I was hoping you wouldn't use it. I can prove it to you that I am telling you the truth, about the collection. Do you wish me to do so?'

Peter glanced at Georgia and nodded.

'Then we have one difficulty. I need you to travel in my car, as I have no wish for you to identify where we are going. However, my car is—'

'Not equipped for wheelchairs,' Peter finished for him. 'In that case, I will follow your car.'

'I fear not. If you cannot accompany me in my own car, then I have to deny you the proof you say you wish, although of course Miss Marsh may come with me.'

'The police will no doubt need to know too.'

'Not without proof that proof exists. Dear me, what a puzzle of logic. I am still willing to take you, Miss Marsh. I should mention, however, that if you *should* decide to follow me, Mr Marsh, I shall merely take you on a circular and pleasant drive through the Kentish lanes. Unfortunately, this inn closes shortly, but there is a pleasant summer house where you may await our return. We shall not be long.'

Peter had hated giving in, but Georgia had signalled to him that he should do so. There was a chance that Douglas Watts meant what he said, and that could be valuable. She comforted herself that she could hardly be at physical risk, as she was fully trained in self-defence. Unless, of course, he had a gun – the gun perhaps that had already killed two people. She firmly put that thought behind her. It was not, she guessed, his style.

She lost count of the narrow single-track lanes that Douglas Watts chose to follow – with unusual care, she noticed. She began to suspect that the route was chosen not only to avoid recognizable villages but any signposts at all.

He eventually drew up outside a house so unattractive that she could not believe it belonged to an antiquarian. On second thoughts, to this particular antiquarian perhaps it could. It was certainly anonymous although unusual in design. It was sturdy, it was functional, not old, not new, once painted white and crying out for similar treatment, and it stood in a row of smaller red-brick houses.

'Welcome to Osborne Castle,' he said. The nameplate at the gate read 'Number 3'. That added up, she thought – it looked suitably anonymous.

Slightly to her surprise he rang the bell at the front door, which was opened by a harassed-looking youngish mother with two small children clinging to her. 'Morning, Mr Osborne.'

'And to you, Mrs Smith.'

This was clearly a well-worn routine, because with the formalities over he simply led Georgia past her, up the stairs, along a narrow corridor and entered a room on the right at the rear of the house.

'I trust this will convince you that my story is fact not illusion,' he said as he threw open the door. 'My den,' he announced.

A den? It looked more like a research laboratory, save for the bookshelves lining the far wall. All were full, with both antiquarian leather-bound books and more modern volumes on art and artists. There was a small sink with running water under the window, with work tops, more shelves with paint, varnishes, sulphuric acid, and paraffin, and behind her was what looked like a state-of-the-art X-ray machine and an ultraviolet light. A large modern table held computers, cameras, a scanning electron microscope and what looked like a magnifier – maybe the jeweller's loupe to which he had referred. There were canvases and frames stored against the wall behind the door, and on the worktops were countless boxes and pots whose contents she could not see save for those with paintbrushes, chalks and pencils in them. Two functional chairs completed the array.

'Are you convinced, Miss Marsh?' Douglas asked politely.

She was determined to remain cool, faced with this overwhelming display. 'Sufficiently, though I'd need more expertise to be sure enough for a court of law.'

'I'm relieved to hear you say so. You will doubtless therefore be informing the police, who will discuss the allegation with whomever they think fit.'

'We shall,' she said evenly, and he merely smiled. She walked over to the shelves to look at the books more closely.

'You referred earlier to *one* of your alter egos,' she said. 'Are there more collections such as the one at Stourdens?'

He smiled. 'Time will tell, Miss Marsh. I hope well after I discover that death is no illusion.'

THIRTEEN

'This,' Peter remarked as they drove back to Haden Shaw, 'is what one might call a humdinger. The sort of tornado that lands us in the merry old Land of Oz.'

Georgia tried to rally her wits, which seemed to have gone missing ever since Douglas Watts had driven her back to the pub to pick up Peter, who was impatiently awaiting them. He had grown tired of the summer house and was back in their own car with his laptop. Douglas had then politely paid his farewells and left. She had to admit that he had behaved impeccably – if there were an etiquette for a situation such as this. He had not sounded smug, he had not gloried in his hoax, he had not shown a remorse that he clearly did not feel.

'*If* we believe him,' she replied.

'Don't you? Rather an elaborate joke, wouldn't you say?'

'He seems to specialize in them.'

'Even so,' Peter ruminated as they pulled off the Ashford Road into Shaw Lane, 'I'm inclined to believe him. Which means—'

'We have to report it to the lovely Diane.' A prospect to which she would not look forward.

'Who may or may not thank us.'

'That's irrelevant. It puts him, as he must be aware, in the front line as a suspect for Laura's murder. She has to know.'

'No contest. If Laura told her loving family – with a query over Jennifer – on the morning of the Gala that the collection was fake, it's a remarkable coincidence that she died before the day was out and moreover that no one has mentioned the question of fakes during the investigation. Not merely did Laura not want to commercialize Stourdens but she had very good reason not to do so.'

'There's another point,' Georgia said. 'Did the interested parties believe Laura when she said she'd changed her mind? Did she tell them it was fake, even if she didn't give Douglas's name? It seems fairly certain that Laura had been convinced by Douglas's story. If the family did know it was fake, though, they've kept unbelievably quiet about it. If they didn't, then they still had reason to want Laura dead, if she was flatly refusing to go ahead with the plans for Stourdens.'

'Perhaps they decided to go ahead anyway. All in all, a puzzle maze,' Peter remarked. 'Fortunately, it's Diane Newton who has to find a way out of it, not us.'

At Mike's request, Georgia drove to Charing Police HQ the next morning, but once again her reception was hardly warm. She had expected detachment – which was the nature of Diane's job – and she had expected her story to be probed. Instead she was presented with a gruelling session with DI Newton which was building up her resistance.

Diane was patently disbelieving. 'Let's get this straight. You can't say exactly where the house is, except that somewhere you remember passing a windmill and a road sign to Ramsgate. Nor do you know who owns the house, but it isn't lived in either by Douglas Watts or by Alfred Wheeler or by Howard Osborne.'

'I believe it's owned by him.'

'Not under either of those three names in the Thanet area.'

Georgia could have kicked herself. Of course it wouldn't

be. Watts would be too careful for that. 'The house was in that general direction,' she said steadily. 'There was a small village nearby which I didn't recognize; the house was outside it in a terrace of six red-brick houses and the one I was taken to was Number Three. It was near a crossroads of two lanes. Here – ' she pushed a sheet of paper across the table to Diane, for which she received no thanks – 'this is a rough layout of what it was like, not that it can tell you much more than I have.'

'You don't think that this man might have been hoodwinking you?'

'Of course that's possible,' Georgia agreed, 'but why should he bother?'

'He sounds like a joker to me. Jokers get their kicks from taking the mickey out of others. You must admit, Georgia, that your investigation into Robert Luckhurst's death must sound ripe for mockery – to some,' she added.

'You're too kind,' Georgia said drily.

DI Newton must have decided to let her off lightly. 'We'll look into it when we've a moment.'

'Cheer up,' Peter said, when she reported back during the afternoon in gloomy mood. 'We didn't expect much else. She's in the hot seat though, because if Watts is speaking the truth, it's undoubtedly relevant to her case and to the Met's. In fact we're in the more interesting position, because the Luckhurst murder is the basic one if all three of them are connected. If Watts was not kidding us, then Bob Luckhurst knew on one level at least that the collection was fake, and so did Amelia and Tanner. Tanner had built up his hopes of exploiting it for the advancement of Edgar Arms, and Amelia for Stourdens. Midnight struck when Bob Luckhurst refused to budge and their dreams turned into pumpkins.'

'That's hardly taking us forward,' Georgia said crossly. 'It merely makes them, as well as Douglas, the obvious suspects for Luckhurst's murder, which we knew already. There were plenty of other people around who might have wanted him dead, though, and in twenty-five years the real culprit could well have died.'

'Tom Miller is still going strong,' Peter pointed out.

'Here we go again. There's no evidence that he had any opportunity to kill Luckhurst.'

'Let's consider again what we know, or think we know about him, and see where it takes us,' Peter said calmly. 'He comes into the folly with his followers as far as the door of the study where Bob Luckhurst was later shot. Tanner is in there with Bob and comes out to see what's happening. Then Bob comes out to challenge Miller. Miller decides to leave – whether peaceably, as he says, or with menaces. He doesn't see Tanner again, telling us that as he goes out, Tanner must have nipped back in. But Miller leaves the folly at the rear of his group, who would not have been travelling in a neat croco-dile formation, but spreading out. If Tanner *is* amongst that group, perhaps on one side where he wouldn't be noticed by too many people, Miller could have decided to make the most of his opportunity. He'd come prepared with the gun, been foiled by finding Tanner present, and now the opportunity reoccurs. Alternatively, Tanner knew about the tunnel and could have returned that way to avoid having to join the protest group with which he's just fallen out.'

'Fine,' Georgia agreed, 'but where does Amelia fit in?'

'Only one person said there was a woman there, and he was a chum of Tom Miller's.'

'We haven't asked everyone on the march,' she pointed out. 'Anyway, it can't have been Barbara's voice, so if there was a woman present it was probably Amelia's.'

'Was Barbara interviewed, I wonder?' Peter mused. 'Perhaps not. She could hardly have been top of the list of suspects.'

'Fancy her for a Lady Macbeth?'

'You'll attract bad luck.'

'I think it's here.'

'You could be right.' Peter paused. 'I'm not looking forward to Thursday.'

'Nor me,' Georgia admitted. The nightmare of meeting Lucien Marques was growing. She glanced through the window as a car drew up outside and her heart sank. 'Bad luck *is* here. Tim Wilson's arrived.'

'Alone?'

'No. Philip Faring's with him.' This did not look good, especially as Jennifer was absent. It was blindingly clear why they had come.

Peter seemed unconcerned, however, even when a tight-lipped, furious Tim launched straight into battle. 'You two have made a monumental cock-up.'

'Have we?' Peter replied. 'Over what?'

'According to the police, who kindly paid me a visit at lunchtime, you have twisted whatever you thought Douglas had told you and come up with a cock and bull story about the Jane Austen collection being faked by him.'

'The police told you it was a cock and bull story?' Peter enquired politely.

'No, but it is, as you must be perfectly well aware,' Philip said angrily. 'Have you given a moment's thought to the implications for Stourdens and for my book if this false rumour gets around?'

'Yes,' Peter said soberly. 'We have. However, as Douglas himself informed us he had faked the collection, we were duty bound to pass the information on to the police.'

'It's bloody nonsense,' Tim said, beside himself with rage. 'I've spoken to Douglas. He told me you suggested a lunch meeting to discuss Bob Luckhurst's death, and that was all he discussed with you. I know you'll have a book to sell, but defaming Stourdens' reputation is not going to be part of it.'

Georgia tried to take in this new blow, and even Peter looked nonplussed. 'He *denies* it? He can't, and therefore we can't omit it. Bob Luckhurst lived at Stourdens, and the collection originated with him; Amelia was his wife, and she has now been murdered. I can't believe Douglas denies telling us anything about the collection.'

'I assure you he does,' Philip said. She could see him shaking. 'And that's because there is nothing to tell. Good grief, I've written a whole book about Jane Austen and Harker. Don't you think I'd have noticed if there was something bogus about the story? Don't you think I've checked it all out? I do have a reputation to consider. Do you really think I would risk that on the basis of something that might have been faked?'

'It's happened before,' Georgia said. 'The best of scholars is sometimes deceived. Think of the Hitler diaries.'

'I greatly resent this,' Philip snapped. 'I take it you aren't accusing me of *knowing* about this fictitious fake?'

'Assuming Douglas was not lying to us, he said Laura knew about the fakes. Did she tell you on the morning of the Gala?'

Both men began to speak, but Tim won. 'All Laura told us is that she didn't feel up to making any announcement about Stourdens that day,' he said firmly.

'Odd,' Georgia said. 'She told Jennifer that she was going to change her will, which sounds pretty drastic.'

Tim's face was bright with anger. 'Leave Jennifer out of this. You've meddled enough in my private affairs.'

'Jennifer and Roy are the beneficiaries, and Douglas the trustee. Not your private affair, Tim.'

'It's Douglas's affair.'

'So you're still going ahead, with or without investigating further to check if the collection is genuine?' Surely he would not be such a fool, Georgia thought.

'Already done,' Philip whipped back. 'I had to be fully confident before I began writing.'

'Using Douglas Watts as your authority?'

'He *is* an authority, and others backed him up.'

'He's also a self-confessed faker, as he told us. Neat.'

'It would be extremely strange if he did tell you that,' Philip said. 'His task as trustee is to promote the story, not shoot it down.'

'Time will tell,' Peter said. 'Does it not worry you that the whole of the Jane Austen world will have its teeth into that collection the moment it's made public knowledge? Every detail will be examined detail by detail. Or are you banking on all publicity being good, no matter whether based on truth or falsehood?'

'Our business, I believe,' Tim said coldly.

'Which will be everyone's affair, once you go public,' Georgia said.

'They'll still flock to Stourdens,' Tim shot back. Even Philip looked aghast at that.

* * *

'Some weeks just don't go well,' Peter remarked as Georgia arrived on Wednesday morning. 'Mike's on his way over, and he doesn't sound happy.'

When he reached them he didn't look happy either. 'OK,' he said grimly. 'Just convince me that the pair of you haven't gone raving mad.'

'Trouble over Douglas Watts, I presume,' Georgia said. It was depressingly likely. She and Peter had been set up and were now entwined in a web not of their making.

'For you, yes, and a fine mess for us. Newton's team tracked down the house in which you said you found the faker's paradise. It's Number Three Beech Cottages, not far from a village called Warmden.'

'So that's good news?' Georgia was relieved, even as it struck her that the long tour on which Douglas had taken her was a drive round in circles.

'No. The occupant, a Mrs Green, agreed she rented the house, but the landlord bore no resemblance to Douglas Watts. The landlord is a woman called Mary Barclay, whose father had lived there. And the father's name was not Watts, or Wheeler, or Osborne. When DI Newton talked to Watts himself, he said you all left the pub together and departed on your separate ways. You told him you had an appointment in Canterbury.'

'But—'

'No point in buts, Georgia. That's it, as far as we're concerned. Mrs Green let the team tour the house to see if they could find whatever it was they were looking for, but they couldn't. They found the room, but it bore no resemblance to the one you described. It was a child's bedroom, with posters on the walls, and nothing more sinister than a teddy bear or two, a chest of drawers, and a lot of toys. There was no sign of the bookshelves you mentioned, or the apparatus or the sink and worktop. The child has slept there for four years. In other words there is nothing to suggest that Douglas Watts is anything other than he seems: a retired antiquarian book-dealer who plays golf and is a responsible citizen. After all,' Mike added, 'you must admit it would be odd to take a trusteeship over something he has faked.'

'Just what Tim Wilson said,' Peter commented.

'And what do you say?'

'That it's not odd at all. Who better to monitor the fake's progress? That's the way Watts' mind works.'

'So why tell you he's a crook?'

'Because he knew no one would believe us, and for some reason I can't yet work out that suits him.'

A pause. 'I'd love to say I'm on your side and believe you one hundred per cent,' Mike said, 'but I can't. You're usually right, and unless you've both had a brainstorm there has to be something more to this. I've nothing to go on though, so I can't call the tune over Newton's investigation. All I can suggest is that you plough on with the Bob Luckhurst line but with a *very* low profile and keep me in the loop. And don't step on the toes of the Met the way you do ours. They're working with Newton over the Amelia Luckhurst murder. Understood?'

'Yes, Mike,' Peter said meekly. 'Last point though. If Watts was telling the truth about the fakes, doesn't it widen the scope over who killed Laura Fettis?'

'It may strengthen it but doesn't widen it.'

'Wrong. You could include Douglas Watts himself.'

To her relief Georgia found Jennifer alone at Stourdens. When Jennifer rang to ask her to come over that afternoon she had feared the worst: that Jennifer might have joined Tim's side over the matter of Douglas and the fakes. Far from it, however.

'It's hell here,' Jennifer said despondently. 'Tim has a face like a thundercloud but refuses to leave me alone. Dad looks hurt beyond belief at my lack of commitment to what was apparently Mum's greatest dream. How can he be so blind? Jake looks as if he has blinkers on, staring only at his film, and Philip like Julius Caesar betrayed by Brutus.'

'I take it you were here when the police came. So you've heard what Douglas Watts told us and what Tim thinks.'

'Both – at length. Why would you lie about it? How can Tim deny it? How can Dad? At the very least Mum told them that morning that she wasn't going ahead with the plans and why. Even if the story didn't fit my memories of Mum in that last day or two I would believe you. But it does. She looked awful that evening after she got back from Canterbury.'

'Have you spoken to Douglas yourself? Does he claim to have been merely spinning us a yarn?' Georgia asked.

'Not in so many words. He says he only talked about the Luckhursts, Georgia. Jane Austen was barely mentioned. That's why I wanted to see you. I need you to tell me exactly what he said and what you saw when he took you on this trip. I've heard Tim's version.'

Jennifer listened carefully as Georgia recounted the full story, including the police's fruitless search. 'And do you believe the police found nothing?' she asked when Georgia had finished.

'I have to.'

'Douglas must have counted on your telling the police and only shown you the room because he knew he could fool them. What's your explanation of how he did it?'

'I haven't got one. I can only think there was some kind of hidden room. But how could you get a child of four years old to lie about where he slept? There has to be an answer and I'll find it. But I'm sorry, Jennifer. It's hard for you being so close to Douglas.'

'I'm not, in fact. Dad is. Mum was pretty neutral about him. I believe he told you the truth. It's too elaborate a story for it merely to be mischief-making and—'

She broke off as Tim came storming into the room, furious at seeing Georgia. 'I thought that was your car outside. What the hell are you doing here?' he demanded. 'Haven't you done enough damage?'

'Georgia's here because I invited her, Tim,' Jennifer said coolly. 'I take it you don't object to my doing so?'

'Then you're an idiot. Douglas is here himself. He'll tell you what a fool you're being.'

Georgia steeled herself as he strolled in behind Tim. 'I'm delighted to see you,' she said. 'It will give you a chance to confirm to Tim and Jennifer what you told Peter and myself.'

Douglas regarded her with amusement. 'A most interesting story you seem to have concocted around that innocent little meeting, Georgia. I hardly recognized myself in such a guise.'

She managed not to retort, realizing that she was again out of her depth.

'Flattered though I am at having such faking skills attributed to me,' Douglas continued, 'I'm afraid I have to deny the story you're recounting. I'm not capable of dashing the Fettis and Clackington dreams to quite such an extent. I'm far too kind-hearted. And I *am* the trustee for Stourdens' future.'

'So as we have all now heard it from the horse's mouth, I take it you'll apologize and leave, Georgia,' Tim commanded.

'Just a minute,' Jennifer interrupted. 'This is my house, Tim, not yours. Mine and Dad's.'

'A house for which Douglas is the trustee and can make all the decisions about it.'

'Not all of them,' Jennifer said coolly.

Tim changed tack. 'Look, Jen, you're going through a rough time. We all are. But this stupid story of the Marshes' has changed nothing. Jake's documentary is going ahead next week, and Douglas has decided we should begin provisional plans for the tours next year.'

'Based on the Jane Austen collection?' Jennifer asked.

'Of course.'

'Even if I denounce it as at least of dubious authenticity?'

Douglas looked pensive. 'I suggest you don't bring my name into it in that connection. You have no proof, Jennifer dear, that there is anything wrong with it. And, of course, I have already authenticated it. There is a law of slander as well as libel.'

'Don't worry,' Jennifer said. 'There's no need to name you, Douglas. As you say, I have no proof of your involvement in any fakes. I shall get it authenticated elsewhere and then act accordingly.'

'Ah,' Douglas replied. 'I wonder, can you do that? The collection is part of the trust.'

Jennifer smiled. 'I'm afraid you're wrong. Stourdens itself is under the trust, but the collection was willed to me alone.'

Georgia laughed at the naked horror on both Tim's and Douglas's faces.

'Is that true?' Tim turned on Douglas, white-faced.

To Georgia's pleasure, Douglas looked genuinely shaken. 'I was not aware of that. I can't believe it.'

'You can safely do so. Dad's been in such a state that he didn't take it in at the solicitors. I did. And Mum told me why she'd done it, too.' Jennifer began to both cry and laugh. 'It wasn't because of you, Douglas, or Dad. She said she loved it too much and wanted me alone to have it. *Loved* it!'

It was happening at last. This was the first time that Georgia had been in the same car as both her parents since Elena had left. The odd thing was that she was feeling nervous not because it felt so strange but because it seemed so natural. True, Elena was unusually quiet and Peter falsely jolly, which was not a normal role for either of them, but considering the circumstances the pressure was at a low level. To Georgia's relief the hotel where Lucien Marques was staying on the South Bank of the Thames had its own large parking lot. The visit would be nerve-racking enough without adding driving problems to it.

Lucien had arranged to meet them in the entrance hall, and they would obviously be easily identifiable. Georgia saw him coming towards them as soon as Peter's wheelchair was safely inside the door, and she had an immediate shock. Rick had been dead sixteen years, and she had therefore expected Lucien to be a middle-aged man, perhaps in his forties or fifties. Rick himself would have been in his late thirties now. But this man looked only in his mid-twenties.

'You must have been a child when the accident happened,' Georgia said, after the introductions and business of settling themselves into a secluded part of the bar.

'I was, *madame*. I was nine years old. I have much to be grateful to Rick for. Certainly for what I am today, and I think also for my life.'

'And what are you today?' Peter was trying his best to seem composed. Elena, however, looked as if her smile were fixed permanently on her face, which made Georgia realize that it would be up to her to help her mother through this.

'I am a musician, a cellist.'

Georgia felt as if she would choke, caught out by the

unexpected. Rick's love of music . . . his happy final weeks
with the singer he had met in Normandy. This man, too, was
a musician.

'He talked of music to me. Nothing but music. My parents
had made me learn to play the cello, but I hated it. It was
difficult, pointless, I would rather be playing football. But
when Rick talked, he made music so alive, so important.' He
smiled at them. 'But I should start at the beginning. You know
where the accident happened?'

'On the Danube near Linz.' Peter had visited it last year
with his then girlfriend and with Josephine Mantreau, who
had told them so much about Rick's last weeks.

'It was dark, and our boat collided with another vessel in
the dark. We had no warning, nothing. Your son—'

'Rick, call him Rick, please,' Elena said.

Hearing the tremble in her voice, Georgia stretched out her
hand to take her mother's in hers. It felt warm and familiar.

'Thank you,' Lucien said. 'We were downstairs in the boat.
My parents had been talking to Rick, and I was listening. Then
it happened, a bang, the lights went out, the darkness came
and then the screams. It was so quick; suddenly I felt water
and Rick's hand grabbing hold of me as it swept us away.
There was no time for lifebelts, nothing. We seemed to be in
the river immediately, just the two of us. Rick sang to me—'

'Sang?' Peter repeated.

'A song. I have heard it since. "Scarborough Fair".'

The choke in Georgia's throat returned in full force.
'Scarborough Fair' had been Rick's favourite song in childhood days.

'I could not see his face,' Lucien continued. 'Rick was trying
to swim, holding me with one arm. I remember that. I was
panicking. "Are we going to die?" I asked him. "No," he said.
"I have to get back for George's birthday." You know this
George?'

Her voice did not seem to be her own. 'He said Georgia,'
she managed to say. 'It was my birthday shortly afterwards.
He said he'd be there, and he wasn't.'

Elena's hand tightened in hers. 'What happened then?' her
mother asked.

'We seemed to be swept away, clear of the boat, and a rescue boat was coming for us. He pushed me into it, but then I think he was swept away and I never saw him again.' Lucien looked at them all uncertainly, perhaps wondering whether he had helped or not. 'But I remembered him. Always I do. I sing that song "Scarborough Fair" to my own babies.'

'Does that finish it, Elena, do you think?' Peter asked during the journey home. 'Is he resting now?'

'In an unidentified grave?' she answered. 'I can't bear it, Peter.'

'Our hearts have to be identity enough. Shall we take a trip to Scarborough, all three of us? Maybe next spring. On the cliff where we took him once as a child. Remember, Georgia?'

She remembered. They all did: she, Peter – and Elena. 'Let's do it,' she said.

FOURTEEN

'Are you ready for the next battle?' Peter asked.

'Which battlefield?' Georgia asked cautiously. In unspoken agreement, she and Peter had abandoned work on their return yesterday and sat with Elena in Medlars' garden.

'Edgar House. The Clackingtons are expecting us at eleven thirty. They're still wavering as to whether they believe us or not over the fake letters. Gerald said he'd ring me back when I first called him, and I got the impression that today was not a good choice.' Peter was amused rather than irritated. 'Something's brewing, and it won't just be cups of tea. For a start, Esther Tanner's going to be there.'

'Maybe Douglas has been invited too and will be sitting there with his inscrutable smile.'

'I doubt it. He's thrown his metaphorical bomb and knows he's on safe ground with Tim and Roy at least. He'll see no need to defend his corner with the Clackingtons. He'll just watch where the pieces fall. What with yesterday and Jill's birthday on Saturday it's going to be a busy week.'

'I wish I could work out why Douglas told us,' Georgia said. 'I'd feel on safer ground. At the moment we could be playing right into his hands again.'

'I would like to say because he thought it would help point us towards Bob Luckhurst's murderer, but it's far more likely he's safeguarding himself. Amelia knew the collection was fake, and he reasoned that she would tell Laura, probably blackmail her and do the same to other interested parties. I reckon he was getting the best of both worlds. Tell us so that he would look good in the eyes of the police – even if they couldn't find evidence – and deny it until he was blue in the face to the Fettises. Clever. No evidence either way except hearsay from two interested parties.'

'What about the publican at the Dryden Arms?'

'No joy there. He simply closed up – and as I was cleverly manoeuvred into the summer house he didn't know I was still there.'

'Any ideas yet on how Douglas made that room disappear? It was a standard house, you couldn't tell it from all the others, and so it wasn't the sort of place to lend itself to murder in the way of magic tricks.'

'Give me time,' Peter said with dignity – which meant he hadn't a clue, she thought. She could hardly blame him – nor had she.

Gerald must have seen their car arrive, because he opened the door even before she had got out of the car. He was hardly beaming in welcome, however, and there was no sign of Dora.

'I'll see you in,' Gerald said neutrally, pulling the door shut behind him and escorting them to the side door. He seemed embarrassed rather than angry at the bad news he'd been given, she thought, even if it did feel as though they were being banished to the tradesmen's entrance. Ridiculous, Georgia told herself. Bad as the news might be for the Clackingtons, she and Peter were merely the messengers, not the evil-doers. Besides, if the Clackingtons doubted what they had been told they had only to get the collection authenticated by disinterested third parties, which would either verify Watts' claim or, hopefully from their point of view, disprove it. Once again she had a niggle over whether Douglas had been telling them the truth or not.

Stand firm and march on, she told herself, a family phrase that had always made her giggle as a child. She could see the lift ahead before they turned towards the living room and she thought of the precious letters lying on their velvet cushions and how fond Dora was of them. Her heart went out to her.

When they reached the living room she could see both Esther and David Wilson together with, surprisingly, John Collier, Amelia's husband. She was immediately wary. For what purpose had they been summoned? To prove the collection must be genuine or to deal with the consequences of its being a fraud?

'We've heard,' Gerald began, preceded by a cough either of embarrassment or self-importance, 'from Roy. As you no doubt know, he had a visit from the police over Peter's story that their Jane Austen collection is not genuine.'

'It was Douglas Watts' story, not ours,' Peter replied. 'He himself told us that he had faked it.'

'Roy assures me that Douglas said nothing of the sort. A mild jest perhaps which you misinterpreted.' Gerald looked hopeful.

'Roy can't know what Douglas said. He wasn't there,' Peter said mildly. 'Have you spoken to Watts yourself?'

'Not yet. Can't get hold of the fellow. But Dora and I had those letters authenticated by him when we came here – sorry, Esther, not doubting you, but that was only reasonable. Watts is a specialist in Austen, so that was good enough for us. The question is where they came from, which is what I hope you can tell us, Esther.'

Esther looked nonplussed. 'I explained when the house sale went through that the Jane Austen connections were Max's department, not mine. He told me he'd found the oil painting with the letters tucked into it and showed it to Bob Luckhurst, who checked out the artist and subject.'

David Wilson seemed puzzled. 'You told me it was Luckhurst who found the letters secreted in the frame.'

'Maybe I did.' Esther looked annoyed. 'Anyway, it doesn't matter, does it?'

'It could,' Georgia said, earning herself a glare from Gerald. 'You said you were both interested in restoring the Assembly Rooms, not just Max.'

'That's true,' Esther replied, 'but I told Max and Barbara they could take care of the history side. Not my thing. Not that it was theirs either.'

'So Barbara was involved in your plans?'

'She was an ambitious young lady. Saw a little nest-egg for herself and decided to make herself indispensable. Behaved like Lady Muck. Same now. She's going into the trade in a big way, I heard. She and that son of hers.'

Max Tanner's? Georgia wondered again.

David Wilson stepped into the ring. 'Seems to me that we're getting off the point. Did Max find the letters here or was it Luckhurst who slipped them into the frame when Max took the painting to him? Seems to me that they must have been planted there, not here. Maybe Luckhurst gave the letters to Max in payment for the painting. Rotten deal if so. They're faked, but from what you say, Esther, that painting was the real McCoy.'

A small moan from Dora. 'Did Amelia mention our letters to you, John? It really seems scarcely believable all that material was faked, and that she knew about it. Of course, I never met her—'

'She knew nothing of the sort,' John Collier replied vigorously. 'And what's more it's unproven as to whether they *are* faked,' he reminded them.

'Did Max believe the letters were genuine?' Peter asked Esther.

'Of course,' she replied immediately. 'He trusted Bob, so he trusted the experts Bob employed.'

Interesting how protective both husbands were, both alert and ready to pounce on any implied slur on their spouses, Georgia noticed.

'I agree with you, David,' Peter said. 'Tanner was probably taken for a ride by Luckhurst and Watts acting together. He wouldn't have known whether the letters were genuine or not.'

'Then it's a question of who put them behind the frame,'

Georgia pointed out. 'If Tanner hid them in the frame himself then he was in the scam. If, as you suggested, David, Luckhurst pretended to find them then Tanner was duped.'

Dora said timidly, 'I'm sorry, John, but I agree with them. I think that Max was deceived either by Amelia or Bob Luckhurst or both.'

David began to speak, but was shouted down by Gerald's yell of fury.

'You're not falling for this line, are you, Dora? After all we've done to this house, and you believe the first crazy story that you're told? It's Douglas's word against yours, Marsh, and frankly, I prefer his, so I'd suggest you leave.'

'Certainly,' Georgia said. Nothing would be gained by their staying.

Dora rose trembling to her feet. 'I believe that I have something to contribute to this argument, and I would be grateful if you could stay, Peter, and you too, Georgia.'

'What the hell are you raving about, Dora?' Gerald was red in the face.

'You're forgetting about Laura,' Dora replied simply. 'I saw her just before she died, Gerald. I'm certain that Laura knew the collection was faked and that Jennifer thinks so too. I've talked to her.'

'You can't believe anything she says at present,' Gerald said sharply. 'She's upset.'

'I can believe her if I think she's right, Gerald,' Dora said with a dignity that Georgia never guessed she possessed. 'And I do. I think that our letters are probably fakes, and we should get another authentication.'

'Are you going to tell Douglas to his face that he's a fraud?' Gerald thundered.

'No, but I can ask for another opinion. I'm sure Peter and Georgia are right.'

'You're an idiot then. They're stirrers.'

'Don't mind us,' Peter said cheerfully. He was enjoying this. Gerald didn't. 'Those letters belong to me as well as you, Dora, and I say you'll do nothing of the sort.'

'That is your right, Gerald,' she retorted, 'just as it's my right to dispute any claim you might publicly make for them.'

Gerald stared at her as though wondering whom he'd been living with for the last umpteen years, but, seeing that he was about to launch another tirade, Georgia stepped hastily into the breach. 'What will you do about Jake's filming? Is it still beginning on Monday?'

'Yes. Happily there is plenty to talk about without mentioning the letters,' Dora replied.

'Is Jake OK with that?'

'I shall ensure that he is,' said the new Dora.

Jill had laid on a massive spread for her birthday, with about thirty guests squeezed into their tiny Canterbury garden. Georgia watched Rosa being lovingly passed from one pair of arms to another, with Elena well to the fore. She had stayed on in a Canterbury hotel so that she could continue house-hunting and had been talking happily about how much she liked the city. She seemed to get on well with Jill, almost as though she, not Georgia, were the proud step-grandparent. Georgia realized with some astonishment that she had herself miraculously become part of a family again, and that Elena was an accepted part of it. Talk of estate agents, instead of filling her with dread, now brought the comforting knowledge that it was a done deal. Elena would be moving back to England and living nearby. What would happen then was something to be dealt with in the future, not now.

'Coming over to Edgar House on Monday to see the fun?' Jake asked as he strolled up to Georgia.

'Depends on what fun you have in mind,' she said cautiously. 'I doubt if the Clackingtons would welcome me. I'm persona non grata.'

'Nonsense. You might have done them a favour, and anyway, you and Peter are most certainly interested parties. Edgar House is hired as my set for the day, so come. We can always fish out a Regency costume for you and call you an extra. Unpaid,' he joked. 'Or if Jill doesn't turn up you can give an erudite talk on Assembly Rooms.'

'On the whole I prefer the latter.'

'You're hired.' Jake went off to get another drink and Georgia went to join Peter, who was talking to a regally clad Jill.

'Ah, Georgia,' Peter greeted her, 'Jill's telling me—'

'All about Assembly Rooms,' Georgia finished for him.

Jill laughed. 'I see Jake's been talking. Phil too?'

'Both, though Peter and I aren't popular with Phil. I'll bring my armour on Monday.'

'Better to be prepared for combat,' Jill agreed. 'He'll have to organize a new presentation, once it's settled.'

'What does it depend on?'

'Jake. Jennifer's taken some of the collection up to London for an urgent evaluation, laid on by Jake and Phil's publishers. Evaluations take time, of course, so this one will be a snap opinion off the record, which will give enough guidance to point the way ahead. If the question mark over it looks serious, then Jake will have to move to Plan B, which means everyone moves to Plan B. Including me,' Jill said crossly. 'Thanks, Georgia. And Phil's not too pleased either,' she added as he and Jake joined them.

'You could say that,' Phil agreed sourly.

'What would you have done in our position?' Georgia asked. 'Ignore it? We had to tell the police.'

'*If* you ever had such a conversation, and *if* you reported it correctly,' Philip said.

'Any reason we should make it up or—'

'Not that I can see,' Jake interposed. 'I told you that, Phil.'

Philip was quick to make amends. 'I suppose you're right. Maybe Douglas said it as a joke and you misinterpreted it.'

So that was the way the relationship worked, Georgia thought. Jake led, and Philip followed. She'd assumed it was the other way around.

'It's one hell of a problem for us, though, especially me,' Philip continued, 'because my publishers have had to be warned. All for nothing.'

'Is it too late to postpone publication and make changes?' she asked.

'It's set to begin printing first week of September, so I hope we can get this mess cleared up by then. If we can't, they might scrap the whole book. It doesn't look good.'

FIFTEEN

When Georgia arrived at Edgar House on the Monday the array of cars and vans drawn up before the house was impressive. It was also daunting, because it brought home to her that the Luckhurst case had stalled. Everyone's attention was on the film. Reluctantly, Peter had pointed out that there was going to be no room for wheel-chairs or lift accommodation today, so she should go to Edgar House alone. Which was a nuisance, he felt, because it would be an interesting day. A phone call from Mike urging her to go but keep a low-key profile reinforced this, but unfortunately neither Mike nor Peter seemed to have any idea *what* they were expecting.

She took a deep breath and went into the house. Not only was the front door already open, but also every door that she could see. Edgar House was alive with sound and energy. Voices, movements above, and a living room apparently turned into a temporary props room. There was no sign of anybody in it, but there was a sense of people scurrying about elsewhere in the house. She could hear voices from the small room to the right of the entrance hall, where Jane Austen had awaited the Godmersham carriage – that much might be true even if the appearance of Captain William Harker into her life had been discredited.

She went into the room and found Dora and Jennifer poring over a script by the window.

'Oh, Georgia,' Jennifer greeted her. 'I'm so sorry – I didn't have time to let you know what was happening.'

'It's been called off?' Georgia asked in alarm.

'No,' Dora said with a certain complacency. 'Very much all on. It's a completely new focus for the film. Poor Jake's been up most of the night. We gave him a bed here.'

'What on earth's happened?'

'I went up to London on Friday and got back yesterday,'

Jennifer said. 'Result: very definite doubts over the collection. Still only doubts, because if they're fakes they're good, including the signatures on the two watercolours. But there was one howler that Douglas could not have foreseen. There was a letter from a Miss Pretty about a visit she paid to Stourdens where she ran into a Miss Jane Austen in the gardens alone with a naval captain, both seeming flustered at her coming upon them so unexpectedly. It was a reasonable risk on Douglas's part, and the Pretty family undoubtedly lived nearby. Unfortunately for him the specialist I saw did know of the Pretty family and was able to check. The sister to whom Douglas had addressed the letter had died in the preceding year.'

'I'm afraid it looks as if our letters are therefore also suspect,' Dora said.

She did not look in the least 'afraid', Georgia thought admiringly. Indeed Dora looked as if she was trying hard not to show excitement over the drama. 'I'm sorry, Jennifer,' Georgia said. 'I know the collection means a lot to you.'

'It did, and in a way it still does. But it's settled now, for me anyway, and confirms what you told me about the meeting with Douglas. But my poor mother – I can't bear it.'

Dora put her arm round her. 'I'll look after you, Jennifer.' And looking at her, Georgia believed she would.

'What about Jake?' she asked. 'How's he taken it?'

'On the chin,' Jennifer replied. 'He was half-prepared for it, but it meant working flat out to recast the working script of questions and answers for the presenter, and Dora, Jill and Phil for the interview questions.'

Georgia grimaced. 'How's Phil taken it?'

'Don't ask,' Jennifer said. 'He's Jake's problem, luckily.'

'And your father?'

'You mean Tim – they tend to mean more or less the same thing at the moment. Answer: let's just say I'm glad Jake's on my side.' Jennifer managed a grin. 'And as for Douglas, guess where he is?'

'A thousand miles away, I hope.'

'Here.'

'I suppose,' Georgia said, when she had recovered her breath, 'it's me that's crazy, not the rest of the world.'

'I'm with you,' Jennifer said.

'And so am I,' Dora said firmly. 'That awful man. And to think I made some raspberry fritters specially for him.'

'What's he doing here?' Georgia asked in bewilderment.

'Believe it or not, Jake's using him as his presenter.' Jennifer caught Georgia's expression and managed to laugh. 'Better to have your enemy within your sights, Georgia.'

'But *presenter*? Is Jake out of his mind? Does he trust him?' Georgia supposed Jennifer was right, however, and she tried to remember she herself was only a visitor here today.

'If he goes off course, Jake has the last word. He won't use the film.'

'So what's the new script about, if there's no Harker and no love affair?'

'It's clever. Jake's concentrating on *The Watsons* and its links with Edgar House for today. There's no doubt that Jane knew the Edgar Arms from her journeys to Godmersham. Nor is there any doubt that the Edgar Arms had Assembly Rooms in Jane Austen's time and that William Harker existed, if Douglas is speaking the truth. *Oh!*' Jennifer's face fell as she realized what she had said, and Georgia laughed. 'Anyway, come and see what Jake's up to.'

Dora hurried them up the stairs to the first floor. She was a stately figure in her chatelaine's outfit for the TV film, a flowing blue chiffon skirt with matching jacket and pearls. When they reached the entrance to the Assembly Rooms, Georgia's initial reaction was that she'd walked into *Alice in Wonderland*, at the point where the gardeners were busy rushing around getting ready for the arrival of the Queen of Hearts by painting the white roses red. The transformation in progress here was just as startling. Someone had performed a miracle by transforming the drab carpet flooring into polished floorboards, candle holders adorned the bright decorated walls, and elegant chairs were clustered along the walls and round the fireside. There was a group of extras in Regency dress, and she could see the camera and lighting crews with their gear hard at work.

Jake came to greet them, looking as if he welcomed a break. 'We've already shot the room before the makeover,' he explained. 'Now we're heavily into 1802.'

'What are you planning to film here?' Georgia tried not to sound suspicious that romance might be about to make a re-entry.

'Nuts, aren't we? But I'd already hired the cast and costumes, so why not use them? It was going to be a gentle, unfocused scene which would blur back to Edgar House today, but now we're planning an in-focus scene of the dance in *The Watsons*, then a dissolve back to the presenter.'

'One of the cast is in naval costume,' Jennifer pointed out.

'Give me a break, Jen,' Jake said wearily. 'I've paid for it, so I might as well use it. And Harker did stay here.'

'So Douglas Watts says.'

'I checked it out with the archives myself. Satisfied? So as long as we don't stray into disputed territory we're safe.'

'And at Stourdens too?' she asked doubtfully. 'What about the love affair there? What else do you have?'

'The visits Jane would have made to Stourdens. Look, I'll *cope*.' Jake sighed. 'Take a look at this lot.' He waved an arm over the Assembly Rooms. 'You can see how much organization goes into one of these days. I've got actors hired, catering fixed, costumes, cameras, traffic, transport – it's a miracle that anything ever gets organized at all, let alone postponed as the whole approach changed like this. I've been closeted with my AD; he's in charge of the schedule. If we are to finish this room by lunchtime that will be a miracle in itself. Douglas, incidentally, is busy with his new script. He's as meek as a lamb.'

With a wolf inside, Georgia thought cynically. 'What are you filming this afternoon?'

'Tracking shots, following the arrival of the Edwards family and Emma Watson from the courtyard then upstairs past Tom Musgrave's room – I've upgraded an extra to pop out of his room as in the novel. Pity the arched entry into the courtyard has been built over.'

At Dora's look of alarm in case Jake decided to knock it down, Jake hastily added, 'Don't worry, we'll manage. I have to be off – they're signalling picture's up. In other words we're ready to go. You'll be next, Dora, but it will be a while yet.'

'Oh dear,' Dora lamented as they retired out of the firing

line. 'It was going to be such fun, but I feel as if we've
unleashed a hurricane.'

'So do I,' Jennifer said bitterly. 'Let's find ourselves a
coffee.'

Georgia excused herself from joining them, preferring to
watch the filming. It was a slow process, however, and having
seen three takes of the Sir Roger de Coverley she decided she
might achieve more elsewhere. She knew Peter would be trying
to reach Douglas by phone today, but it was far more likely
that she would find him first. Whatever his function in the
film, he was a captive here, and for once not in control.

She passed Gerald as she walked along the corridor to the
stairs, but he said nothing, merely acknowledging her presence with a curt nod. When she poked her head into the room
where the letters were kept, however, she was rewarded – if
that was the right word – by seeing Douglas. He was calmly
reading a newspaper. Not his script, she noted, and furthermore
there was no sign of the showcase containing the letters.

He promptly rose to his feet. 'Ah, Miss Marsh, enjoying
the fantasy?'

'Which fantasy?' she replied lightly. 'If yours, I'm afraid
not.'

He looked reproachful. 'I was referring to Edgar House
dolled up as an early-nineteenth-century pleasure palace.'

'I'm told you're the new presenter for today's filming. Isn't
it hard to reconcile that role with the one you boasted about
to my father and me?'

'A mere fantasy on *your* part, Miss Marsh. However, I did
enjoy our lunch with your father. Such a pity I had to leave
early.'

'You haven't won yet,' Georgia said, 'so don't be too
confident.'

'Dear me, I am terrified.'

'I hope with reason.' Georgia was surprised to find herself
shaking and remembered all too clearly that Douglas Watts
might be a murderer – twice over. 'I shall work out how you
managed that trick with your studio.'

'Shall?' Douglas queried. 'That word implies that no doubt
exists. But I think it does. If you'll excuse me, I have a script

to present. Oh,' he added as he passed her, 'by the way, Esther Tanner is here with her current husband. Nice chap. She deserves a bit of luck after that skunk Max.'

He looked highly pleased with himself, Georgia noted. Not for long, she vowed as she went back to the ground floor. If she were Jake, she would be very worried about what Douglas might slip into his presentation. Or Philip, come to that. She made allowances for Philip, however. He must be shattered at the news that Jennifer had brought. Far from being a careful interviewee, he must be considering his options if his publishers took the same view as Jake. Better safe than sorry.

Why were the Wilsons back here? she wondered as she walked through the living room. Just visitors, as she was, or was Jake going to give Esther a grilling over the forged letters? And it was odd that Tim hadn't turned up, or Roy.

She made her way to the kitchen, where she found Barbara and her team laying out the lunch ready to take into the garden and courtyard. She'd seen her van in front of the house, so the hard work was probably done at home in the new purpose-built kitchen. Today it was not Jane Austen food, however. She could see delicious-looking quiches, salads and plates of sandwiches. She didn't want to interrupt the flow and was about to retreat when Barbara noticed her and waved.

'How's it going?' Georgia called, and Barbara came across to her.

'Good, thanks. Funny being back here. I nearly went into the old kitchen. They've changed it around. It used to be right behind the bar, but it's a storeroom now.'

'Craig not with you?'

'No, it's a dry lunch. Odd for an old pub, but Jake said he wasn't taking any risks. No relaxing. It all has to be shot today. Like the old days, it is, only it's Jake shouting the odds and not Max.'

'I'm told Esther Tanner is here.'

'Is she?' Barbara looked interested. 'I'll look forward to seeing Madam High and Mighty at closer quarters. See that photo outside in the corridor? Stuck-up cow, she was. It's one of the photos Max took every New Year of staff and a few regulars. That was the last one, 1985. His idea of our all being chummy.'

'I'll take a look at it,' Georgia assured her, kicking herself for never asking the Clackingtons if they had any pictures of the old pub and staff. 'Right now,' she added, realizing she was holding Barbara up.

The photo was taken in the front of the pub with a grinning Max (she presumed) in the middle. He was a tall, stocky man, with an easily recognizable Esther at his side. A young Barbara was on his other side, with a man's arm round her shoulders. It took a few minutes for it to dawn on Georgia that it was Tom Miller, then a good-looking flaxen-haired young man, cocksure and arrogant, the leader of the pack. He had not changed much in that way. For some reason Barbara had wanted her to see this photo, Georgia realized – could that reason be Tom Miller?

She was still thinking of him as she went in search of Jennifer again. The filming must be behind because the crew was still in the assembly room. She could see Jennifer, standing with Phil, in the corridor – that couldn't be a happy conversation, unless they had talked out or postponed their differences.

'Have you had your moment of glory, Jennifer?' she asked as she joined them.

'Not me,' Jennifer answered. 'Phil's had one, haven't you?'

'Did it go well?' Georgia asked him.

'Thanks, yes,' came the brief reply – although not, Georgia thought, antagonistic. Perhaps he'd faced facts, or rather fakes.

'Phil did a good job,' Jennifer assured her, 'keeping to Jane's visits to Kent and how she travelled and Edgar House's role in that.'

'And Douglas,' Phil added meaningfully, 'did well on the Harker side, talking about the Napoleonic wars and his staying in the Edgar Arms with his brother, and how he later married Lady Edgar at Stourdens. All true, of course.'

'I'm sure Jake will be monitoring it,' Georgia replied sweetly, but was taken aback when Philip flushed and did not reply. Not so hard-boiled then. 'Were you happy with the new approach, Jennifer?' she asked.

She replied without hesitation. 'I don't think Douglas would dare go off script now. Tim popped in to see him earlier. Tim's been as good as gold. He told me he had in fact suspected there might be an authentication issue, but didn't want to face it. He agrees that we and Jake should keep off dangerous territory.'

'Lucky for some,' Philip said ironically.

'I'm sorry about your book,' Jennifer said, 'but we really don't have any choice.'

Philip shrugged. 'What do you expect me to do though? Tell my publishers that one daft female and just *one* expert have bees in their bonnets and maybe they should scrap the book?'

'Not so daft,' Georgia rejoined. 'And perhaps the mistake was yours in building a book's thesis on one opinion.'

'Find twenty-four experts and you'll have twenty-four opinions,' Philip exclaimed with disgust. 'I can't get Jake to understand that.'

Jake must have heard his raised voice, because he promptly came over to them. 'Georgia's right, Phil,' he said quietly. 'I have to act on the verdict that Jen's been given, even if it's not set in stone yet.'

'Whose bloody side are you on?' Philip exploded.

'Mine, and all these people I'm employing at vast expense. I realize I'm luckier than you, because I can switch themes, albeit with difficulty. You can't.'

'My problem,' Philip replied wearily.

'Is there nothing I can do?' Jake asked.

'Yes. Show some guts,' Philip retorted. 'You were eager enough to scent a scoop at first. And nothing has happened to change that.'

Shaken, Jake did not reply, but Jennifer did. 'Something *did* change,' she whipped back. 'My mother was murdered, Phil, just as she was going to put a stop to this fantasy. Then Amelia Luckhurst was murdered. Coincidence? I don't think so.'

'I'm sorry.' Philip shook his head, perhaps in disbelief at what he'd said, and walked unsteadily away.

'He'll come round,' Jake said, 'once he's sorted this mess out. I'm afraid this is the end of a beautiful relationship though. I told him yesterday that I was moving out and did so right away. I've been thinking about it for some time, and this Austen business has brought it to a head.'

'What will you do if he pulls out of the film?' Georgia asked.

'No problem. I'm pretty sure he'll go on with his other

scripted pieces, but if he doesn't I'll get Jill to do the lot at the Stourdens filming. Don't worry about it, Jen,' he added. 'We'll be there as planned.'

Jennifer leaned forward and kissed his cheek. 'Thanks, Jake.'

'All in a day's work.'

'And for you and Phil?' Georgia asked.

He pulled a face. 'The land of lost loves is heavily populated. I'll recover. So will he.' A pause. 'Look, Jennifer, I'm going to have to tell you, it's gone too far not to. Your mother did tell us that morning that she had just been told the collection was fake and that she was going to talk to you about it afterwards. We truly didn't believe her and thought we had time to discuss it with her.'

Jennifer stared at him aghast. 'Then why did you, Phil and Tim attack Georgia and me over whether it was faked or not?'

'Because Laura didn't name Douglas. She just said she had good reason to believe it was all faked and so was not going ahead with the Stourdens' plans. Tim nearly went spare. Roy was yelling at her, and Phil and I were just poleaxed.'

'And no one remembered to tell me – or the police, come to that?' Jennifer asked angrily.

'We thought the jury was still out, that's why,' Jake repeated. 'Tim said he knew Amelia Luckhurst had been to see Laura, clearly bent on making mischief. I began to get cold feet and decided I needed a plan B. I was still thinking about it when Georgia came into the picture with her story. Phil was sure it was more of the same baloney, but it all began to make terrible sense for me. What better mask for a faker than to be a specialist in the subject? I'm sorry, Jen. Roy and Tim were adamant that I shouldn't tell you, it would be the last straw and I wasn't thinking straight. It never occurred to me – crazy though this might sound – that it could have had anything to do with Laura's death.'

'And did it?' Jennifer asked quietly.

'I don't know. I just don't.'

Jennifer said nothing, perhaps because the facts were so clear, Georgia thought. Only the fakes linked both deaths.

Lunch in the Edgar House garden offered a welcome interlude, even if Georgia's ideal choice of companions wouldn't have been

Esther and David Wilson, Jennifer's presence notwithstanding. They were a curious couple, she thought. She spoke to them and received replies, but without getting much impression of the kind of people they were. Barbara and her helpers had laid the buffet out in the kitchen for everyone to help themselves, but every so often she appeared in the gardens. As now. Georgia could see that not surprisingly she had her eyes fixed on their table. Barbara can't take her eyes off Esther, she noticed, and wondered again what had gone on between the two women in 1985.

'Well, well, well,' Barbara said. She looked almost shocked as she came over to the table. 'Quite like old times.'

Esther seemed equally taken aback. 'No one told me Barbara was coming,' she accused Jennifer when Barbara moved away.

Jennifer stared at her in amazement. 'She has the catering contract. Why should I have told you?'

The moment passed, but even so when Georgia went to the kitchen to return dirty plates, she was concerned at how white Barbara still looked. 'Are you all right?' she asked.

'Just seeing Madam again,' was the reply. 'It's made me feel quite faint.'

Georgia was uncomfortably aware that Barbara's eyes followed her out to the garden again, and that when Barbara next emerged into the garden herself she was still staring at them. The Wilsons seemed ill at ease too, when Georgia returned to their table.

'Tim told us about the faked Austen letters, Jennifer,' Esther said. 'I hope you don't think that Max and I knew they were faked. Or that Max was scheming with Amelia and Bob in any way. To him everything was genuine.'

'That seems unlikely,' Georgia pointed out. 'Amelia knew they were faked, and Bob did too. So did Douglas Watts, and Max Tanner doesn't sound to me an ingenuous person, though I can well understand he might have let you think they were genuine.'

This annoyed Esther. 'There's no way Max would have been in some kind of conspiracy. He thought it was real, he really did.'

'Isn't it possible that he found out it wasn't, realized he'd been duped, and went storming up to the folly to have it out with Bob?'

'Whatever he went there to do, Amelia got there first, through the tunnel.'

A dead silence, and Georgia broke it. 'You mean she killed him?'

'Of course,' Esther said. 'Who else?'

'You did know about the tunnel then? You were rather vague about it when we last talked.'

'Lots of people knew about it,' Esther flashed angrily back. She was on the defensive, and Georgia could see her husband becoming agitated on her behalf.

Georgia cut in before he could speak. 'Why didn't Max speak out at the trial and say Amelia was guilty?'

'He did. No one listened, because he had no proof,' Esther said.

That could be so, but Esther was hiding something. She must be, Georgia thought. This didn't make sense. Amelia could not have killed Bob before Max (and then the protesters) arrived, so did she hide in the tunnel?

Georgia knew she must keep the pressure up. Esther was looking to her husband in appeal now. 'Isn't it more likely that Max and Amelia were working together?' Georgia shot at her.

'No, it bloody isn't,' David Wilson intervened on her behalf.

Push or not push? Georgia debated. Push, but not too hard or she'd lose the momentum. She felt her voice losing control and fought to regain it. 'How would you know that, David? Your wife—'

David interrupted her, red in the face. 'Because I'm bloody Max Tanner, that's why.'

SIXTEEN

'I should have guessed,' Peter said bitterly. 'We've been fools.' He had been steaming for the last hour over the fact that Max Tanner had been effectively right under his nose. Georgia had rung Peter immediately in the hope that he could reach Edgar House quickly enough to speak to Esther

and David. It was still easier to think of him that way. As she
clicked off, however, she saw them already driving out of the
forecourt. Fortunately, she'd been in time to stop Peter leaving.
Jennifer had followed her, and she too had watched her
prospective parents-in-law leave.

'They're probably going straight over to see their darling
son,' Jennifer had ruefully suggested. 'It's beginning to look
as if it's Stourdens that Tim wanted to marry all along.'

Georgia had reassured her, even though she thought Jennifer
was probably right.

Back at the office Peter shared her view. 'Why didn't it
occur to us that Elspeth could have remarried him under another
name? And having fooled us, why did he suddenly decide to
tell the world?'

'That's easier,' Georgia said. 'Barbara had recognized him
despite the beard and ageing process, that's why. He'd taken
the risk, and it hadn't worked.'

'Did he admit to knowing the letters were fake?'

'No way,' Georgia replied. 'His line is that it was all a plot
by the Luckhursts.'

'Did he support Esther's claim that Amelia killed Bob?'

'No. That's weird, isn't it?'

'Indeed it is. Does he still claim he's innocent? And if so,
who does he think was guilty?'

'Guess who? Tom Miller.'

Rather to her surprise, instead of growling in frustration,
Peter looked interested. 'I've got something to contribute too.
Suspects Anonymous.'

She groaned. 'Not again. It's software, Peter. It doesn't
know what's outside the box. Which in this case is an ugly
black monster sitting on your desk.'

'And therein lies its value,' Peter said smugly. 'It sees everything objectively and together. No prejudice.'

'What has the Great Box produced this time that is so
relevant?'

'Craig Hastings.'

Georgia began to laugh. 'He's an old chestnut. What's
Suspects Anonymous's thesis? That he popped up out of the
cradle to kill Bob Luckhurst?'

'He wasn't in his cradle if you remember. He had burst upon the scene nearly two years earlier. I got his birth certificate fast-tracked to me, courtesy of Mike.'

'What made you ask for it?'

'Suspects Anonymous.'

'Silly of me to have asked,' she said resignedly.

'It pointed out that as a player in the 1985 murder, Craig was a loose thread to be followed up.'

'We knew that,' she said impatiently. 'Who was the father?'

'Tom Miller.'

She immediately remembered the photo of Miller's arm around Barbara's shoulders so carelessly and possessively. He'd claimed only to have visited the Edgar Arms occasionally, but the photo implied he was a regular. 'Would an apology for stupidity placate Suspects Anonymous?' she asked.

'None needed,' Peter replied graciously. 'I've double-checked that Barbara was still Barbara Merryweather when Craig was born. Miller was already married and clearly preferred to stick with what he'd got. But where does this leave us on the murder? Miller had a pretty solid alibi. Even if theoretically he could have managed it, it would have been one hell of a risk.'

'Barbara couldn't have been the woman involved, although Amelia and Tom seem unlikely conspirators.'

'Only one person talks of a woman's voice – Tom's chum in the pub,' Peter pointed out. 'A staunch chum who perhaps has no objection to throwing in a red herring. And what about the gun? It was Max's.'

'Max claimed Tom could have pinched it, knowing it had a silencer on it, and that he seized the opportunity to get rid of Bob once and for all.'

'Doubtful,' Peter said. 'Opportunism and planning don't sit easily together.'

'He said Tom knew where the gun was kept, and the drawer was unlocked. Tom could easily have nicked it on the way to the Gents and just as easily thrown it down in the cellars afterwards.'

'He couldn't,' Peter came back instantly. 'He was at the Bat and Trap.'

Georgia was only thrown for a moment. 'We don't know when the police checked the cellars.'

'Barbara could have picked the gun up for him.'

'Risky. And there's motive to consider, Peter. Surely murdering someone over a footpath issue isn't very likely, especially as Miller would have had no guarantee that Bob's successor Amelia would take a more lenient view. She didn't strike me as a soft touch.'

'Would you say from our brief knowledge of him that Tom Miller was an intelligent man?'

'No,' Georgia said immediately.

'Easily led?'

'Easily influenced,' she amended. She shot a doubtful look at him. 'Barbara again?'

'With young Craig,' Peter added. 'An ambitious lady with a son's future to think of.'

'She might have stolen the gun in the first place,' Georgia agreed. 'Killing Luckhurst might or might not have solved Tom's footpath problem, but what she wanted was the development of the Edgar Arms. That adds up, Peter. Barbara was good-looking and capable.' Then she saw the flaw. 'Problem: she might in theory have had a good future ahead at the pub, but not if Max Tanner went to prison for murder. So why should she return the gun which would point right to him?'

Peter looked taken aback, but then rallied. 'Esther was the current licensee. With Max in gaol she would need a deputy, and Barbara was right there.' He glowed in satisfaction. 'It fits, and there's only the simple matter of proof to find.'

'Hold on. What about Douglas Watts?'

Peter looked blank. 'You mean criminal charges for fraud?'

'You had him slotted in as a suspect for Laura's murder. Doesn't the same hold true for Bob's?'

'Very tempting,' Peter said crossly, 'but although I would put him high on the list for Laura's death if I were DI Newton, I'm told he was still living in south London in 1985, and he doesn't seem to have been interviewed by the police at the time.'

'He *told* us he was at a camp site in Clacton when Bob was murdered.'

'How about going to the Bat and Trap tomorrow?'

Georgia blinked. 'Why so suddenly?'

'Because Douglas Watts rang. He'd like to meet us there. I didn't tell you earlier in case you exploded before we had talked Tanner through.'

The cheek of it. 'Too right I would,' Georgia agreed. 'We're not going, are we?'

'If we don't, we play into his hands.'

'If we do, we play into his hands,' Georgia said crossly. 'Suspects—'

'*No.* Absolutely not, Peter. *We* decide, not a machine.'

'Let's go. Craig and Miller might be there.'

The Bat and Trap was crowded, but Georgia quickly spotted Craig and Tom Miller. Both seemed ostentatiously busy, however. Douglas Watts was by the window at the same seat as before.

Peter immediately joined him. 'May I buy you a drink?' he asked him politely.

'Thank you. A pint of bitter would do me nicely.'

All very civilized, Georgia thought, although she would have liked to have thrown it over Douglas's smug civilized face. She left Peter talking to him and went to buy the drinks.

'Film going well then, Craig?' Tom conversed at the top of his voice as she reached the bar.

'Suits Mum OK, but this Jane Austen stuff's a right bore. Dressing up like kids.'

'I'd like to take their precious collection and ram it down their smug Fettis throats.' Tom looked pleased with himself.

'Steady on, Tom,' Craig said uneasily, with an eye on Georgia. No doubt he was thinking of his future career, she thought.

Tom was not to be steadied, however. Young though the day was in pub terms, he had obviously partaken to the full and over.

'Leading us up the garden path, they were,' he roared. 'And your mother, Craig. Telling us what big things were going to happen. Nothing has and nothing will and that's all we've got – nothing. Not now they've changed their high and mighty minds about what to do with that pile of old stones. I'd like to rip the living daylights out of them.'

'No talking like that, Tom.' The landlord came hastily over, though Georgia wouldn't mind betting that it was only because of her presence and Peter's. Tom spat elegantly at her feet and walked off.

When she had finally returned to the table with drinks, Douglas thanked her, then added, 'I should offer you an apology, Georgia. And you, Peter.'

'Why not?' Peter said encouragingly. 'Now it's generally accepted that the Austen collection is fake.'

Douglas considered this. 'Not quite. It depends on whom Jennifer has consulted.'

'Immaterial,' Peter answered. 'We know it's fake, because you told us yourself.'

'What exactly did I tell you? I recall talking about poor Bob Luckhurst during our delightful lunch together, and I believe I might have mentioned his and my common interest in Jane Austen.'

'Do you recall driving me to your tenant Mrs Smith's home, Number Three Beech Cottages, where you keep your faking studio?' Georgia asked politely.

He frowned. 'I'm afraid not. I can't think where you got that idea. I do have tenants, but I don't recall visiting them with you. It must have been so dull for the police having such a wasted journey.'

'And so will we have,' Peter said impatiently, 'unless we stop talking about our last visit and talk about this one.'

'Excellent idea, Peter. Very well. I have decided to admit that I did do a little work for Bob Luckhurst to fill in one or two gaps in his already existing collection. It is possible that Laura Fettis and you yourselves gained the erroneous impression that the collection was all by the hand of Jane Austen and her friends, and that my additions were not the pure fantasy they were created to be. There is no proof to the contrary, and so I consider it is generous of me to go as far as this.'

'Not far enough, Mr Watts,' Georgia replied. 'Not only we but Jennifer need to know exactly how much and what you did fake. Remember that I did see your studio.'

'Now that is a creation of yours, Georgia,' he remarked good-humouredly.

'It existed and it will be found.'

'I doubt it, but even if it is,' Douglas said, 'has any crime been committed? If anyone had any legal cause to complain it would be Jane Austen herself. I merely carried out a commission for a *private* customer who kept my work in a *private* collection for his own satisfaction. No one else's. Any preliminary enthusiasm I displayed about wider publicity can be disregarded. My work has no commercial value at all, unless it were to be used against my wishes as part of the Stourdens' plans for its future. Plans which dear Jennifer has apparently scuppered, and thus it remains *private.*'

It was an unexpected holiday. An afternoon for enjoying the garden. Peter had wanted thinking time before the filming at Stourdens the following day, which he was determined to attend. There were no lifts necessary at Stourdens, and invited or not she and Peter would be present. Her plans for the afternoon, however, changed with a phone call from Jennifer. Could she come to Medlars and see her urgently – and if Peter could be present too that would be even better. That implied her visit was work related and not private, Georgia realized. Peter forgot about his thinking time and came over right away.

As Jennifer arrived and Georgia took her through to the garden where Peter was waiting it was clear that she was under strain.

'Tim, Dad and I went to see the solicitor this morning,' she began immediately. 'I needed to know where we stood if we wanted to sack Douglas from the trust. He's looking into it, but the snag is that even if we could prove what he told you about the collection, it doesn't affect the trust, so it could be tricky. Luckily, Dad's gradually coming round to my side.'

'And Tim?'

'He's being amazingly meek ever since we found out about his father. He's busy sorting out the new film schedule with Jake. You know he based the filming at Edgar House on *The Watsons* – well, Jake's got a whole new line for Stourdens now, based on a paragraph in *Northanger Abbey.* He's planning to use the tunnel, so Tim's helping sort that out. As for Tim and me, it's a bit of a facer.' Jennifer hesitated. 'I think it might sort itself out in time, though. I have a good feeling about it.' She looked at them. 'Does that sound crazy? If taken with care over the winter?'

'Can we ask what Tim told you about his father?'

'Of course. That's what I wanted to explain before I get caught up in the filming tomorrow. He's told me that his father is a dreamer, who had this notion that he was meant for greater things. That he had been fixated on Stourdens, partly because Amelia had been so scornful of him, after having earlier buttered him up to be on her side in persuading Bob to commercialize Stourdens. Max really thought that they were all going to work together and put both Stourdens and the Edgar Arms on the map. Then when he came out of prison he remarried Esther – Tim knew all about that at the time – but Max wasn't happy at living in a house just like everyone else's. He never forgot Esther and he never forgot Stourdens, and then fate played into his hands when Tim met me, so it all started again. I imagine he saw himself as the power behind Stourdens. Tim had other ideas though.'

A house like everyone else's, Georgia thought. Why did that phrase seem significant? She searched through her memory, and at last it came to her. Someone had used it in conversation about the row of houses to which Douglas had taken her. Isn't that exactly what she had thought about Beech Cottages – and what DI Newton's team would have thought? Was that the point? Had the police somehow searched the wrong house?

She tried to subdue rising excitement and think logically. If so, that meant Douglas must have planned it. It could not have happened by chance. Was there anything to make Number 3 stand out from its neighbours? As far as she remembered they were all painted roughly the same colour. Only the number plate drew attention. That big Number 3 stood out at the gate. Had the other houses had similar number boards? She hadn't looked. Of course she hadn't. Suppose . . . Suppose . . .

Georgia felt as tense when she arrived at Stourdens for the first day of filming as if she and Peter were playing starring roles. Thankfully they were not, they were only spectators, and she didn't have to climb into Regency dress or talk before the cameras. Peter had fallen on her theory about the Beech Cottages house number like a dog with a particularly attractive bone and told her he would be along later after he had discussed

it with the police. Luke too was delayed but would arrive with
Mark by lunchtime, although Jill was already on set. Georgia
was glad they were all coming because their presence would
make the event seem more of a family occasion, masking the
work element. She knew DI Newton would have a couple of
men present, but not what they were expecting or whether
they would be uniform or CID. Did Diane hope that today
might jog memories about Laura Fettis's murder?

Jennifer had suggested Georgia come to the house first, but
she was not surprised to find that Jennifer was not there
but already in the thick of the filming. The vans were parked
on the forecourt, including Barbara's again, but there had been
no other sign of life there. Filming had been due to begin at
seven a.m. so it must be well under way. As she walked through
the gateway to the terrace, her first reaction was that it looked
like the day of the Gala. The significant difference was that a
uniformed policeman stopped her to ask for identification, and
recorded her name.

Jennifer spotted her and came up to the terrace to greet her.
'No Regency dress for you?' Georgia asked, seeing her classic
skirt and blouse.

Jennifer smiled. 'This is my lady-of-the-manor outfit. I don't
have to look learned, just posh and confident. That's not easy
right now.'

'You'll do fine,' Georgia assured her.

'I don't feel fine. You name it, I'm worrying about it.'

'What's top of your anxiety list?'

Jennifer hesitated. 'Silly, I know, but it's the collection. It's
still in the folly, and I'm stuck with doing my presenter's bit
here with Jill. I'm worried because I don't trust Douglas any
more. I'm afraid he might torch the lot. Most of it I'd be only
too happy to lose, but the watercolours and the oil painting I
feel strongly about. I had a threatening phone call last night,
and though it didn't mention the collection and wasn't
Douglas's voice it wasn't reassuring.'

'Is that why the uniformed police are there? I heard Tom
Miller making threats in the pub yesterday.'

Jennifer paled. 'He's in the catering tent giving Barbara a
hand. Craig's there too.'

'I'll have a word with the police,' Georgia said uneasily. What was Craig doing here when again it was probably a non-alcohol day? It didn't sound like Craig to be eager to help out his mum unnecessarily. 'Is the folly open?' she asked.

'Yes, Jake's filming inside now. He's got this great idea for the tunnel too.'

Georgia shivered. 'What's the idea?'

'It's where *Northanger Abbey* comes in. Jake wants to film inside the tunnel, and his crew's prowling along it now.'

'What's the connection with the novel though?'

'Catherine Morland and the Gothic angle. When Henry Tilney is trying gently to coax her out of her fixation that every corner holds a dark and dangerous secret he teases her about a secret subterranean communication between her apartment and the chapel of St Anthony scarcely two miles off. Jake said there's mention of a small vaulted room too, with a dagger, mysterious chest and a few instruments of torture in it, so he's seized on it as his way out now the love affair is off limits. The stuff is safe enough in the folly at present, and I'll collect it when he's finished.'

By lunchtime Jake must just have finished at the folly because he arrived complete with crew to grab a quick sandwich. There was still no sign of Peter or Luke, or even Mark, and Jill had gone to join Jennifer in the house because filming was behind schedule and that's where Jake was heading next.

'How's it going?' Georgia asked as Jake stopped to have a word with her on his way out.

'Well, thanks.'

'Have you finished with the folly yet?'

'Yup, all done in the folly itself and we'll film in the tunnel this afternoon. I want to get the house done first.'

'Has Jennifer taken her watercolours out of the folly yet? She was worried about them.' When he shook his head, she thought this at least was something she could do for Jennifer. 'Tell her I'll collect them for her.'

'Will do.'

She hesitated. 'Is it all going OK with Douglas and Phil?'

'Haven't seen Douglas, but Phil's doing fine on the revised

script. What's more he said his publishers have agreed to postpone publication so that he can rewrite or rejig the text as necessary.'

'That's a relief.'

'He's looking his old self again.'

'But that won't change—'

''Fraid not,' Jake said. 'But he's happier about it now. And, thankfully, so's Tim. I thought he might have thrown a wobbly with the revelations about his father, but no. And Roy's happy too. So it's on with the show!'

Could it really be as simple as that? Somehow Georgia thought not.

SEVENTEEN

Georgia was all too uncomfortably aware of how close she was to Abbot's Retreat, and her steps towards the folly quickened. The sooner she was back at the house the happier she would be. In her casual offer to Jennifer via Jake she had forgotten one thing. When she went into the folly, she would have to run the gauntlet of the 'fingerprints' again. Added to that, images of Laura's death refused to go away.

Peter had told her that now there was corroboration that the Austen collection had been faked, the police were working on the line that Amelia Luckhurst had killed Laura in order to prevent the truth emerging after she had unsuccessfully tried blackmail. Georgia had mixed feelings. It would be a relief to agree with the police, rather than to think of Laura's murderer still being at large, but she was not convinced this was the answer. How many others had Amelia tried to blackmail, one of whom might have killed her?

Georgia tried to fix her mind on the rest of the day ahead. By the time she returned to the house Peter would be there, and probably Luke too. Peter might even have Elena with him, and perhaps the detour to pick her up from her hotel had caused his delay in arriving.

As she approached Abbot's Folly she could still hear voices, snatches of music and distant sounds floating across the gardens, which made this shady path seem lonely. Being so near the Retreat did not help. Jennifer had talked of making it a memorial to her mother, renaming it Laura's Garden, when 'everything was over', as she put it. What was 'everything', however? The filming? Laura's murderer behind bars? Jennifer's marriage to Tim? The Luckhurst case solved? Or just today? At the moment Georgia would settle for that.

When she reached the folly she was relieved to see that the door was open, which implied that at least someone else was here. Probably Jennifer had not yet got the message that Georgia was fetching the watercolours and had sent Roy or Tim. Or – and sudden fear – was it someone else? Tom Miller? Then she relaxed as she remembered she had seen him in the catering tent, far too busy to have reached the folly before her. Douglas? Could she cope if so?

As that unpleasant thought struck her, the fingerprints overwhelmed her as she stepped over the threshold.

'Roy!' she shouted. The door to the archives was open, but there was a scurry of movement in the study so she went straight there.

And stopped, transfixed.

There was no Roy. No Tom. No Douglas. It was Philip, looking as stunned to see her as she was him. She only fleetingly registered that, however, as he pushed past her and was effectively blocking the door. Most of her attention was on the terrifying sight before her.

The study was in chaos. Paper and books were strewn everywhere, savaged, ripped and torn. Emptied drawers lay around, shelves had been swept clean, prints taken from the wall, torn and their frames and glass smashed. The watercolours, she immediately thought in panic, then remembered thankfully that they were in another room and so was the oil painting. Had that too been vandalized? Then her eye fell on the piled-up desk, where the two watercolours lay out of their frames, waiting for the next onslaught.

She wanted to cry out, but that would only encourage him. Take your eyes away, she told herself, or the watercolours will be next. Her eyes took it all in, but her brain could not cope with what was happening and what it meant.

'What,' Philip said from behind her, 'have you come for?' His voice was dispassionate and cold, as though she had interrupted a tutorial.

'Jennifer sent me to fetch something for her.' She tried to sound matter-of-fact.

'The watercolours, I suppose. I'm taking them,' Philip said. 'Jake wants them.'

'Good . . .' she began. She could feel herself trembling and could not stop herself. 'What's all this mess?' she cried. 'Did you find it like this? Who's been here?'

'I did it.'

The words chilled her. It didn't take much to realize what danger she was in. She disciplined herself to turn round slowly and saw the gun in Philip's hand with little surprise. It was pointing at her. No need to ask him why he'd trashed the room, nor why he happened to have a gun with him.

'You killed Laura.' She listened to her own words disinterestedly. She could think about them later – if there was a 'later' for her.

'I had no choice.' Philip sounded as though it was of little interest. 'The woman had no compunction at all about proposing to announce that the story of Jane and William Harker's affair had no basis. That's what she told me when I went to see her that afternoon. She didn't care a damn about my book or reputation. Amelia thought I'd buy her off when she rang me to say she was going to tell Laura it was all faked, but I don't have that kind of money. That's why I'd no choice. My father taught me to shoot, and so I took his old gun with me to the Gala in case I couldn't make Laura see sense. I couldn't, so I told her I'd found evidence in the folly archives that the collection was not fake and she should come with me to see it. It had just been Amelia making mischief. Now the whole lot's worthless: this collection, my book, my future.'

Keep him talking, she thought desperately, aware that the hand holding the gun was moving nervously around. 'Jake told me your publishers had a plan to save it.'

'Sure they have a plan, but not to save it. They're scrapping the whole edition if the third opinion they've taken comes through that most of the collection is fake. And it will. I know that now. Douglas thinks it's funny. I suppose you do too.'

'No.'

'You and your self-satisfied publisher husband. They're all the same, publishers. Where is he, by the way? I haven't seen him. Nor will you. You could try to run away, but it wouldn't be any use.'

Her mouth went dry. He was serious. He was *serious*.

She seemed to be watching herself from somewhere very far away, wondering why Georgia Marsh, happily married woman, was facing a maniac with a gun.

'I don't want to kill you,' Philip said reasonably. 'I'm going to shoot Jake, and then myself. But you're here now, and you'll do nicely as a hostage. If I let you go, you would warn Jake, but if you did I'd have to shoot that smug husband of yours instead. I don't like him. Your choice, Georgia. Makes no difference to me.'

Think, think, *think*. But her mind was jelly. Unrelated thoughts bound together only by the gelatine of terror. 'Let's talk about your book, Philip.' She really sounded quite calm, she told herself. 'There are always ways round problems, and I know about the publishing world. I write books of my own. I'd be an objective eye on the situation. I can *help*.'

'No. Let's go.'

'But you can't . . .' She heard her voice getting shriller and tried to calm it. 'You can't just walk through the crowds with me as a hostage in order to shoot Jake. You'd be bounced on from behind. And there are police here. Luke is on his way too.' It sounded weak even to her but she had to keep fighting.

'We're not going outside,' he said. 'We're going through the tunnel. Jake's meeting me there for the tunnel shots in fifteen minutes' time. There will be real shots though.' He laughed at his joke. 'One, two, *three* of them. We'll all go together. One for you, one for Jake, one for me. I'm taking the watercolours with me, and I'll make you tear them up in front of him. Jake is fond of them. He was fond of me too once, but that's gone. I still love him though, and that's why I want to take him with me. That's reasonable, isn't it? And if that husband of yours turns up, you can take him with you. That's only fair. Four shots.'

She had to go. If she didn't this crazed man would shoot her in the back, and if by any chance she escaped he'd stalk Luke to kill him as well as Jake. Her brain was ice-clear now, she had no choice. With luck, as a hostage she might escape. Jake was his real target. If Jake saw what was happening in time or if she yelled out a warning, he would retreat – and Philip might rush after him, without her, and they'd both escape. No, that wouldn't work. So much that could go wrong. Talk, talk, *talk*, she told herself. The only hope, but such a slim one.

'Did you kill Amelia too?'

'Yes.' Philip sounded quite pleased with himself. 'I had to. I think she guessed it was me who killed Laura, but even if she hadn't I couldn't risk Amelia spreading the story of the fake collection. But then you did,' he added.

'And I told the police too.' Georgia knew she sounded scared. Stop, *stop*. 'It was Douglas who started it, however. He did the faking.' Better.

'Doesn't matter. It was your fault. I quite liked you, but I do need a hostage.'

His voice was trembling, and his grip on the gun increasingly uncertain, but if she risked grabbing it . . . Self-defence training or not, a gun was a more formidable opponent than she could manage.

He must have seen what she was looking at, because his face hardened again. 'We're going. Now. Move.' With one hand, he picked up the watercolours from the desk and pushed them at her. 'You carry them.'

'What about light?' she asked as she clasped them. 'Do you have a torch?' Please say you do, she prayed. It might help distract him, and the dark might prove her friend this time.

A giggle. 'Jake's gaffer has kindly lit the whole tunnel, so that I can see to fire straight.'

She looked down the steps into the darkness of the tunnel and the claustrophobic atmosphere rose up to meet her. She had no choice though, and she picked her way gingerly down the uneven steps. The tunnel ahead was indeed lit, but it somehow looked even more sinister. Think survival, she told herself. I'm going to survive this. I *must*. There's Luke, Peter and Elena and Rosa. I have to get through it. What would Peter and Elena do if I was taken from them, just like Rick?

'Aren't you worried about the effects of shooting in the tunnel?' she asked inanely. She stumbled, and the gun poked impatiently at her back. Her fear gradually steadied as she progressed a little further.

'Why should I?' he answered. 'I'll be dead. It can bring the whole roof down for all I care.'

What to say next? 'Where are we meeting Jake?' It came out as half choke, half mumble. 'By the Abbot's Retreat exit?'

'No, that's where I took Laura. We were going to the folly where she thought I'd show her my new evidence, but I changed my mind. I told Laura that if she sat in the gardens I'd bring it to her, because she was looking a bit peaky by then.'

'But where are we going?'

'There!' Philip's voice rang out almost in triumph as the grotto came into sight. 'What a backdrop for an orgy of killing.'

'Jake's not here.' Alarm bells began to ring in her mind. Was all this Philip's fantasy?

'He will be. You'll see. He'll realize he loves me.'

Waiting, waiting . . . every second a minute, each minute an hour. There was no sound except the steady drip of water.

'A leak in the roof,' he said dispassionately. 'The roof's weak here. You're right. The shots may bring it down. That would be dramatic, only I won't be here to see it. Nor will you.'

Still no Jake. 'He said he'd come,' Philip muttered.

She could hear his ragged breathing; he was beginning to panic. 'Perhaps he's changed his mind. We could—'

'He will come. I know he will.'

The silence continued. Georgia tried to empty her mind of everything but the need to focus on that gun, but there was too much . . . too much . . .

She felt the pressure leave her back and hope flickered as he walked round in front of her. But the gun was still trained on her as he peered for one brief instant into the arch of the grotto. 'Put the watercolours on the table as an offering to the gods,' he giggled. 'That would be a nice touch.'

'Would it?' she said wearily as she obeyed him. There was

no sound, no sight of anyone else in this godforsaken tunnel, only the two of them.

'Perhaps you're right. He's not coming after all,' Philip said. 'That's the trouble with Jake. He keeps changing his mind. No organization. Not like me. So Georgia, I'm sorry, I really am. But it's got to be you. I can't go alone.'

He's mad, Georgia thought dully. The atmosphere was beginning to choke her, a tomb for the living. *I shall survive, I shall survive*, she repeated silently like a mantra, but could not believe it.

'First you, then me,' Philip said, raising the gun. Any second now he would pull it and it would be over. One instant of pain and then . . . what? *Survive, survive* . . . The word was meaningless as his finger rested nervously on the trigger. She felt her eyes closing and struggled to open them.

Then came the noise. The world exploded around her, and she opened her eyes to blood and Philip's body sprawled in a sea of red. More noise, more, and then more dust and small bits of stone as the noise intensified all round her. She threw herself to one side as the roof of the grotto began to crack and crumble. Then came pain and nothing more.

Pain, and more pain. She was conscious, then nothing, then conscious again. She could feel someone holding her – hands on her, perhaps checking for broken bones, carrying her with her pain, and then mercifully nothing. Then she was conscious again, lying on some kind of bed in a tent, Luke there, Peter, and at her side Elena, smiling as she used to, stretching out her arms to her. Georgia sat up with difficulty and went willingly into them, aware that she was crying. She might have been talking too because she heard someone say 'Mummy'. Or perhaps she was wrong.

'A sprained wrist and a bruise or two. Not bad, eh?' Georgia managed to joke, when Luke collected her from the A and E department in the small hours. She seemed to have been checked out by every machine known to Wallace and Gromit, plus a few human beings into the bargain.

'The word miracle comes to mind,' Luke said quietly. 'If only I'd got there earlier.'

'You couldn't have known I would run into a maniac.'

'Knowing you, I could.' He hesitated. 'Sweetheart, do you feel like talking to Mike and Diane Newton tomorrow morning?'

'Is there an alternative?'

'Only my taking you to a nice cosy police station.'

'Medlars it is then. You'll be there too?' She felt weak asking for his presence.

'Chained to your side.'

In fact, the ordeal was not as great as she had feared as she related her story to Mike and Diane and answered questions as best she could.

'Something else, Georgia,' Mike said when she had finished. 'Douglas Watts.'

Diane promptly looked very po-faced, and Georgia wondered what might be coming. 'You know about the opinion Jennifer received on the collection?'

'Yes, but that's not what Diane wanted to tell you. Go ahead, Diane.'

Diane actually smiled. 'You were right, Georgia. You guessed how our friend Mr Watts fooled us both. He owns two houses there, adjacent ones, three and two. The Number Three you saw was in fact Number Two, and we checked an entirely different house. Simplest solutions are best. The number boards were switched as and when needed. The unwary, like us, would simply think from Number Three's position that the houses carried odd numbers only.'

'Are you bringing charges?'

She shook her head. 'Difficult to prove. But now Watts is in our sights, I doubt if it will happen again.'

Georgia was not so sure, but she must have passed out again, because it was late afternoon when Luke gently woke her. 'Jake's here,' he said, 'and Jennifer too. Do you feel up to it?'

'I think so.' Did she? Yes, because it was something she had to do. Sitting in the living room at Medlars made it easier, because she couldn't have faced Stourdens again so soon.

'I'm sorry, Jake,' she said as he kissed her.

'Not half as sorry as I am. I realized Phil was going off his rocker, but I didn't enquire further when he said his publishers were OK with the book. I was too relieved that I didn't have to cancel my film, I guess. Serve me right. I knew I didn't want to live with him any more and never asked myself why. I get a bit carried away with my job, but the result is that you've taken the brunt of it. I don't know whether to be glad or sorry I was late getting to that hellhole.'

'Glad,' Georgia said stoutly. 'It saved your life and mine.'

'That's a nice way of putting it, but I still blame myself.'

'What's happening about the film?'

'We're being British,' Jennifer said. 'Carrying on. More re-scripting, more reshooting, more scene changes. Barbara's turned up trumps over the catering, and Jake only has to pay for the cost of the food. She says it's only right after what you went through. She seems to have a soft spot for you – we all do. So it's a case of us all mucking in.'

'And before you ask, Georgia,' Jake added, 'we've no references to *Northanger Abbey* and tunnels now. We're using the folly instead, which luckily is outside the disaster zone decreed by Health and Safety.'

'I'm beginning to feel like a queen holding court,' Georgia said weakly, 'with my privy council telling me what's going on.'

'You are a queen,' Jennifer said fondly. 'No doubt about that. Even Tim was rather overawed. He said he was pretty nasty to you in that tunnel.'

'Tell him a queenly veil has been drawn over it,' Georgia said.

'For me too. It's too early to be sure, but I think we'll still get married in due course. I do love him. And he stood by me stoically at the end. I was raving at first when I heard about you and Philip, and I said I would have nothing to do with any plans for Stourdens at all. That I was going to get that trust dissolved, get Douglas charged with fraud, and Stourdens could fall down for all I cared. Then I calmed down and we came to an agreement. There's so much furore about Phil's death and Jake's film that we're going to let the dust settle for a few months. The book's publication is cancelled, of course, and the film won't be shown until next year.'

Georgia could not resist the temptation. 'Are you really going to pursue Douglas in the courts?'

Jennifer grinned. 'I doubt it. He seems to have made himself scarce. He's good at fading into the background. He's resigned as the trustee of Stourdens, anyway, but we hope to keep the trust going.' She hesitated. 'We have a new trustee in mind.'

'Who's that?'

'You, Georgia. Could you bear it? Or would it be too painful?'

'*Me?*'

The idea initially appalled her, but then she thought more carefully. Painful? No, it might be the cure. Looking after the future of Stourdens, something positive to replace the awfulness of the past. 'I think . . . I think . . . Yes, I'd like to take it on.'

Jennifer beamed and hugged her – carefully to avoid the bruises. 'That's wonderful. Well, your first job is to come to Edgar House with me when you feel up to it. Bring Peter and Luke too. The more the merrier.' Another pause. 'And let me know when because we want Tim's parents to be there. *Both* of them.'

'Nothing like throwing me in the deep end,' Georgia joked. Could she face it, knowing that far from being solved, the truth about the death of Bob Luckhurst might never be known?

'You flourish on deep ends,' Luke said comfortingly.

Did she? For such a meeting the shallow end looked distinctly preferable.

'You don't mind, Peter?' Georgia asked him later. 'The trustee job might have suited you nicely. You've a better financial head than I have.'

'Which will always be at your service. Don't worry. I shall have my hands full,' he said. 'And not only with Marsh and Daughter.'

'Oh?' She had half expected this.

'I shall have Elena to look after soon. She's decided on a house.' He looked both anxious and pleased at the same time.

'To look after?' she queried.

'I want it that way, sweetheart. I get sick and tired of having to be cared for. That's what went wrong between Janie and me. Now I've got a chance to care for someone else, emotionally if not physically.'

'Is the house in Canterbury?'

'Actually it's closer.'

'Haden Shaw?' she asked with foreboding. He was looking shifty.

'Not a million miles away. Next door. Your old home.'

Edgar House was beginning to feel like home, Georgia thought. Gone was the hostility Gerald had earlier displayed, and Dora seemed complacent at having proved her independence. It was a cheerful occasion, for which Dora must have spent a long time preparing. Raspberry fritters were well to the fore. Georgia had wondered just why Jennifer was so keen on this gathering and had assumed it was to reassure the Wilsons that David-Max's revelations were an accepted fact in her relationship with Tim.

Georgia had been wrong.

'We have something for you,' Jennifer said to Dora and Gerald. 'It's on the large side so Tim's fetching it in.'

Georgia turned curiously as Tim came back bearing a large wrapped object whose shape made it clear what sort of gift it was.

Dora saw immediately as Tim pulled off the paper. 'Oh! The oil painting of Captain Harker.' Her delight was evident and her and Gerald's thanks profuse.

'It needs to live here,' Jennifer said. Georgia was aware that Max's eyes were glued to the painting. With wistfulness or avarice? she wondered. Was yet another plan running through his mind?

'You know,' Dora said, 'I really love that painting most of all, although the watercolours were very pretty. I suppose they really have gone for good?'

'A few scraps have been found,' Jennifer said, 'but I realized I could never look at them now without remembering everything that had happened, so I've destroyed them.'

There was a silence, during which Dora looked lovingly at the portrait. 'I suppose,' she said thoughtfully, 'it is just possible that Captain Harker and Jane Austen met here.'

No one spoke, so Georgia decided to break the silence. 'It is,' she said cheerfully, 'but I don't think we'll ask Douglas to prove it.'

It was a convivial gathering after that, and very enjoyable. So much so that Georgia realized that neither she nor Peter had talked to Max Tanner. 'I'll ring him some time soon,' Peter said as they left. It was unnecessary because Georgia turned back to see that Max was following them out to the car.

'Did you talk to your police chums about Tom Miller, Georgia?' he asked.

'No, David.' She would continue to think of him so, rather than as Max.

'Why not?'

Peter answered. 'Because he was innocent. As you know.'

'Do I?' He didn't look surprised, only somewhat hurt.

'*You* killed Bob Luckhurst.'

'That's only what the jury said. They were wrong.'

'You'd just found out that not only were your precious Austen letters faked, but also the whole collection – and what was far worse was that Bob refused to exploit them, anyway. He wanted to treasure them alone.'

David looked at them speculatively. 'I've served my time.'

'We know that,' Georgia said. 'Care to tell us what really happened?'

David considered this, then grinned. 'Why not?' he said. 'Between us, and don't bother your police chums over it, it was like this. I had all my plans ready for the pub; Amelia told me the Stourdens' plans were agreed and they'd be going ahead any moment. How was I to know the stuff was fake? Bob paid me a few quid for the painting and then generously presented me with the letters he said he'd found there. He said it was a surprise to him too, and maybe it was – Watts could have poked them in there. I didn't know about that gent at all. Amelia and Bob kept quiet on that score. But the bastard kept delaying doing anything about the Stourdens' plans and wittering on about being the keeper of the Jane Austen heritage. At last Amelia told me the whole lot was a scam, and I went berserk. Thought I could get Bob to change his mind. I took the gun with me to frighten him a bit, but Miller and his gang came barging in. I didn't know about that. I said I'd go and come back later, but I stayed in the other room just to see what was happening, and then came back once the mob had gone. Blow me if Bob didn't accuse me of bringing Miller and his gang there to steal his precious collection. I reminded him it was fake, and I thought he was going to hit me, so I raised my arms, his arm shot out and the gun sort of went off.'

'But you still kept saying you were innocent.'

'I said the jury was wrong, and so it was,' David said indignantly. 'They said I killed him because of that licence, but that wasn't the reason so the whole trial was a mockery. That's bloody British justice for you.'

'Why didn't you say anything about the collection being fake at the trial?'

'Given me more of a motive, wouldn't it?' he said practically, then added: 'Besides, I didn't know Esther was going to sell it. I reckoned one day I might get a second chance.' He grinned.

'There's one good thing emerged from this mess,' Georgia said thoughtfully as she drove Peter home. 'At least Suspects Anonymous has been proved fallible.'

'Conceded,' Peter said reluctantly. 'Although—'

'It was wrong,' she repeated. 'It pointed to Tom Miller.'

Peter gave in. 'If you say so. Georgia, I asked Jennifer if she'd mind if we visited Abbot's Folly on the way home. Could you bear it? There's one loose end . . .'

Her heart sank. She knew exactly what he was going to say. 'The fingerprints.'

'Yes. I'd like to see if they're still there.'

'They can't be. Max Tanner killed Bob Luckhurst, and whatever he says justice was done.' Nevertheless, she knew how he felt and was also aware that she was arguing against his suggestion only because she didn't want to go near that place so soon.

Peter glanced at her. 'Jennifer said we could use the tractor path behind the folly and get the car nearer to it. There's a gate through to Stourdens and the track is wide enough to get the wheelchair along once inside. Does that help?'

She looked at him gratefully. 'Yes. Thanks. I'm not crazy about seeing the folly, but the tunnel is still the real nightmare.'

'It won't take long, I promise.'

It felt strange to be here on their own in the early evening, and, with the setting sun, she felt that some of the peace that the Mad Abbot must have loved seemed to have returned. Ahead she could see the woods near which the huge hole left by the falling tunnel masonry must lie, but she could turn her back on that. She would concentrate on the fingerprints.

The door into Abbot's Folly was closed but unlocked, and the ramp was still in place. Georgia pushed open the door, prepared for she knew not what, longing for it not to be just as it was the last time she had come here. Peter followed closely behind her.

'Nothing,' he said. 'There's nothing here.'

He was right. It was an empty building. *Completely* empty. Empty of its vandalized contents, and empty of fingerprints.

In silence Georgia struggled to take in what this meant. She saw Peter look up at her, and she met his eye, knowing they were both thinking the same thing.

Peter cleared his throat. 'Those fingerprints weren't left by Max Tanner or by Bob Luckhurst, were they?'

'No,' she agreed.

A long silence, then she said diffidently, 'You don't think that they were left by someone who felt betrayed and that justice had not been done?'

'Impossible,' Peter said hurriedly.

'Either because of the collection, or – ' she steeled herself – 'because of an unhappy love affair?'

'Sheer fantasy.'

'It's not.' Georgia put it into words. 'The fingerprints could have been Jane Austen's.'

AUTHOR'S NOTE

Jane Austen paid many visits to Kent and in particular to Godmersham Park, between Canterbury and Ashford, which at the time of this novel's sub-plot was owned by her brother Edward. As a boy, he had been informally adopted by the Knight family, who owned Godmersham; he had married into the Bridges family of Goodnestone Park and come to own Godmersham himself, taking the name of Knight in 1812. Jane Austen and her sister Cassandra were indeed staying at Godmersham during most of September and October in 1802. They were living in Bath at the time, and their former home at Steventon in Hampshire was currently lived in by her brother James and his family. It was there that Jane and Cassandra travelled after leaving Kent, and during their stay at Steventon they paid a visit to friends at Manydown where Jane accepted and instantly regretted a proposal of marriage from Harris Bigg-Wither. So much is fact, but Stourdens and Captain Harker, and the story and characters of this novel, are all fictional. So too is Edgar House. Although Jane and Cassandra would have hired post-chaises to reach Kent, the inn in which they awaited the Godmersham carriage for the last stage of their journey was not the Edgar Arms. For background information I am indebted in particular to David Waldron Smithers' *Jane Austen in Kent,* to *Letters of Jane Austen* edited by Edward, Lord Brabourne, and of course to the novels of Jane Austen herself.

As always, my thanks are due to my agent, Dorothy Lumley, and to my publishing editor, Rachel Simpson Hutchens, together with Severn House's expert and friendly staff.